IF ONLY FOR A SEASON

ANARCHY AND DESPOTISM IN CRIPPLE CREEK

A Novel

RAY WHITE

IF ONLY FOR A SEASON

Chapter One

May, 1895
Freighter's Route Around Pikes Peak, Colorado

MICAH AND CALEB HAD evidently thought it a novel idea to stand atop the wagon's thin rattling tailgate for a better look over the rocky edge. And I'd bet a dollar little Caleb had suggested it.

And why not? From a six-year-old's perspective, the view off the edge of a four hundred foot mountain must have been irresistible. You could practically see Kansas.

Patricia popped the four leather reins while I scouted afoot up the rugged mountain trail. Dragging two mules hitched to the loaded wagon, and heaving for breath in the thin alpine air.

A good head of foamy lather dripped from the mule's withers and shaky legs as we fought over rock ledges, washouts, and crumbling edges. I didn't even want to look over that edge.

"Up, up. Rosebud, Black Jack, up. Up, now. Git up that ledge, Rosebud."

Four hundred feet below lay a fine field of red boulders, some larger than the home we'd left in the open country of Randall's Flats, Missoura. Rock outcroppings erupted from the valley floor in an odd array of shapes and colors, challenging the eye to believe what it was taking in. And scenes up the mountain pass offered less comfort. Snowcapped pitches thousands of feet above us banished any sense of personal safety. This was no time for a leisurely twist of chewing tobacco, and no time for curious boys and their shenanigans.

Just the recipe for disaster.

Rosebud suddenly dropped to her knees and let off a piercing bray right into my ear. She broke through a shelf of decomposing granite and fell. A second time. And this time the right foreleg snapped in one quick motion.

"Patricia! Draw those reins," I shouted, diving for the black harness behind me. "Get her off that loose rock."

Flailing hooves fought for purchase in a haze of dust while Patricia dragged back on the reins. She could not control the powerful animals.

Dirt and rock flew into the air.

A ragged bone ripped through the hide, throwing Rosebud into a wild panic. I practically hung from the harness to hold her down. Blood sprayed across my thigh and up to my neck. I knew in that one instant I'd have to put her down.

But Rosebud would not go down.

The old wagon lurched forward and back, pitching Caleb off the back and down the slope he'd been eyeing so excitedly.

"Caleb!" Patricia cried. She tied off the reins and threw herself back across the tail of the wagon to rescue the fallen boy. "Caleb, wake up!" she demanded, slapping his face harder than necessary. Although a woman of strong constitution, seeing her baby tumbling toward eternity proved too much to bear. After a few sharp slaps Caleb awoke in her arms, and she bolted back up the slope for the other one.

"Micah, get off that wagon right now!" She juggled Caleb in one arm and patted his bloody forehead with the other. "Micah, right now!"

"Patricia, get those boys up that hill," I shouted, gasping in the thin air. A high-altitude nausea dogged me as I finally wrestled down the flailing mule. But just as I did, Black Jack reared up in fits and starts, wrenching the wagon again and inching its rear wheel closer to the rocky edge. Another six inches, and we'd lose everything to the dizzying wilderness below.

"Rosebud, Black Jack, just stop! Lay down!" I hollered, heaving the harnesses while minding my own footing on the rolling gravel.

Seasons of punishing weather had pried away granite chunks which rolled like marbles off the rock ledges. Every lunge became another gamble for life as the crumbling granite sent the iron-shod hooves skidding for the edge.

At fifty yards from the crest I had a downed animal in a pool of blood, and no way to turn back.

"With this busted leg, she'll never make it up that hill. She's lost. But we got to get off this ledge." Rosebud was bleeding out, clearly a hopeless case, and Patricia knew that as well as I. She grasped the boy's necks and took up her apron to cover her mouth.

A sweaty chill of shame came over me.

I could not escape the thought that my own selfish ambition had led us here. I had pushed my family from our home, fleeing what I considered an economic panic in the South. With waves of others, we had pushed hard for the Colorado gold rush hoping for something better. But even stupefying squalor might be better than this place, standing on the threshold of eternity.

"That old man in Colorado City warned us," I said, digging Rosebud's tangled leg out from under her belly. "Only the bullwhackers and jack trains use this trail now, and most of them take Ute Pass. I'll bet their stock and trade isn't sliding over cliffs to the rocks below."

Even with cooler air flowing down from the high country, sweat covered my face, streaming onto my lips and mouth. Spit and sweat sprayed out together. I finally pried out the mule's twisted leg and jumped up, only to stagger around like a drunkard in the light air.

Rosebud quit thrashing and now clung to the edge of the crumbling granite ledge, hanging by the harness straps alone. Her left hind leg flailed over the empty edge, still searching for a foothold, but without the strength for another lunge. The nervous animal threatened to drag the entire rig into the aspens below.

Black Jack must have gotten a fresh snort of that blood. He brayed and reared back as if a coyote had just darted out from behind a rock. Rosebud slid another foot.

"Patricia, git back down here and calm these danged mules," I hollered, unsure when the big iron wheel might slip the edge. "And get some blinders on these mules or throw a sack over their heads."

Patricia left the children at the top and skidded back down the rock slope on leather soles no wider than saplings. Delicate in stature as she was, she was still no shirker of difficult tasks.

"There now, Rosebud..." she whispered, covering the animal's wild eyes with her apron. "There now... calm down, now."

Rosebud and Black Jack responded to her gentle touch but still shifted nervously on the rocky edge.

"Mama! Come back!" Micah and Caleb cried from atop the incline, stamping their feet and reaching out with little hands. Only their mother could comfort them now, but she was busy with the mules.

Despite their cries, calm returned and I got hold of my own weary nerves. The mules finally settled down but Rosebud was hopelessly stranded. After setting the brake and chocking the wheels, I unhitched the thirty-pound harness, bit, and bridle from her heavy head. A puddle of blood ran down the rocky ledge. The twitching leg dangled over an empty edge and her struggle slowly gave way to acceptance.

Disaster had struck so fast.

"Go on up to the top, Patricia. You won't want to see this."

I pressed a sugar cube into Rosebud's mouth, and caressed her ears and jaw. "You're okay now."

Her breathing slowed.

I cocked my .45 caliber Peacemaker and stood over the gentle beast to speak my final words. She had been like a friend on the rich acres of Missoura. Rosebud and Black Jack were a matched pair, bred for the plow since my youth. Trained by the best Missoura muleskinner there ever was, my own granddaddy, back in Jackson County. We had worked the black earth season upon season as endless acres gave way to corn and crop, repeating the cycle year after year. For a decade and a half I had followed the routine, harnessed strap and rein to these gentle laborers. The loss was more than a mere pack animal.

A black cloud of squawking ravens lighted from their perches high in the Ponderosa pines as the roar of the heavy Peacemaker echoed over the open valley. They sounded loudly in protest as Rosebud slipped over the edge and out of our lives forever. Silence settled on the mountain.

It was just Black Jack and us now.

Man-hauling five hundred pounds of belongings to the top of the incline fell to me. Purple fingers reached down from the western pass just to remind me what trouble might await us up the muddy mountain slope. But I was in no mind to be pushed.

Black Jack finally managed the lightened wagon to the top where we sat in disgust at the terrible waste. Rosebud was gone. Quaking aspens flickered in the light air. No one spoke a word.

But as God would have it, Patricia became so distracted by the unspoiled beauty of the place that she stood to remark of it. Her pained eyes had brightened, and nothing could divert them from the tumbling valley hundreds of feet below. And those quaking aspens. And the romance of a new life, with all its adventure and expectancies.

Patricia's eyes kindled. "Oh, Honey, what a view! I could live here forever," she said, waving her arms in the crisp air. She had just set Caleb down on a big rock where he had forgotten his bloody affair and dug up what he considered buried treasure in the form of a spotted salamander. The hot Colorado sun danced on her wavy auburn hair and little freckles, ministering revival from the awful event. Her delicate white fingers waved in the soft breeze. "It's like another world," she beamed. "Isn't it grand?"

"Well, no," I shot back in hot disgust. "Didn't you see what just happened? How can you dance around like that? I guess I married a gypsy woman."

Patricia's arms fell. "Jeremiah. I—"

"What did we come here for anyways? To kill off our livestock and die in the wilderness? I hate this place. I left twenty dollars of good work in Randall's Flats, not to mention a half-paid McCormick plow at Boyd's Mercantile. Thirteen dollars and it would have been ours, and then I could have done some real work. But look at us now. We'll be lucky to last the night in this place. Don't get used to it. We're leaving for home in the morning."

"I am sorry," Patricia answered softly, running the tips of her fingers over my shoulders and sliding the tight braces off. "I meant no offense. You have done a fine job getting us up here, so don't take so much to heart. We'll get there."

She turned back to the boys with some concern. They were exploring the wonders of a rotten log.

"But I will confess a concern for those sons of yours. I wanted Micah to start school in the fall, and Caleb the year after. Folks say a quarter of the country has been out of work since '93, but I say half in the South. Do you think those boys had any future in Missoura? Could they have even made the eighth grade in a place like that? I just don't think we could have stayed another year, and I cry when I think of those poor little boys still there. Rotten teeth and rags. It was just no place..." She lifted her hand to her cheek. "I know Rosebud is lost..." Another pause and glance over the valley. "But we'll be up on our luck again. I know that. I hope you can see that."

I just dragged my hat down over my eyes.

"Jeremiah, I trust you. And I will follow you wherever you take us. Even if I have to turn gypsy and put rings in my ears," she said with a teasing little twist. "I wonder how gypsy women keep their men so happy?"

Patricia's words came with some comfort, enough to lighten my thoughts, but not enough to change my mind about leaving. Not that much.

"I understand how you feel," she said, dropping down beside me and nodded up the mountain pass. "What do you reckon's up there? Up in Cripple Creek?"

I shrugged. "I don't know."

"Do you think they have a proper schoolhouse? A church with the Spirit of God? I just picture it full of savage Indians and no place to live at all. Is that the sort of place to raise boys?" We both sat quietly under the unanswerable questions. A half-hour passed with Caleb passing through the full length of that rotten log eight times, and coming up blacker each time.

The shady stand of elk-chewed aspen seemed a likely place to camp for the night. Cowboys had carved interesting messages into the smooth white bark, telling of water holes, and hard snows of winters past, and huts just ahead. And just as Patricia had pointed out, we had a breathtaking view of the valley full of evergreen, aspen, and red rock outcroppings. Clouds of light-green pollen lighted from the Ponderosa pine as swirling winds swept up the mountain pass.

A herd of elk edged up the draw into the high country for cooler temperatures, grazing in quiet contentment. With no natural enemies save the occasional mountain lion or bear, the huge herds flourished in the wild country. An ample count of bulls with proud spring racks commanded the herd in yearly migration to and from their high tundra habitat.

That alone was a sight.

Minus the threat of certain death, this country was indeed a beautiful place, even if I could not admit it to my little gypsy wife. Our big granite rock on the plateau gave a full view of a hundred-mile domain, with the dreary Kansas trail just a memory on the distant horizon.

Despite the intoxicating beauty, I still felt inclined to leave at first light. Even Patricia's words could not change that. Our first day in the Rocky Mountains left me sick and disgusted. How could such splendor and cruelty dwell together in a single place? But with only a little disgust, I stood up to finish the day's work, driving the menacing thoughts from me.

By now I could make camp with a toe sack wound over my head. Our trek across the windswept plains of Missoura, Kansas, and Colorado had been a dreary continuum of daily ritual. Break camp at dawn, drive the team into the dying sun, and set up for the night – twelve miles a day for two months.

After the day's events, I welcomed the mindless chores to relieve my aching head.

The boys had reluctantly given in to the duties of stacking firewood, clearing a circle and conjuring up a flame with flint and steel.

Of course, boys do love fire. The purple fingers had finally reached us and flurries began whirling through the camp.

"Fetch a little extra, boys. It looks like this isn't letting up," I said, feeling the chill and eyeing what could be seen of the western skies through towering Ponderosa's.

"Aw Pa, it ain't blowin' hard," they complained, scrunching up their noses. "We wanna climb on the big rocks one more time."

"Micah, Caleb, you best do as your father says," Patricia warned, intervening before I could find the words, "And don't sass, or I'll skin you to within an inch of your lives."

The words were no idle threat. Micah and Caleb scampered for the extra wood, not wishing to test their mother's resolve.

I hoisted our tent over some level ground, leaving the mouth open to a growing fire. Thin yellow baling twine tightened white canvas to nearby aspens. It was a simple bivouac that suited us fine for now. After scraping the ground and digging out a few hip holes to lay in, I put down a bed of pine needles and a layer of canvas. A two-gallon cook pot hung from an iron triangle, waiting for Patricia's potato stew. Filling the pot with water proved more difficult than expected.

"I'm not having any luck with these witching sticks," I complained, after trudging up the mountain in search of snowmelt runoff. "But, it looks like you found some. I never expected such a dry place. Where are the lakes and rivers?"

Patricia dropped two sloshing wooden buckets and panted. "Yep I did, right up that gulch about fifteen minutes. There's a little spring."

"You just won't quit on Cripple Creek, will you?"

She smiled and wiped her forehead. "Nope. Guess not."

"That's your mother's Southern grit. Mrs. Branson, from Missoura. She was one tough old gal," I joked. "Now didn't she capture the James gang after the Pinkerton boys failed so miserably?" I said with a light smile, hoping to make up for the earlier outburst.

"Funny boy. Yep, my mama is a hard woman. She would have tanned me good if I sat down and played in the dirt. I guess I learned right."

We hugged and kissed and sat together. Patricia played in the water buckets like a girl.

"Jeremiah, I know you have doubts. So do I. We don't know what's over that mountain, but we'll face it together." She would not talk of turning back especially with our goal just over the hill.

"Alright! Well, let's get a stew on," I said. "I'm going to get me some."

I threw off care with a steaming tin plate in front of Micah's fire. Sparks and pops flitted into the evening sky. With mind and body free of the day's calamity, I pulled a wrinkled yellow paper from my breast pocket, sliding easily into dreamy thought.

Brightly colored handbills like the one I now studied told of million-dollar mining claims practically free for the taking. Advertisements touting the rich lands of the West circulated widely in Missoura, drawing pilgrims into the new territory.

And of course I was one such pilgrim.

I had plowed and planted fields, sharecropping and hiring out my labor and mules to keep my family in beans and cornbread. Lured by the multiplying handbills, but without a lick of experience, I still supposed I could learn the mining business and make a new start. Anything seemed more attractive than plowing the black Missoura bottomlands for two dollars a week. But time and opportunity passed quickly.

Night and day the pioneer trains pressed west, wagon upon wagon, making it hard for a prairie dog to pop up for a quick look. Witnessing their adventure as they rumbled past the farms left an empty hole in my own life behind the plow. I dreamed of holding the reins of a Conestoga rather than a pair of sweaty draft mules. Colorado offered that opportunity.

By the summer of 1895 it would seem everything outside Randall's Flats was in a state of constant change. New industrial inventions emerged every year. Machines existed today that my granddaddy would have no understanding of their function or purpose. New ideas. New places. New people. Something loomed on the horizon. Something big. Everyone knew it.

Of course gold and silver had been struck in the western territories since 1849, and from time to time animated fellows galloped into our quiet little town with news of another strike, riling citizens to head west. Reports of Colorado gold strikes had reached a head, and I would not wait for another before partaking of the riches myself.

But perhaps not everyone shared that blind enthusiasm.

"Howdy, Pard," a man said, startling me from my thoughts. He had come around the bend, obviously headed for the lower elevations of Colorado City. The man hiked alone toting a big black knapsack quite possibly with all his worldly belongings. Twine ropes bound the heavy load to his tall, wiry frame. He was the only soul on the old deserted trail.

"Howdy!" I replied, glad for an opportunity to talk. So many conflicting thoughts crowded my mind that I needed someone to talk to – someone other than Patricia. "Where you headed?"

"Down Colorado City. Jes left Cripp' Creek. Had my fill and movin' on," he said with a sniff. "You?"

"Well, we were just heading up that way. That is, until today. I'm so disgusted, I ain't sure no more. Aimed to open a gold mine. These yellow handbills claim they're getting rich up there. Millionaires, they say. Any truth to that?"

"Reckon some," the man allowed. "You'll see the glory holes. Bob Womack struck gold in '86 down in Poverty Gulch. Winfield Scott Stratton made some money up at the Independence. And I guess those at the Mollie Kathleen are still doing okay. Stratton may be a millionaire by now, but I don't 'spect too many others have made a go of it. Well, there's Penrose and Tutt at the C.O.D, and you do hear of a few new ones every so often. But, I never got nothin' but enemies up there. I'm headed back down to Colorado City. Figure I'll pick up some work in the processing mills," he said, glancing down the trail with some impatience. "Standard Mill. Portland. One of them, I reckon."

I smiled. "Well then, it sounds like there's some truth to what I've heard."

"Oh yes, Cripple Creek has probably produced... oh, maybe... fifty million in gold in the last ten years, and of course that leads some to holler about making it the new state capital, but that's just wild talk. I don't put any stock in that; they said that about Leadville."

"Fifty million dollars! How many people are living up there?" I asked in surprise. The handbills hadn't said. "We figured only a few hundred. Maybe a thousand at best," I added. Would we be latecomers like the hordes that had poured into Sutter's Mill in California, back in '49, I wondered?

"Well, they're practically coming in two to a mule," the man said. "There's got to be twenty thousand by now. But it still ain't no place for women and children. Yep, popped up from the soil overnight, just like Tombstone and Deadwood. And just like them camps, a man's life ain't worth a dog's hind leg. But yes, some are getting rich. I'll give 'm that. I just never struck no gold, so I'm headed out."

"Sorry to hear that. Say, is there an easier route into Cripple Creek?" I asked, as Caleb crawled up my leg. "They told us Ute Pass was twice the distance, so we took this road instead."

"Well, twice the distance, but half the climb," he explained. "They're drivin' Texas longhorns up the Ute Pass every day. Supplying all the mountain towns. Even got standard gauge up through it now. I'm surprised to see a family like yourn on this old skid road. Yer not from around here, I can see."

"No, sir. Came in from Jackson County, Missoura. We lit out within a Sabbath of our decision," I said, hoping to expand the conversation. The man fidgeted so much it seemed impossible to get a jaw started up. "Tied down this here wagon and cut out. Nothing to hold us there."

"And Pa's gonna open a gold mine and get rich!" Caleb added excitedly, sporting a big dirty bandage over his forehead. "There ain't nothin' that can stop my Pa! He can lick anyone."

"Can he, then?" The man's eyebrows rose, which only invited little Caleb to more bravado.

"My Pa can kill a bear with a sword!"

"Thank you, Caleb," I said, patting his head. "But I don't know now. This is some kind of territory. Never expected this. Can a man make any kind of living in these wild territories?"

11

The man shrugged without reply. He cast looks down the twisted trail, his eye returning only for brief conversation, and then back again. With the sun waining, and worsening weather, he seemed eager to reach town. I couldn't blame him.

"If ya 'spect to get rich up there, good luck," he said with a doubtful smirk. "Few have. Well, I got to make Colorado City. Snow's comin'. Jes watch out for the rough element in Altman, and I hope you know what you are doing. Evening, now."

With that, the man tipped his hat and started trotting down the trail to civilization. But I wondered what he meant. Of course I knew what I was doing.

Or so I thought.

During the dusty months on the trail, I had scratched out a fine plan for success in the gold fields. Common knowledge in Missoura, mostly based on those handbills, held that gold could be found lying about the hills of Colorado, and that a man could become rich by just picking up the nuggets. They said other nuggets lay just below the surface, and could be had with only a pick and shovel or a plow if you had one handy.

This whole mountain glittered with flecks of color, surely a sign of greater wealth up in the high country. Just eyeing a handful of the silvery dust lifted my spirits for what lay ahead. But why bother with paltry flakes when nuggets lay up the mountain? When we reached Cripple Creek, I would stake a claim and become a millionaire, just like that Stratton fellow. According to the yellow paper in my calloused hands it was just about that easy. No "rough element" in Altman would bother me, I thought. I'd seen enough of that in Jackson County.

But with the territory we'd witnessed so far, I questioned whether we were suited for it. Were we sowing the wind, only to reap a whirlwind of regret?

Just as I pondered the new information a wall of snow dropped in over the mountain and jarred me back to the present. Thick ice-fog swept in from the west, slicing temperatures down another thirty degrees. A velvety blanket soon covered the ground scrub, thick enough to hide a dead marmot twenty yards across the plateau. In the excitement of the moment, the boys played and swiped at flakes just as I realized we faced the real danger of exposure. The few sticks we'd gathered would be inadequate.

I ran to the wagon for our winter coats, splitting open a crate with an iron crowbar. Just as I turned my back, gales tossed me over, and then blew our canvas tent to the far end of the clearing.

I could only curse and wonder what new calamity this hostile place had ready for us. Were Missoura flatlanders forbidden in a place like this? Would we be shooed away like a few prairie hens? With my indignation for this place renewed, I determined to leave as soon as we could. Maybe I, too, could get work in Colorado City.

What was it? The Standard Mill. Yeah, that place.

We scrambled to tie down the flapping canvas. Would twenty hemp ropes do? No, twenty five. And a spool of drawn wire. Sideways snow attacked our eyes. Fingers, toes, and lips became unworkable blocks of ice. Winds tossed the cast-iron cook pot over. Its hot contents sprayed across the white ground. Only when the slashing winds tired of their little handiwork would they permit a moment's rest.

With the tent finally wired down, I pointed a stiff finger at Micah. "Get some wood on that fire!"

"Yes, Pa," he said, and then immediately pulled Caleb into the job.

With the fire roaring twice as high, we dived into the tent for a little relief. I opened my coat and stretched it around Caleb. Patricia did the same for Micah. Four sets of eyes peered out the canvas slit into an opaque whiteout.

"So this is Colorado!" I said, warming up the boys. Within minutes, we were asleep under a pile of wool blankets.

I slumbered in a dark world of swirling dreams as powerful winds lashed the mountain pines and craggy heights.

Morning came with a thick blanket of warm sunshine, and thirty inches of new snow. Light powder had drifted up to six feet. Other spots were windswept and barren. Deep snow buried our little tent. A deep hole remained where the big fire had burned all night.

The spring snow suffocated massive Ponderosa pines, pulling their lowest branches to the ground, and producing plump satin pillows on their boughs. Down in the valley, miles of evergreens glazing with layers of ice could be taken for a sea of cotton. Sparkling crystal lay over every tree, bush, and rock, multiplying the sun's rays. It came up at us like a winter wonderland, the likes of which I had never seen, even in the picture books.

The children romped like puppies in the new-fallen powder, unaware of the conditions for our departure. As high noon passed, with play-tunnels dug and snowmen fought and conquered, I understood that we would not be leaving for home today. Jackson County, or Colorado City, would have to wait. Even with this beauty, I wanted no part of this country and would leave without a tear. I could not abide this jealous place.

But maddening days came and went. Nothing moved on this mountain. Except the budding aspen. Daily thaws and nightly freezes produced what might pass as a bulletproof shield of ice. The bogged load would not move no matter how hard I lashed the mule in anger.

"I'm getting tired of this," I complained loudly over breakfast. Patricia only shrugged, returning to her chores. "It's overcast again this morning and it froze again last night. Look at that snowdrift."

She didn't even turn.

So I yanked the Peacemaker and blew a half-dozen holes into the bulletproof ice. The reckless act was too much for Patricia, who lit into me like a schoolmarm with a chokecherry switch.

"Put that away! Is that the way you want those boys to handle a weapon? Like cowboys on a Saturday night? Can't you see they're watching every move their daddy makes? They got eyes. Stop feeling sorry for yourself and put that nasty old pistol away."

"Well, I can't stand this. What are we doing here?"

"All right then. If you're so dead set on leaving, then we'll go, but I told you what I think," she said, stamping off.

But time passes even in a place like this. Self-pity slowly melted into new visions of the gold fields up yonder. I even lost the will to rebuke myself for the blind ambition that had landed us in this awful place. A double-minded man is unstable in all his ways. Every warm afternoon found me dreamily returning to my mining operation in all its glory. With healing time, we left our little aspen resort and headed up the trail again.

We soon learned that five hundred pounds of dry goods exceeded one tired mule's capacity. I reluctantly unloaded another hundred pounds of our belongings onto the roadside. My mind flashed back to the littered alkaline plains of Kansas, where luxuries slowly bleached in the scorching sun, awaiting their owner's return. We would either make it light, or die in the effort.

Pikes Peak or Bust!

Black Jack faithfully trudged up the mountain road under the heavy load. With the mule's strength nearly gone, we ascended the last onerous ledge of granite where we could see the Mollie Kathleen headframe a mile in the distance. Civilization lay within reach. The relief was enormous.

"Look Pa!" Micah shouted, scrambling higher onto the rig for a better view. "What is that big wooden thing? It's so huge! And what's that wheel on top?"

"Take your seat, son, before you fall off like Caleb. We'll see soon enough. But I reckon it's one of those mines they tell about. You just take your seat and we'll see."

"Pa's going to get rich and buy the place!" Caleb put in.

The massive wooden headframe used to hoist ore from the depths of the mine drew us in with excitement. It towered a hundred feet into the sky, peaking over the tallest Ponderosa pines – the tallest thing we had ever seen. Long green timbers formed a large open structure, like the new oil derricks that had begun to pop up in the South. We could scarcely take our eyes from it.

As we drew up, a small sign pegged to a sprawling wall of wooden cribbing read, "Altman 2 Miles." Next to it a rutted switchback led up another mountain to the south, presumably to the town of Altman. But we pressed the mule onward for that grand structure ahead.

As we passed the little sign, a wince of worry struck my eyes as if some harm lay up that twisted mountain road. The hurried man on the

15

trail had mentioned his enemies in Altman, and the mere sight produced a quick lurch in my gut. I was happy to pass the sign and be on our way, pushing the premonition from my thoughts.

We reached the top of a summit near the Molly Kathleen where the view opened up again. This time it included a vast network of civilization bristling with activity.

From that new vantage opened a fifteen-mile swell of white canvas, railways, glory holes and headframes. We saw with what strength remained the lively gold camp that was to be our new home, Cripple Creek, Colorado.

Chapter Two

A FIFTEEN-MILE RING of mountains on the back side of Pikes Peak meandered along like the eroded rim of an ancient volcano. The Cripple Creek mining district lay in the basin below. It was a grand sight to be sure, the reward of two months on the trail, and a passel of tribulations.

"Patricia. Just look at that place," I said. "I never expected so many people. Just like you, I pictured jagged mountains, some renegade Indians, and a whole lot of empty space. But it's so busy. I guess the man on the trail was right."

My jaw practically hung open as we studied the mining camp six hundred feet below.

Patricia's eyes widened. "Yeah..."

"There must be a thousand tents and twice as many cabins and buildings down there. Are we going to make it here?" I asked, shifting a little in my seat.

In the sea of activity, mule teams hauled lumber from the dense eastern hills. Steam engines arrived and departed without interval. Supply lines to and from the camp may have even exceeded those of the Union Army at Gettysburg, of which my granddaddy had made notable mention. Three dozen stamp mills pounded out a rhythm, filling the valley with a roar unmatched by any industrial operation I had ever seen.

17

"Make it here?" Patricia said. "I hope so. Look at all those mines. Do you think you'll be able to start one with all those others? And where will we live? In one of those bleached white tents?" We both sat in silence at the overwhelming bustle and commotion.

Hundreds of glory holes dotted the hills, staggering the imagination for what riches lay within them. A twisted and rutted wagon trail led down from the Mollie Kathleen, through switchbacks to the center of camp. Winding around piles of mine tailings and wooden cribbing, we passed through thick clouds of smoke, rife with the draft of coal and wood-fired furnaces. A broken wooden sign read 9,494 Elevation.

Makeshift rail cars and strong-backed men ferried cargo to unknown destinations. But I saw nothing special in the rock they guarded so carefully. It looked exactly like the Pikes Peak granite we had seen on the old freighter's road. No sparkle? No gold? Just rock, as far as I could tell. What could the trained eye see that I could not? How could a man tell good from bad? And what of the nuggets strewn about the territory? These questions dominated my anxious mind on the slow descent into town.

We passed the Colorado Midland Terminal situated at the east end of Bennett Avenue. Smoke and steam blasted from the enormous engines, which slung cars along delicate mountain ridgelines, departing with precious loads of ore bound for the Ute Pass and Colorado City. No sooner did one engine steam up the pass than the next chugged in to take its place. The industrial efficiency alone thrilled us, especially after months trekking through the Kansas and Colorado grasslands.

A right turn at the Midland Terminal, and we were heading straight down the main street.

Bennett Avenue.

Tall square-façade pine-board structures jostled for choice spots along the angled street, where hordes of citizens scurried about, busy with important matters. Busy building their own empires.

Endless black-on-white advertising seemed to call out as if to say, "Stop here weary traveler! Get your supplies here. Open an account here."

And it was not just the advertising that cried out for attention. Peddlers and pitchmen sought to engage with carefully crafted messages, mostly selling want over substance. One such fellow called out as we lumbered up the avenue amidst a rank odor from his establishment.

"Greetings, traveler!" the man hailed. "I'm Johnny Nolan! I've got the best Irish whiskey in camp. Come on in for a free taste. That is if ye can leave the wife and wee sprouts a spell. Aye, and there's a fine match of fisticuffs about to commence. If you don't see some black blaggard's lips fly off, then you ain't seen the best Irish boxing in Cripple Creek. Dynamite Dick and Lew Joslin, the 'Leadville Blacksmith' is both here today. Come on in."

He waved broadly. "It's a bucket o' blood!"

I just smiled, touched my hat, and passed by without a word. I'd never seen a man dispense free whiskey, or any such means of entertainment. I figured if a tenth of the men passing through took him up on the offer, he emptied no small number of barrels. Mr. Nolan must have been a man of means to offer it so freely. But the sights of Bennett Avenue were enough for me today.

Rows of shiny red shovels peered out through rippled supply store windows. Picks, axes, hammers, bits, nitro, and all manner of mining implements waited for enthusiastic fortune hunters to snatch them up. One mercantile offered deafening exhibitions of nitroglycerin out back. A restaurant displayed a neatly painted shingle offering fresh Alaskan crab and New England lobster. Pushcarts with hot beefsteaks and onions, roasting goober peas, and assorted cooked candies vied for consideration. Even a dog team with a little musical calliope trotted past, towing a large billboard-cart advertising necessary goods for the smart prospector. It was more like a carnival than the main street of a respectable town. In every direction, hotels, saloons, cafes, and assay offices thrived on Bennett Avenue, each competing vigorously for the eyeballs of its busy citizens.

"Pa! Look!" Micah entreated. "Caleb wants one of those big red lollipops. They're only a nickel." He practically pulled me off the seat to consider a purchase, although, I could see Caleb just waking up from a

19

long nap in the back. With our tight finances, we had no room for such extravagances. Food and shelter would be our priorities.

The contrasts to rural Missoura became immediately evident, and I too could hardly keep my seat on the wagon as it rumbled up the busy street. Missoura had been a lean existence where most folks lived on a dirt-floor with scarcely a change of clothing. The folks I knew lived off corn pone and sow belly, not crab and lobster. I'd never actually seen a lobster, and considered the slippery critters inedible. Still, there they sat for sale on the same street as the latest Paris fashions. I could only imagine that the folks in Cripple Creek must be a far sight richer than the country folk of Jackson County. Perhaps one day my efforts would treat Patricia to a taste of that life. But for now, we enjoyed the sights of modern civilization quite capitally.

Perhaps my senses were only temporarily overwhelmed, but a nervous energy surged through me as though positioned at the starting gate of some grand race, being surrounded by so great a cloud of witnesses. Would I have the fortitude to win such a race, or even finish with the laggards? Could I compete with the likes of these lobster-eating city folks, with their education and expertise?

After taking our fill of Bennett Avenue, Patricia spotted a wide place to spin the rig around. We needed a place to stay. As I wrestled the wagon, a half-dozen well-dressed men greeted us at the west end of town. They sported new derby hats, fine cravats, and brightly polished shoes. The leader quickly approached the dusty and creaking wagon to speak.

"That's a fine rig, Pilgrim, but you appear to be minus a mule. You here to stay or just passing through?" He smiled widely enough to expose a perfect set of pearly teeth, a rare sight in my part of the country.

His black hair flowed smoothly with an ample supply of hair tonic, and his chiseled face was clean and groomed. From his direction came the fine scent of French toilette water. Could have been a politician.

Indeed the harness intended to yoke a pair of animals to the wagon visibly drooped to the left, obviously missing half the mule team.

It was a sore spectacle to anyone with an eye to see, but had gotten the job done.

"Mister, you smell," little Caleb put in, still groggy from the nap and unable to identify the unfamiliar odor from the man.

"That'll be enough, little man," Patricia corrected, flushed with embarrassment at the forward child. "You'll speak only when spoken to. Now, take your seat before you get a whooping."

"Yep, lost a mule down the trail," I answered. "It was a grim incident for sure, but we made it. And we're here to stay. Say, has this town got a rooming house with a bath?" I asked, hoping to satisfy our necessities for the evening. We'd been on the trail for more days than I could number, and it was high time for a little comfort.

"Yes sir, fourteen of them," said the man. "And you'll find any one a pleasant convenience."

I tipped my hat. "Thank you. Which do you—"

"Say, Pilgrim, I'm looking for a good man, and I need him in a hurry," he burst out, turning the conversation to his own apparent needs. "If you'd consider rounding up a few cowboys and signing on with me, I'd see you get a replacement for the missing animal and a fine bed."

"Well—" I began, but the man wasn't listening.

"I need some work done fast, and I need a little muscle behind it. I'll pay cash on the barrelhead."

My eyes flinched.

Even while perched atop the big wagon, at least three feet above the well-dressed man, I still felt a little lower. He was a gentleman of stature and made that clear, but I just couldn't take a comfortable angle to the man. His sudden proposal of cash money rang a little hollow for my tastes. Although I suppose it might have sounded pretty inviting to most fellows coming into camp and looking to get established.

"No sir, I make my own way. But thank you just the same," I said, forcing myself to stay the course I'd laid out. Employment with another outfit would only jeopardize my plans. We came here to open a gold mine and make money, and that dream would never happen at the beck and call of another. If I was to pull myself up by the shoe leather, it would be on my own terms.

21

"Well ain't you an independent fellow!" he said with a snap of the head, glancing back to the other men who all agreed quickly. "Well good luck to you then. But once you get settled in and signed on somewhere, we'll swing by to sign you up for the miner's union. We need good men like you. My name's Chuck Moyer. I make sure all the men sign on with the union."

Chuck Moyer. Yep, could have been a politician.

I reached down to shake hands. "Jeremiah Clark. Thank you for the offer. I guess we'll be gettin' on. Gonna open a gold mine."

"Gold mine, eh?"

"Yessir."

Moyer's lip twitched.

"Listen Pilgrim, you aren't going to be any trouble, are you? Since that incident last year, we've run a tidy little operation up here, and we aim to keep it that way. We put those mine owners back in their place and things are operating just fine now. Watch your step up here. That's just a small piece of free advice from someone who knows."

Another flinch. "Thank you, sir."

"Well, have a pleasant afternoon Pilgrim. We'll be seeing you," he finished, signaling the lower minions to cross the wide dirt street in search of the cowboys he evidently needed.

Although he had missed the mark with me, he seemed a determined man, used to getting his way. He'd find the men he sought, one way or another. But it didn't concern me. I wouldn't be signing on with anybody, including Mr. Moyer.

I soon learned a thing or two about lodging in Cripple Creek. A rope bed in a lean-to could run a dollar a day, while a straw pallet or an empty bench or a pool table went for fifty cents – if you were fortunate enough to find one. After weeks on a dusty trail tending a team of lathered mules, we were determined to have a proper bed and bath. I soon learned there were none to be had.

But Patricia would not be put off.

"Jeremiah, I don't want to be a bother," she said shyly. "You've worked so hard to get us here, and I appreciate that, but I want a bath tonight. My hair is an owl's nest, and just look at my black fingers. I hate being dirty, and I hate this old wagon. And I won't sit in front of a dirty campfire another night. I just want a room with four walls, and I don't care how much they cost. They must have something we can afford. Let's keep looking, can we?"

Patricia's words riled my feelings, and I could not refuse her unhappy eyes. We'd find one, and before the cock crowed for sundown. I would see to that.

And then like a miracle, only one block south of Bennett, we stumbled into a beautiful new parlour house named The Old Homestead, where as newcomers I negotiated an entire room for a dollar a night! It had been vacated only an hour ago. The beautiful ladies at the house were so accommodating that we felt at home. They considered our Southern ways quaint and doted on us like kin, fetching water and soap, and exotic foods I'd never even tasted before. That night we learned that Myers Avenue was not exactly a family-oriented place, but accepted the room as a blessing, and stayed a week.

In beds!

We had arrived in Cripple Creek with a grubstake of $128 in Double Eagle gold coin and federal script borrowed from every family we knew. So, even big red lollipops for a nickel were out of the question. Paper brought only seventy cents on the dollar. Here, gold coin was king. And if a man were foolish enough to produce an old greenback or Confederate dollar, he'd be laughed to scorn. I hoped the grubstake would last six months, and planned to produce the yellow magic as soon as possible. But I quickly learned that my gold mining ideas were as bad off as the old mule.

"That ain't gold," Pearl de Vere at the Old Homestead informed me, eyeing a bag of silvery dust taken from the freighter's trail. "It's nothin' but mica. We got lots of that. And there ain't no nuggets in this whole territory."

I adjusted my hat. "No? But what about panning that creek, yonder. Any gold—"

"What, Cripple Creek? That little ditch?"

I pointed to the little creek up the gulch. "I could pan that—"

"Look, mister, this here's a hard rock mining camp. They blast solid granite to get the gold. And there's only about an ounce in every ton of ore. They don't pan gold here neither. I'm sorry for what you was told in Missouri."

"Well, where do you recommend I start?"

"Try the Lonely Lode Saloon. You'll get plenty of advice there. Just stay clear of Altman and Bull Hill. Somethin' ain't right up there."

The news stung; it was nothing like the handbills in Missoura had claimed. I never imagined scratching through a ton of rock for a single ounce of gold. Was that even possible?

"Pa, you and I'll start up that gold mine," little Caleb offered eagerly. "It don't matter what them ugly old hags said. Besides, they got funny dresses that show their underbritches. They don't know nothin'."

"Thank you, Caleb," I said, rubbing his head and smiling. "You sure are an eager one. You get that from your mama?"

"Yeah, I guess." He grew bored and looked around for some fun. "I'm going to play in the ditch now!"

Micah cocked his head. "Ma says them ladies is just advertising, and not to look. What's that mean, Pa?"

I laughed. "I guess it means not to look, son." I mussed his hair, and he walked off as confused as ever.

All I knew was that I was finished with the poverty of the plow. And determined to succeed, regardless of what the ladies said. I figured I only needed a little advice to get started, which is how I came to meet old Sam Whitman at the Lonely Lode Saloon. He was the type that liked funny dresses and lady's underbritches.

"Ha! You best go on and git yer sleep, boys. Cause you ain't whippin' this old coot tonight. These hearts an' diamonds is as red as a tinder box," Sam hollered, flinging a winning hand onto the saloon table for all to admire.

It was hard to miss Sam.

"Yeah, y'all go on and git yer mama's ta tuck ya in now, cause I ain't no nursemaid to a peck a early risin' church boys!"

I soon learned that saloons outnumbered hotels four to one, and that they were the only places to learn the mining business. In between hands, Sam set me straight on gold mining and camp customs. He had turned the dirt with Ed Schieffelin down in Tombstone in '88, and dealt Faro with the Earp brothers at the Crystal Palace. He claimed to have been shot on two occasions during the war, and then again in Tombstone, freely offering this as evidence for an awkward limp.

"I'll whip yer one-legged granny in a footrace any day but Sunday," he had boasted with a wide grin. "Fetch her on out here!"

What he lacked in mobility, he made up for in rough-mannered magnetism. With an old gutta-percha cane and a confident swagger, he rode herd over the green cowboys at the all-night poker tables. The ladies loved him, and he loved the ladies. Sam could attract a crowd anywhere, producing tall tales of daring feats from bygone times. He was a product of the Wild West, which by now seemed like another era. After all, we were about to enter the twentieth century.

I learned that Sam had lingered about the saloons of Cripple Creek for the past few years on little more than quick wit and an abundant supply of companions. Upon meeting him, I wondered why he had not staked a claim of his own and gotten rich like the rest. He certainly had a nose for sniffing out the profitable claims and ditching the losers, and offered ample advice to the hordes of grubstake prospectors like me. They all found their way to old Sam just as I had. By this time, his advice had likely produced a million dollars in gold profits, and men freely offered drinks and meals at every saloon.

Perhaps this life of ease had stalled his entry into the gold mining business. He simply did not need to work, and perhaps that suited him just fine. He could have hung out a shingle, but why go to the effort? Business came to him.

But I knew Sam kept an eye peeled for a venture that suited his pleasures. I believe he offered his advice for that very reason, scouting for a partner and a challenge to sharpen his teeth on. And as with all prospectors racing into town at this time, Sam Whitman offered his advice to me. I received it at 3 AM, a week after pulling into town, the only time I could catch Sam alone.

Sam moseyed up to the bar. He raised an amber glass and proclaimed loudly, "Juice fer me joints!" and threw back the drink with expert precision. He turned a blinking eye to me and asked, "What can I do fer ya', son?"

"Well, Mr. Whitman, you offered your advice on the business," I reminded him. Sam had been busy at cards all evening, and requested I stop by when the playing was done. That was nine hours earlier. "How do I stake a claim?" I asked.

"Oh yes!" he said. "Claims are registered at the assay offices on Bennett Avenue. That's the big street you came in on. The property is staked and roped, then registered at d' office."

I straightened up to listen. "Okay."

"Any claim unattended for even an hour is considered abandoned and fair game, and will sure as your knickers be registered under a new owner. You got to watch fer claim jumpers. Don't hesitate to put a bullet into one of 'em, but whatever you do, keep 'em off your land. They know to stay off another man's claim so you got the plain right to shoot 'em. You hear me?"

"Yessir," I said, although I didn't care much for the shooting part.

"But if ya find yourself dead and lookin' up at the pearly gates of Saint Peter, then you know you was the one doin' the trespassing. Ya understand? It's a simple rule."

"I don't have a lot of time for prospecting," I said. "My grubstake won't last long. Only got about–"

"Yeah," he said, rubbing his bearded chin and cocking his head to spit. A sign above the bar said "No Spittin on the Flor," and Sam was careful to mind it.

Tink.

Sam's dark stream hit the brass spittoon from a distance of two and a half feet.

"Normally, a man'll prospect for years lookin' for mineral traces what suggests a possible ore lode. Like old Bob Womack done. But don't waste yer spit. And don't waste time with assays and geologists and so-called experts that'll jus rob yer last dollar and leave ya suckin' yer thumb. That's the mistake they all make. That gold is in the ground, sure 'nuf, so git out there and git you a piece o' that land, 'fore it's gone. I learnt that at Tombstone, and I learnt it here too. Jes get some land, anywhere in this here territory."

"Okay... Assuming I can, what's next?"

"Well, git ya a four-pound hammer and a dozen bits from McGunthry's Hardware and commence ta drillin. When ya got a twelve inch hole, load her up with nitro. Ah, got tobacco? Stuff 'er in your ears and turn yer head while she blows. McGunthry will give ya a lesson if ya don't know how. If ya dig your way to China, then ya know ya gone too fer. Look for grayish rock and pink crystal, and show me a piece of what ya find. I'll let ya know when ya strike the motherlode."

I edged in, expecting more.

Sam's expressions cooled. "That's enough for now. Now git out thar or you'll be lickin' yer chops somethin' fierce come winter."

Indeed, it was enough to get started. Finished with the lesson, Sam turned back to the saloonkeeper with an angry stare. "What is this dark swill, sheep dip? What happened ta the good stuff y'all had last week?"

The bartender shrugged and walked away.

I took Sam's advice, but staking a claim was no trivial undertaking. Months of studying claim charts and stomping the rugged territory yielded nothing but blisters. Summer passed into fall, and still nothing. At least we had a rented shack for winter. That is, if we could still make the payments by then.

Patricia was happy for that. She finished dinner on the little potbelly and sat down with us to eat.

"Caleb, you need to let me know when you're going to be gone so long." she warned. "You stayed out all day today."

"I'm not a baby, mom. I'm six, you know."

"Oh, okay little mountain man. Eat your beets, now." She turned to me and forced a smile. "Any luck staking a claim today, Honey?"

I stirred the beets. "Tomorrow's another day!"

Chapter Three

WITH TIME RUNNING THIN, providence finally came from the
most unlikely source – little Caleb who had busied himself hunting
squirrels and rabbits all day long. $128 didn't last long in a place like this.

"Pa! You'll get a lickin' with them muddy boots." Caleb warned,
pointing down. "Ma says you might just as well drop your britches. She
took a green switch to me when I done it."

"Well, alright! I reckon you're right about that, Caleb. Ma don't
wait around for explanations does she? Come outside and help me scrape
'm clean, son. You've just saved me from the mean stick," I said,
mustering a faint smile but exhausted from another fruitless venture into
the barren hills. Maybe Patricia was right. Maybe we'd be up on our luck
soon, but I saw no evidence of that. This territory held no sympathy for
would-be prospectors without the will to survive.

"I know what you're looking for, Pa," Caleb said, poking a stick
into the deep cracks of the old boots, carefully prying out the stubborn
muck.

"Well, good son, help me get all the mud out so we can get some
of Ma's vittles before they get cold. She don't cotton to late arrivals."

"No, not your boots, I know what you're looking for up there."
Caleb turned and pointed. "I killed a rabbit up the hill a piece, and I

found the gold mine. I know where it is, and I'll show you. If you don't believe me, I'll show you tomorrow."

I looked up the hill, hiding my disbelief.

"Well, I'll take you up on that, son," I said. "We'll go right out tomorrow morning 'fore the chickens leave the roost, but right now, let's get some grub. Ma sure can do miracles with rabbit stew."

While Micah attacked his pages with a burning fury, Caleb evidently became quite a little man of the field. I suppose for every hour I tramped the rugged hills of Cripple Creek, little Caleb did the same – maybe to emulate his daddy.

And just as he had promised the day before, he had not only found the spot, but it seemed the only unclaimed wedge of property in the area. I couldn't believe my eyes – he had done it.

I quickly staked off the tiny spot and documented its location on one of the old yellow handbills for proof.

"That's it, boy! You've found it all right."

Situated up the hill from the town of Independence, almost to Altman, the claim sat three miles southeast of Cripple Creek. The town of Victor lay a mile and a half south, and Goldfield was a stone's-throw down the hill to the east. I could see all the mining camps below, including the big headframes at the Independence and Teresa Mines.

Scrub oak covered the little sliver of land that appeared good for nothing but a hedgerow and garbage dump. Struggling past the tangled brush and rusted cans where Caleb had killed his rabbit, I realized he had somehow hit the jackpot. This was my lucky strike. Or, our lucky strike, in fairness to little Caleb and his rabbit hunting skills.

I saw no gold on the surface, but Sam had said "If ya find a little crystal rock outcroppin' with a gray streak, thars yer gold." In these times, you took a few things on faith. You grabbed your piece of the action and believed. Who knew what riches lay beneath the soil? You just had to believe.

Monday morning found me in line on Bennett Avenue. Fifty anxious men stood shifting foot to foot in the early morning air, eagerly waiting for the metal doors to fly open. Some would file claims; others held bags of ore for testing or to be cashed in for a little whiskey money.

I was so excited I must have looked as bouncy as a three-legged puppy on a short leash. In a few short minutes I would be in the gold mining business. My fears of failure would end, and I would make good to the kinfolk who had waved us out of town in disbelief.

I opened a hand, and in slid a pick mining claim.

Strutting proudly out of the office, I went straight to the saloons to find Sam. After months of searching and without a Morgan dollar to my name, I offered Sam a tenth share of the Black Jack Mine up on Battle Mountain where Winfield Stratton had struck it rich.

"Battle Mountain?" he asked.

"Yessir," I said. "Battle Mountain. Is that good?"

Sam rolled his eyes and turned back to the curious bartender who raised a bushy gray eyebrow in obvious interest.

"Well, they say them tenderfoot miners is pullin' out gold with pitchforks and plows up 'ere."

Sam was not impressed. "I was the one that spun that yarn. It ain't true."

I pressed for an answer while he considered the offer. Independence on Battle Mountain was definitely a good location, and if I'd actually staked a claim up there then he wanted in, but he wasn't about to gush over it in front of me. All the big mines were up there – the Portland, the Vindicator, the Independence, and the big Theresa Mine. It was the hottest spot on that mountain. Sam would definitely want a piece of that action.

"Come back tomorra' son, and I'll let ya know," Sam answered dryly, as he turned around, winking at the bartender. "Bring a little more of that rock outcropping, and I'll think on her a piece."

Sam was an honest man, and after some maneuvering I had a willing partner. He was at least twenty years my senior, and as a younger man had taken his fill of wild living after the war, and later in the silver mining business. He reminded me of Uncle Olin. In Tombstone, Sam had been a millionaire on paper, but I had no idea what that meant.

We studied the claim together and decided our next order of business would be getting underground before the snows.

"We got us a partner," I whispered, slipping into the cornshuck bed at a quarter to four.

"What?" Patricia slurred, still half asleep. "A partner? That's nice, dear. Sam agreed?"

"Yep, start work on a windlass tomorrow. And you can operate it with Black Jack if you like. I want the boys to learn a trade, and this is as good as any."

"Well okay, if you want," she whispered, and then moved on to another subject that had evidently caught her interest. "I heard of a fella living in Colorado Springs who knows the Cantrell's back in Randall's Flats. Isn't that amazing? I want you to meet him."

I kissed her and settled in for sleep, secretly hoping for a few more kisses. "Okay. Who is he?"

"He's a big Yankee general. A Blue Belly, but someone who actually knows your uncle. I don't know how. But I'm dead tired, so leave me be," she said, immediately falling back to sleep.

I pondered this Northern general for a while, deciding it didn't matter now; I'd be hoisting buckets of gold come morning!

I knew that Cripple Creek miners were deeply suspicious and vocally opposed to any women on mine property, not to mention operating a hoist. Most simply would not tolerate it, especially the Cornish who claimed to see Tommyknockers and interpret their knocking within the rock walls of the mines. I supposed there wasn't much point in tempting fate with things known to be bad luck, and a female on mine property was one of them. Nevertheless, it was my operation, and I'd run it any way I liked.

I worked as the Black Jack Mine powdermonkey, mixing nitro at night and bunking with the solution to keep it within stable temperature range for the next day. I quickly found that nitro in the bed has a way of keeping a man lonely at night. But those were the sacrifices one made for fame and fortune. And like a fool for adventure, I gladly accepted the hazardous duty. Of course, I never gave a thought to the danger it posed to my family.

Too much adventure.

Sam posted a sign for a workforce I soon learned we could not pay. He said it made the operation look legitimate, and had obtained some literary help from Winfield Stratton who came up the hill to greet us. Sam didn't read or write.

He stood back to admire their work. "Right purty, ain't she?"

The sign read:

> "Men wanted: $3 a day, 8 hours. Bring your own equipage: candles, candle picks, hammers, bits, muck sticks, and picks. Powder and fuse cords free."

"It's nice to meet you, Clark," Stratton said. "If you need anything, I'm spittin' distance down that hill. See that cabin next to the Independence headframe? That's me. I was the first one up here on Battle Mountain. Besides Bob Womack, that is. But he was down in Poverty Gulch, up a piece from Myers Avenue, you know. I've made a good living, and I 'spect you will too. It's rich country."

I extended a hand. "Thank you, sir."

"Most of these men up here are common folk just like me. I was a carpenter in Colorado Springs. Spencer Penrose, Charles Tutt, Bob Womack – all common folk – herdsmen, blacksmiths, horse traders, and the like. That's what makes this place great. They've gotten rich out of sheer luck, although one could argue, a dogged tenacity to fight for a thing worth having. If you got grit you'll make it up here too. Again, you let me know if you need anything. Good luck to you now."

We made our initial descent into the earth with little more than blind faith and optimism. For the first fifty feet, I swung a four-pound hammer, singlejacking twelve inch holes, and stuffing them with a powder charge and fuse cord. I twisted the bit a quarter turn with each stroke, and rock slowly gave way to blasting depth. When finished hand-steeling a hole, I set powder to blast. Packing a moist twist of tobacco into each ear before a blast, I pressed downward, foot by bloody foot, repeating the endless routine in ever-increasing agony.

Broken knuckles. Skinned fingers. Blisters.

While the hard work put me out as soon as my head hit the hay, Sam maintained a vigorous nightlife. A tenth share at the Black Jack Mine would certainly not preclude that, although he was apt to find himself in a scrape or two at the establishments he frequented. Sam shared the story of one such evening, as he sat gabbing with a saloonkeeper. Two tough customers had come in looking for Sam, and they weren't there for cards.

Above the big mirror at the Lonely Lode Saloon hung a tattered Confederate Stars and Bars flag. Sam liked it there, mostly because of that ratty old flag. He claimed it flew over Valverde and Apache Canyon, but I didn't know where that was.

The men had burst through the door. "Hey old man, we understand you got yourself a new claim up on Battle Mountain. They say you got a new partner. A sodbuster from Missouri, we hear."

"Yessir," Sam replied cheerfully, spinning on the stool. "We're haulin' fortunes out of a big hole up thar. But if you boys are lookin' to get a piece of the action, I ain't the man to talk to."

Sam eyed the men from head to toe and finished wryly, "But you 'ol boys don't look the type." Sam could see the two were not there to obtain shares in the Black Jack Mine. They had other business on their minds. Judging them quickly, he just spun back around and resumed his drink.

"Listen here, you old coot. We ain't finished with you yet," the lead man said, irritated at Sam's maneuver. "You two ain't joined up with the union yet. Ol' Billy Johnson down at the Golden Spike says your man came struttin' out of the assay office like a day at the picture show, and he ain't even checked in with Mr. Moyer yet. We're here to see you two boys get signed up. You got plans to take care of that piece o' business anytime soon?"

Sam turned back around with an impatient eye. "No sir, we ain't. We may hire a few of your ignorant ore muckers. Or maybe we won't. How's that suit ya, sonny? Now quit yer jabbering and get to the horsemeat."

Sam didn't ordinarily go out of his way to offend, but when he saw a fight coming there wasn't any point in dawdling. You might just as well get to it.

The lead man tipped the blue-steel barrel of his Winchester up, intending to proceed with his threats until he got the job done. He had employed such tactics before, and they worked well with other men of lesser resolve. No one did business in Cripple Creek without the miner's union.

No one.

But Sam was no man for intimidation. He simply jerked the weapon from the man's weak grasp and slapped him across the cheekbone with the flat side of the wooden stock. The swift blow knocked the man over, and sent the other back a step in surprise. Sam had learned a few treacherous maneuvers in the war as a younger man, and was no hombre to mess with.

The man bent down to pick up a tooth.

"Now listen here, fellers," Sam said, raising his voice only slightly. "I came in here for a drink and some lively conversation. That's about all. Now you 'ol boys can join me if you like, but I will not tolerate such behavior. But, I don't reckon yer here fer that. I seen yer type in Tombstone, and I ain't yer kind a customer. So, if you got nothin' else to say, gents, I expect you'll trot on out o' here and leave me to my pleasures."

The men eyed him angrily but stood down.

"Don't come around here again, or you'll git a belly full of what yer coddlin' fer. Is that clear as spit?"

Satisfied the men had gotten the message, Sam offered the weapon back to the lead man, who accepted it with one hand while favoring his bruised cheek with the other. They shuffled out the door without a word.

Sam had handled the men like any pair of ruffians spoiling for a bar fight. After all, any two healthy men picking a fight with an old man deserved what they got. And Sam was only too happy to oblige. For him, it amounted to little more than swatting gnats on a hot afternoon. It was all part of the nightly routine.

The next day, Sam returned to the mine without a word of the incident, which to him was not worth mentioning. I learned the details later when he shared the story, but for now I was too busy nursing bloody knuckles to care. Sam simply went back to his duties, instructing me on the business and offering his encouragement for the work ahead.

"You'll know the high-grade when you see her, son," Sam said. "It's dull gray, and packed with the milky white. Maybe a little purple, even. A thin vein of color no wider than a man's finger is an assayer's dream. Watch how she widens out."

"What'll we get for it?" I asked, rubbing my bruises.

"High-grade ore 'll fetch forty bucks a ton in Colorado City, and a one-ton bucket is pretty danged small. We'll be pullin' out a thousand dollars a day when we hit her. Jes keep yer backbone and don't let anyone take it from ya. No matter how rough they look."

I never doubted.

This was a golden era of promise and we couldn't help but strike it rich. I was sure of that now, but it took Sam and Patricia's optimism to get me there. Even so, I still understood little of the process we would follow, and only Sam could help with that.

"I'm still confused," I said after weeks of work. "What exactly is in an assay report? You said we needed them to finance the operation, but why? Can't we just borrow money or sell shares like the other outfits?"

"Clark, you are a New Boot, ain't ya? It ain't that hard. Jes bring a bag of ore down ta the Golden Spike Assay. They'll take yer twenty dollars and hand ya a report the next day. That report will list the parts of gold per ton of ore. They jes weigh it, crush and smelt out the gold, then weigh it again. Simple enough for ya? Well now ya got yer fancy pink paper, and it only costs ya a week's pay."

He paused impatiently. "You got an extra week's pay?"

I knew I didn't.

"But there ain't no processing mill in Colorado City what'll take yer ore 'til ya got a few o' them reports, see? They ain't wastin' mill time on low-grade ore, son. And I don't reckon you can afford to ship it down thar neither. Ya heard what the freighters charge, right? So, ya got ta ship high-grade with the assay sheets, or you ain't doin' no bidnez at all.

"Once you done that fer a while, then yer speculators and banks'll talk. Not until. They ain't got money ta throw at a lame horse. Ya understand, son?"

Sam had just laid down the unwritten laws of gold mining, and it was obvious you couldn't bend them. At least I couldn't find a way. And you couldn't continue operations with a worn out Missoura draft mule and a Civil War cripple neither. Sure, we'd make the hundred-foot level, but only with the necessary capital to back us.

Good luck was also a requirement for any new venture in the gold fields of Cripple Creek, and some said the harder you worked the more you'd get. Given that theory, I was due a little luck of my own, woman or no woman on the premises. Maybe I'd spent all I was due nursing nitro, but I still figured I was owed. Maybe I'd die there in the hole, or I maybe I'd be a millionaire tomorrow.

Chapter Four

"PRAISE JESUS AND REPENT, for the end is near!" thundered a black-clad preacher atop a bandwagon. "Repent of your sins and be ye saved from eternal damnation and fire and brimstone," he shouted as the wagon proceeded down the dank alleyway called Myers Avenue. "Wine is a mocker, strong drink is raging; and whosoever is deceived thereby is not wise!"

I stood there wondering how a gold camp of twenty thousand hard-rock miners managed to muster a monthly parade of thirteen tuba players, ten bass drums, a dozen horns, and two hundred marching men to proclaim the coming of the Lord.

In the face of withering public ridicule.

I had been in camp long enough to know these Myers Avenue types were a scornful bunch. They were not to be trifled with, and they would not permit this intruder an inch of welcome – not in their territory. Without a touch of luck from the Almighty, the man would be dragged from the platform and beaten mercilessly for his words alone. They stood for no preachers on Myers Avenue, and definitely not on a Sunday morning, their only day off.

Strained harmonics from the marching band, now blending with the morning's yellow rays, urged red-eyed men from saloons, opium dens, pool halls, alleyways, and prostitution cribs along the avenue. Men staggered from the night's debauchery and mustered rank and file at the road's edge for a look at the brave souls passing by. I was there for the same reason – minus the night's debaucheries. While up on Carr Avenue, I had weaved across camp to Myers to catch a glimpse for myself.

Pretty awesome.

The men had dozed in their places of depravity for only a few short hours, if at all. They were in no mood for parades. The previous night's activities consisted of wild drinking, riding the oriental dragon, fistfights, exotic shows, and sampling the soiled doves of the evening. It was everything the Women's Temperance Union had warned us of, and despite their pleas for temperance in the camp, the unbridled scenes repeated every Saturday night. And the more the miner's union brought them in, the more intense it got – worse than a Plains cow town. Although a pointless battle, the beleaguered women refused to yield to the forces of darkness.

Skirmishes broke out at the avenue's edge as the band proceeded past. Intoxicated men fell into the path of the oncoming procession but quickly scrambled back to their places of safety. They brawled over an accidental shove, the opportunity for a better view, or a tug off a whiskey bottle loosely clenched by a staggering drunk.

Those men still in the shadows shivered in the morning chill that soon gave way to the Colorado sunshine as it crept into the corners where they stood. Streaks of light now breaking over the heights of Independence and Altman and spilling into the long basin of Poverty Gulch, tortured their weary red eyes. It pushed some deeper in, while drawing others out for an angry look.

It seemed the fiery figure atop the crudely ornamented parade wagon could slay a man with his very gaze. In one hand, he wielded a black leather Bible, and in the other a swagger stick to ward off attacking drunks. He held complete command, acutely aware of the wild crowds on Myers Avenue. I sensed from his words that he had been, in times past, a partaker of the very sins which he now condemned. This was no crimson-robed minister to the wealthy.

He bellowed above the instruments and rabble of the noisy men, "Jesus said whosoever will come after Me, let him deny himself and take up his cross and follow Me! Whatsoever a man soweth, that shall he also reap. Ye are of your father the devil, and the lusts of your father ye will do. Repent therefore and be saved!"

His words sliced like a two-edged sword, dividing asunder soul and spirit. He spoke directly into the hearts of his listeners, bypassing their intoxicated minds as if they were of no account. One dare not make eye contact lest he too be slain by their piercing influence, and surrender his ways to God. While most turned away in disgust, others stared helplessly into his eyes. I stood there too, with a keg of nails in one hand, a coil of rope in the other, and a staggering amazement that one man held such sway over the hearts of men.

Known criminals sank to their knees and pleaded for salvation as the marching band cut a swath through the crowd of onlookers. Mocking bystanders cast derision and tobacco onto the marching men who held ranks as if stoic legionnaires. But not fifty feet passed before another man fell to their gospel spell. Just like the song they now sung, they were "Christian soldiers marching as to war," and no measure of ridicule, mockery, or taunt dissuaded them from their ranks.

From the west side of Myers Avenue to its eastern end deep within Poverty Gulch, in the space of a half-hour, a dozen hardened men abandoned their lives to Jesus. I had witnessed this for the past six months, and each month the marching men increased in number, confounding those who remained to mock.

The procession passed by with all its homespun pomp, ending in the gulch just past the Midland trestle where depravity had reached its zenith. I pondered the man's words on the long walk up the eastward trail to Independence.

Those fallen were the lowest of men: the high-graders, thieves, drunkards, miscreants and malefactors – the ilk of a territorial prison. In the western frontier, such men drifted with the tumbleweed from town to blistering western town, festering as an untended cancer, eating at the flesh of society. During my short time in camp, drifters from the bankrupt remains of the silver busts of Leadville, Aspen, and Tombstone poured into Cripple Creek. They were desperate men seeking a little work and some sinful living to ease their pain after the Panic of '93. With such a flood, I began to fear for the safety of my family.

In addition to these, an army of criminal and rough element deported from the mining camps of Coeur d'Alene, Idaho had seen fit to occupy our gold camp. Sam had warned me of them earlier, as had the man on the freighter's road coming in.

"Back in '85, them Western Federation boys was blowin' up miners in Coeur d'Alene," Sam had said. "Booby traps... infernal devices... satchel charges... They deported six hundred of 'em while I was still in Tombstone. Been ten years but I reckon most are here in camp now. They follow the strikes, ya know. Got a taste for licentious living. You stay clear of 'em."

With Cripple Creek now a boomtown of historical magnitude, Charles Moyer and his Western Federation crew gladly signed them up. These were the cowboys Moyer sought when I met him on Bennett Avenue a year ago. They were the type he could use. That is, until they fell spellbound to the words of a hellfire preacher atop a parade wagon. After that, they were ruined for his purposes. Men like this, and a good share of honest ones had settled into steady employment at the lucrative Cripple Creek mines by 1896.

A kneading-trough of mining labor.

Times were booming and the Black Jack Mine was poised to hit paydirt in the countless underground drifts and veins we had worked for months. Being a God-fearing man myself, I stayed clear of the entertainment opportunities on Myers Avenue. I stubbornly hammered day after day through solid granite to reach the fabled one-hundred-foot level, where the Independence, Portland, and Christmas mines had all struck good ore. At that level lay a meandering paper-thin ribbon of gold just waiting for the first rays of sunshine. And after a few false starts, Sam and I were there to discover it. It had been a long haul.

"Thar she is!" Sam said, pointing down at a thin gray line of rock. "That's what yer lookin' fer. It don't look like much, but that's the high-grade, and it'll fetch them bankers like a beehive."

I scratched my head. "That? I've seen more of that. Look over here."

Like Sam said, it didn't look like much. But maybe the ancient volcano had looked forward to this day and laid up seams of richness beyond our imagination. Tiny strands of yellow-gray gold mingled with milky-white quartz secretly spidered through nearly impregnable granite. A billion tons of jealous granite guarded a single seam of precious metal, and it was our God-given duty to extract it.

"Cart about fifty tons of that thar ore down to the Carlton Samplin' Mill," Sam instructed. "They don't take the big loads like the Colorado City mills. But, fifty tons'll give you a good assay value, and they'll pay ya fer it, just like the big mills."

"How much can we get?"

"If that load assays out at $25 a ton, yer in bidnez. That's over a thousand dollars, and I reckon it'll feed dem hungry younguns for a week or two."

Sam spat on the ground, happy as ever.

"They're going to shut that Carlton Mill down, I reckon," Sam said. He took off his hat and scratched the back of his head.

"Them high-graders walk off their shifts with everything including their butts plugged with this here stuff." He replaced his hat and spat again.

"Of course, the Carlton cashes it all in, and them high-graders are sappin' the profits out of every mine in this district. And, its gittin' so they don't prosecute like they used to, not when the high-graders are union men. I don't reckon that mill will stay open with that goin' on. But, you just get on down thar, Clark, and see what's she's worth!"

Our fifty-ton load at the Carlton Sampler assayed out at $85 per ton. We made the newspapers the next day. Word spread to Colorado Springs, Denver, and even as far north as Cheyenne, drawing even more hungry men into the region.

"Bonanza at Black Jack Mine," the papers read.

"There ya be, Clark, you ol' egg suckin' dog!" Sam howled in delight. "Now you can git yerself a proper henhouse."

I loaded hundred-ton ore cars for Colorado City. Each car fetched $9,000 in gold revenues. Minus the transportation and processing fees at the Standard Mill, we netted enough to employ a four-man crew for six months. The strike played out exactly as Sam had foretold. We'd be walking in tall cotton, and it was high time for a few of Micah's big red lollipops.

Chapter Five

ABOUT A MONTH AFTER the lucky strike, at exactly six o'clock, I sounded the hoist bell to raise workers from the shaft. They had been extracting high-grade during their eight-hour shift. The sharp ding signaled Black Jack to hoist the wire cage to the surface. The first men of the shift were pressed into the crowded cage, waiting a hundred feet underground in pitch blackness. With the cage door shut, and men squeezed together skin to skin, it was an uncomfortable experience for any person. I had been there many times.

I expected Black Jack to begin trotting down the narrow mule lane with the wire cage in tow. But I heard nothing, standing inside the blacksmith shop. Although occupied over a red-hot forge, I suspected something amiss. I listened for the rattle of the little sheave wheel and hoist cage rising to the surface. Nothing.

I sounded the bell again. No sound, no movement. A third time. Nothing.

"Danged ol' mule…"

Angry words came from the hole, casting obscenities and threats to the distant surface. "Clark, git this cage moving. Now! Or we'll beat you with pick handles. Clark? You up there?"

Men in the hole expected exact hoist schedules. Any deviation brought panic and vocal displeasure. I learned early that my timing above all else must be faultless. Even Black Jack knew the exact bell timing and protested noisily when I failed to execute at the precise hour. Yet Black Jack had not moved. The hoist was dead.

"Hang on," I yelled down the hole. "We got a problem."

One glance at the hitching post told the whole story. Black Jack lay in a crumpled heap beside it. A pile of offal, blood, and urine, evidently emitted from the animal cast an undignified pall over its years of service. I quickly realized what this could mean for the Black Jack Mine. And it made me sick.

The loss of a hoist animal was nothing. Mules were replaceable. But the sensational headlines this could generate presented a greater threat. I saw the morning papers in my mind's eye as they read, "Men Stranded at Black Jack Mine," or "Black Jack Mine Disaster," or "Death at the Black Jack!"

Sam had warned me of the socialist-leaning journalists at the Victor Record Newspaper. Since the Black Jack Mine was the newest darling in the public eye, the press would never pass up the opportunity to report it as capitalist neglect for the workingman.

"Them newspaper boys 'll cut yer throat as swift as any road agent," Sam had said. "A shirt, tie, and a pair of specs don't make 'm saints. They can drive yer worth down in a month's time. All it takes is a little envy and some wrong thinkin'. Watch yerself. They love a good tragedy, and they'll be layin' fer it. 'Specially now that you got yerself a little strike."

I knew what could happen. Five daily papers and twenty weeklies were the principle means for citizens and investors to learn of the events at the Black Jack Mine. They'd be on this.

In a panic, hunched over the deceased mule, I felt like throwing up. Micah and Caleb ran up to Black Jack.

"Pa! What's wrong with him," Micah asked.

Caleb reached down to pet his head.

Before I could answer, a clattering horseless carriage caught my attention. It effortlessly drew my thoughts from the boys' questions and the dead mule. An experimental automobile bounced up the mountainside toward the mine.

"Hang on boys," I yelled down the hole. "I think we got some help coming."

The little red machine rattled over the high-mountain tundra like a loose collection of tin cans on a string. It was no more than a carriage with a miniature belching power plant. Large bicycle wheels bounced over ditches and melon-sized obstacles, surprisingly fleet. Up it came, picking through the piles of waist rock with the grace of a prairie gazelle. At first I dismissed it as a blacksmith's misguided tinkering, but stood captivated by this novelty of modern invention.

Micah looked up at me. "Is that—"

"It's Ma!" Caleb cried out, running down the hill toward the little machine.

Where had she gotten such a contraption, I wondered. And when had she learned to drive the clattering thing? In all our years, I had never seen such a performance.

With her successful summit, and with a flick of a smile and faux calmness, she hitched the hoist line to the rear of the carriage and leaned over. "Hi Honey. Look at me! While you were in the shop, I fetched a little help. Mr. Stratton was kind enough to lend his motorcar and teach me the little black levers. It's not hard. And I thought you could use the help!"

With just a little pride in her well-timed achievement, she puffed confidently down the mule lane, hoisting the anxious men to the surface.

I stood there for two minutes with a wrinkled grin as Caleb and Micah laughed and cheered.

"Ma looks like a steam engine driver!" Micah yelled, rolling on the ground and using the distraction as an invitation to punch and abuse his little brother.

She had evidently seen the mule fall, and ran down the hill to the Independence Mine for Winfield Stratton's help while I baked in the oven of hot coal. She had saved the day.

A skip full of anxious men thanked her. Even if it was illegal to be on mine property.

And even with the situation promptly resolved the news shot down the slopes of Battle Mountain to waiting newspapermen. The

Victor Record scooped the story and exploited it exactly as I had feared, and exactly as Sam had foretold. They loved a tragedy, even if this was far from one.

Readers of the slanted piece came away with the shocking impression of mismanagement and disregard for the safety of the men, an impression quite far from the truth. I loved those men like brothers, but the sensational story added nothing to complete the picture for unsuspecting readers, nor did it mention the amazing recovery by Patricia. But it did bring the union representatives out for a little social call.

Ding. Ding.

A dozen men arrived the next morning. They circled the hoist house with Charles Moyer leading the mongrel pack. Moyer had a way with those men like the preacher on the bandwagon. He found me in the blacksmith shop pumping the bellows, where I still spent a good deal of time.

"Howdy neighbor, my name's Chuck Moyer," he said with a big smile and friendly handshake. "These are my business associates Bill Haywood and George Pettibone."

"Glad to meet you all," I said apprehensively. "Name's Jeremiah Clark. We've met."

"Oh, yes. And as you know, we operate out of Altman. Just up the hill. We run the union in these parts. I guess you and I met about a year back as I recall. You'd lost a mule on that old freighter's trail. And as I remember, you went independent, didn't you?"

I tied off the bellows and counted men. "Yessir."

"Well, it looks like things are working out well for you. From the looks of things, you've built this operation up right nice. Good for you, Pilgrim."

Moyer glanced back to the others with a hint of irritation. He flicked a condescending wink and a bitter smile.

"Well sir, I've got a little problem," Moyer continued. "Maybe you can help me out. My sources tell me you've had a little accident up here. Word is, you've had some safety problems with your conveyance, putting your employees in a little danger. Had some trouble with the hoist I hear?"

"That's all cleared up." I nodded at the new apparatus.

"Well, there's still a problem, you see. The workers you employ are union men. My men. And as such, they are entitled to a safe environment. And I'm responsible for that. We'll need to bring in some union inspectors to check you out. We can't have this sort of thing happening every day. I'm sure you understand."

"Mr. Moyer, I said it was taken care of."

Moyer looked down.

"Clark, unfortunately I'm forced to suspend your operation until we can guarantee the safety of those men. And as much as I hate to do this, I've also got to fine you $1,000 for the safety infractions. Now don't get riled, there's no jail time. I just need to bring your operation into line, that's all. So, if you'll oblige me with the keys to your operation, I'll see to all the details. You'll also need to vacate the operation while the certification is carried out. But don't you fret; I'll see you're back in business as fast as my office can manage. You have my word on that."

Fingers tightened.

Moyer swaggered about as though he owned the place. In his mind, bringing the Black Jack Mine under his authority was a foregone conclusion, provided I sheepishly handed over the keys. The back-up men practically guaranteed his expectations. Not a man was under two hundred and fifty pounds, all rough as convicts. But I wasn't having it. Until now, I had had no beef with Moyer, and found the measures shocking to say the least. Especially the thugs at his side.

Mules and oxen were a common form of hoist power for new operations without the capital for expensive equipment, and they gave up the ghost like any other beast of burden. Moyer knew that. But as long as I was here, he would not be riding roughshod over the Black Jack Mine.

I lifted my head from the anvil to face Moyer. My hands and face were black with coal soot, and every muscle tightened like bands of iron for the grueling work. I was in no mood. Hired thugs or no.

47

"Mr. Moyer," I said, lowering my arms and looking him straight in the eye. "I need to tell you a little story to help you understand something. This news comes as a shock, so please hear me out."

Moyer gestured for me to continue, tightening his lips and looking around. He expected to wait only long enough for my story to end before pushing for final resolution, forcing me to vacate the premises. He was not there to listen, but to act. But he failed to recognize the manner of wrangler he faced. I began my story with a solemn look, hammer in hand.

"Down South there was a little family. They had a good life on a quarter section of land. 160 acres. It was barely enough for most to make a living, but good enough for them. They didn't need a palace. The land was handed down from father to son, beginning in 1799 when a man came out from Boston to homestead it. The family owned it for many years, and improved it with cleared fields and nice hedgerows."

Moyer's eyebrows rose in feigned interest. "1799?"

"Through a series of unfortunate events the family fell on hard times. In fact, the whole region did. There was a terrible war in which a quarter of the men-folk were killed, and another quarter came home morphine addicts from wounds inflicted upon them. Perhaps you remember that little war?"

Moyer shrugged.

"Well, there was not so much as a mule to skin for a hundred miles. The family was starving. One morning, a group of finely dressed carpetbaggers with bowler hats and fancy canes came to visit the remaining widow. A boy stood by her side. They claimed to own her property now, purchased from the bank for the cost of back taxes, which the widow could not have hoped to pay. The woman and her starving children were forced to leave.

"That thin teenage boy watched as his mother was driven from their family home and forced into a life of squalor for the rest of her days. And that tender young boy swore he'd kill any man who tried such an act again.

"There's an old saying, Mr. Moyer," I concluded coldly. "God created all men, but Samuel Colt made them equal."

Click… pause… click.

The Peacemaker swung up from under the workbench and concluded the story in convincing fashion. Six haughty men fell back. I would not be vacating anything except the breach of that hog leg. That is, if Moyer and his men missed the message. I was in no mood for a roaring lion seeking whom he may devour.

Moyer, who was not heeled for a fight flinched in alarm. "Simmer down now, Pilgrim," he said. "You can take your finger off that pepperbox, son. I see where your story is headed. I take your meaning."

"Well, I told you before."

"I'll tell you what I'll do. I'll check with my office and see if we can waive that suspension and fine. From the looks of things, you may already be back on track. It looks like you've already replaced the mule with a new ten-horsepower donkey engine, and you've got a good start on a new headframe. That'll be a seventy-footer, if it's an inch. Good for you, Pilgrim.

"But you've got to understand one thing: as far as the workforce goes, I am the Son of God around here. Understand? I decide who works for whom, and for what wage. I also ensure the operations are safe for my men. I make the law, and I enforce it. Keep that in mind when you employ my men. There are rules in this business and I'm here to enforce them."

"I understand that. But—"

"One more thing," he said. "That old man you've partnered up with is causing no small stir downtown. He's a pockmark on an otherwise fine operation. One more altercation with my men, and he's a dead man. I don't think he understands how things work around here. My advice: drop him as fast as you can. That is, if you and I want to do any business together."

He paused and stared.

"We may have cleared our differences for today, but we'll be seeing you again, Pilgrim. You can count on it. Good luck on the headframe," finished Moyer, as he tipped his derby and mounted his gelding for the short lope up the hill to Altman.

Chapter Six

April, 1896

"FIRE! LOOK, CRIPPLE CREEK is on fire!" shouted a group of boys smashing bottles and scrounging trading valuables from the Independence town dump. "Look at that smoke down there."

Straddling a large wooded beam at the top of the new Black Jack headframe, I turned to see a thick column rising out of the basin below. This was no pile of burning leaves.

The streets of Cripple Creek, Goldfield, Victor, and surrounding gold camps were plainly visible from my position. Beyond the muddy streets rose the snowcapped slopes of Pikes Peak and the Sangria De Cristo Mountains. With all this in view one might assume the god-like powers to skip from mountaintop to hilltop to valley below. In three big steps over Bull Hill, Wild Horse, and Gold Hill, I could be in the hollow of Cripple Creek. But in reality all I could do was sit and stare at the rising smoke like it was some curious circus attraction.

My thoughts turned to the camp below.

On any given day, some two hundred new buildings were under construction in Cripple Creek. Twenty-five thousand citizens in four thousand structures filled the six-mile area. Few of them could see what I saw now.

Tightly connected businesses, shelters, and wooden walkways made Cripple Creek a virtual tinderbox of enormous scale. And it was all

50

suddenly at risk. Every square inch of real estate was fully exploited, dovetailed together for maximum economy of space.

The butcher shared a wall with the assayer, who shared with the banker, who was next to the livery, and adjacent to the stock exchange, which connected to sawdust saloons beyond count. And so it went from one end of the camp to the other. They had connected the entire camp nail-by-nail, plank-to-plank, and wooden structure to haphazard wooden structure. A child could trace a chalk line from the first building to the last without lifting his tender hand.

The entire city was clearly at risk.

"Patricia! Look," I shouted from the headframe. She and others had poured out of the buildings and pointed to the gray column in disbelief. "Do you see that? Must be a fire. Where's Micah and Caleb?"

"Caleb's in the office doing his bookwork, but Micah is staying with the Burnses. He's studying for the spelling bee. You remember," she stammered anxiously.

I yelled down, "With the Burns family?"

"Yes, the Burnses. You remember... the spelling bee is next week."

I had forgotten.

"Can you go find Micah? I'm scared," she called up, pacing a little and lifting her hands to her face.

Doctor Burns owned a home in the northern heights of Cripple Creek on Galena Avenue, but Micah and his friends could be anywhere. Of course, they were studying their vocabulary for the spelling bee, but Mrs. Burns allowed breaks. The boys could scamper down to the soda fountains and candy shops with any small opportunity. There was just no way of knowing Micah's exact whereabouts.

"You stay here with Caleb. I'm headed into Cripple Creek to find him. I don't like the looks of that smoke," I said, still struck by the sight of the awful gray column.

The swelling plume pushed a stream of white ash into the breeze. Soft flakes fell like a spring flurry. Residents of Colorado Springs would soon see the smoke expanding over Cheyenne Mountain and Pikes Peak, and question what had befallen their neighbors to the west. Telegraph lines would crackle with inquiries just as concerned operators in Cripple Creek fled their posts.

Under new orders from Patricia, I practically fell from the headframe, leaving my tools hanging from the wooden beams.

Cripple Creek lay less than three miles as the crow flies, but well over ten by road. I started off on a dead run, picking through fields of glory holes and mine shafts. It was a footrace against the clock.

While flying afoot to Cripple Creek, I reflected on my choice of travel. Motorcars could rumble no faster over the rutted mountain switchbacks. And charging a horse into a burning camp was not a wise idea either, even if I had had one available.

Lungs burned and ankles twisted in protest. Rusted machinery. Blind holes. Mine shafts. More than once I crashed onto the rocky deck only to thrust my aching body back into service. I would not stop to pamper the flesh when my son's whereabouts remained unknown.

Wild Horse cleared… Gold Hill ahead.

Coming up over the last rise at Gold Hill, I could begin to see Poverty Gulch down at the east end of camp. At the end of Myers Avenue.

The Gulch had evolved into a shantytown of sorts, invoking the ire of the Midland Railway. It had not been named for the tumbling array of houses of ill-repute lining the valley but certainly lived up to its prophetic name. Dilapidated shacks and prostitution cribs extended east from Myers right under the Midland trestle. If not a fire hazard, it was at least bad for business. The Midland wanted it cleaned out and today appeared to be the day it would happen. Because that seemed like the source of the smoke.

With knees still trembling, weak from the scramble down fifteen-hundred feet of elevation and over three mountaintops, I landed across the valley to begin a staggering search.

I step up to the Trade and Transfer building next to McLeary's Assay and discovered the camp in turmoil. Citizens scurried like angry ants on a damaged hill. Some ran for fear, some to rescue loved ones, but everyone ran. Toddlers stumbled in the smoky confusion. Frantic mothers scooped them up to their protective bosoms. Men raced to help.

Cattle stampeded with wild eyes. The camp was a virtual beehive of panic and anarchy.

"The drunken fools kicked over a lantern at the Loose Slipper dance hall," a man hollered, as he ran east from Myers, now clearly the source of the thick smoke.

"Well, that is a careless place," I said, catching my breath enough to survey the murky avenue a block south of Bennett. Rows of tiny cribs on the Old Tenderloin housed a multitude of unhappy prostitutes, with the Loose Slipper right in the middle. Not a week passed without news of another morphine overdose. The painted ladies of the half-world lived hard on Sin Street, and it seemed only a matter of time until something like this would happen.

Especially at the Loose Slipper.

I still needed to cross town and get up to the Burns house on Galena Avenue, but decided to scan the candy stores just in case. I knew Micah had at least two bits in his pocket, and that couldn't last long with such attractions so nearby. I spotted Sam emerging from McGunthry's Hardware while racing up the wooden plankway on Bennett Avenue. I skidded to a stop just in time.

"Sam, have you seen Micah?" I shouted breathlessly across the busy avenue. "He was at the Burnses."

"No, Chief, I ain't seen him. I jes came down for a crate o' nitro and fuses, but I ain't takin' it now. I'm headin' back up the hill unless you want me. I ain't no good in this here smoke, and I ain't totin' no crate o' dynamite through it neither. If you don't need me, I'm headin' out right now."

Sam was right. He was too old to chase down missing children or fight fires with the young men. Although plenty tough, this thickening air was no place for old Sam.

"You go on ahead. I'll track him down."

My lungs rebelled at the thick smoke swelling over Bennett Avenue. Even a good handkerchief didn't help. But I navigated well enough to reach the Burns house at the top of the hill. I saw them all standing on the porch pointing and estimating the size and direction of the fire. All the neighbors were out anxiously debating a course of action.

The fire raged only six blocks away, but they could scarcely see a thing. I sprinted up the steps, heaving for enough air to warn them.

"Doctor, you best get out of town," I said, still drawing hard breaths from the smoky air. "The winds are up from the south so you ain't got much time. I just came through Poverty Gulch and across Bennett, and the fire is coming this way. It's a nuthouse down there."

The doctor strained to see through the thick haze. "Oh yes, you are right. Where did it start?"

"Myers. Now listen, I'm taking Micah up to his mama in Independence. Y'all are welcome up there, but you gotta get out of here now. You ain't got but a half hour."

"Well that sounds like the prudent thing," the doctor said, still pondering his options like the rest. And not moving as fast as I expected. He was not a man for rash action and considered the idea longer than I thought sensible. "I suppose we will go with you. But Jeremiah, there's something you ought to know."

I shifted anxiously, looking around for Micah. "Make it quick."

"Last night I treated a woman at the hospital when a well-dressed man came in hollering at the staff. The Sisters of Mercy keeps a quiet ward. At first I thought he had been shot, but when I discovered no visible wounds the orderlies escorted him out. He was just drunk. He kept shrieking about the mine owners needing a lesson if they thought they were running things around here. When finally shoved out the door, he continued shouting something about labor inequities and anarchy in the camp."

I stood there eyeing the rolling smoke. Doctor Burns didn't seem anxious, but he hadn't seen things downtown.

"I don't suppose it has anything to do with this fire," he continued. "And from what I've heard about where it started… down on Myers you said… I'm sure it doesn't, but I just thought you should know."

"Okay," I said, tapping my fingers on the porch rail. Micah and the rest of the family emerged from the house with their belongings. I hugged Micah and grabbed him by the hand.

But Doctor Burns kept right on talking.

"This man was no drifter. Obviously educated and well-heeled. I just don't know what to make of it, especially in light of what happened today. It sounded awfully spooky."

"Well, Doctor, I'll keep that in mind, but right now we've got to go."

With that, we started for the foot-trail at the east end of town. The same trail I had just come down.

Even with a half-dozen children in tow, we soon caught glimpses of Sam who trundled up the hill to Independence on his bad leg. Sam had made the two-hour climb dozens of times and usually passed the hours whistling The Bonny Blue Flag and enjoying the mountain views.

He wasn't whistling today.

"Sam! Wait up..." I hollered from the rear, trotting up to meet him. "Can you take Micah and the Burns family up to Independence? Take Micah to his mama and tell her I'm safe. I'm not going back right now. I need to stay and help if I can. I'll see you tonight."

Kneeling in haste, I kissed Micah, left him in Sam's capable hands, and dashed across the gulch and into the smoke.

Chapter Seven

THE CAMP HAD AT least two dozen horse-drawn water pumpers and volunteers to man them, but I had just run past two fire stations that were still shuttered. Same with the fire whistle. Silent. The loud blast normally heard every day at noon hadn't gone off. In theory, the system could be mobilized at a minute's notice, but had sat idle during the mayhem. City supervisors finally rushed in to open fire stations and muster crews.

"Right here, Clark," one said. "You and these other nine guys. Get this pumper up to the Palace Hotel." The man pointed to the rear of the firehouse.

In the back under a layer of dust, sat an old pumper as ancient as Pharaoh's chariot. We grabbed the ugly contraption and began dragging it up the avenue. Would it even work? Rusty axles squeaked and groaned as dried dirt clods clung to the heavy iron wheels. Our crew of six hand-pumpers, two hosemen, an operator, and a foreman barely got the thing moving. I was to be a hosemen. We continued westward on Bennett Avenue and prepared to enter the flaming remains of the Palace Hotel.

Hundreds of miners poured into the camp from surrounding regions. Men boiled out of the hills, scrambling down Poverty Gulch from the Mollie Kathleen, and more off Globe Hill and Signal Mountain. Pumper crews raced out of the newly opened fire houses while other men began their own efforts to contain the threat. Our crew arrived at the hotel and pumped wildly to build pressure.

The rear of the Palace Hotel shared the back side of the Ajax Saloon. Both wooden structures. The hotel burned in brilliant fury – a looming giant before us. A blast of sparks showered over my face, singeing my eyebrows. The blaze quickly consumed the roof and rear of the structure, exposing flaming rafters to a clear blue sky. We lifted the hose and released a thin stream of water at it.

The light spray from the little pumper barely made the fiery beast blink. We'd need to get closer. The team forced our way into the structure and up the stairs where blistering wrath surrounded us. With burning faces and choked lungs we scarcely extinguished one wall of blazing framework as ten others burst into angry flame.

Feather-filled mattresses with freshly pressed linen exploded into hot beds of fire. Printed wallpaper flashed into crispy ash. Horsehair plaster-and-lathe burned like stove-wood kindling, determined to reduce everything in its line of assault. Faux marble... oak mantles... door frames... everything burned.

It all went up in golden hues of fury. Even the crystal chandelier, once the pride of the hotel staff crashed to the floor, signaling the end of service for the lavish accommodations.

"It's a total loss," I yelled.

We retreated back down the stairs into the front parlour, out the elaborate archway entrance, and into the street. A hundred pumpers could not save this house of livid fire. A relentless inferno insisted upon having its way and would not be satiated by any means known to man.

My last memory of the grand hotel, which seared an imprint on my hazy mind, was the red-velvet upholstery in brilliant flame. O, how the mighty had fallen.

Just then a huge explosion erupted from the structure, and suddenly the vision was gone.

As a rude thank-you for my efforts, the hurling force threw me into the center of Bennett Avenue. I lay in the street blinking up at the falling structure. Minutes passed in slow swirling motion. Like in a milky dream, I was uncertain of anything before me. All sense of duty vanished as I lay before the fiery structure.

Struggling to regain my wits, I saw men running in dreamlike motion about me, fighting for a cause now foreign to me. I could hear nothing but the sound of my own ragged breath. My fingers and toes rang with numbness. My vision dimmed. Had I lost an eye? I could not tell.

Beside me lay a man skinned of his clothes, his scalp aflame. Although not entirely in control of my senses I managed to rise and extinguish the flame. He thanked me and fainted. I gaped at the freakish sight. Surely my dream would end and everything would be right again. None of this could be real.

When I finally managed a blinking stare it became clear that helpful citizens had dynamited the two buildings adjoining the Palace Hotel in an attempt to create a firebreak. Blasts like the one I had just survived now roared from all parts of the city. Hard rock miners were certainly handy with nitro, and quick to offer it for any solution.

Flaming timber flew into the air. Splintered beams burned like hot kindling roaring out of control. The dynamite seemed to set more fires than it prevented. A hundred yards up the street another blast blew down a dozen citizens, killing an old man and his donkey. The dazed bystanders fled with faces of splinters, bloody and seeking medical attention.

Panicked livestock trampled a disoriented woman in a wild bid to flee the blast. They nearly hit me. Three brightly-painted trade wagons flew aside, throwing fresh seafood into the muddy street. Across the street, the latest Paris fashions burned with the same disregard as refuse from a nearby livery stall. A twelve-inch gash in my pumper allowed precious water to escape into the gutter.

I started up the avenue, recovering my balance. My pumper crew had vanished, leaving me to fight on alone. After tottering up the street for several minutes, I rejoined as best I could.

By late afternoon, the business center of Warren, Myers, Bennett, and Carr Avenues were totally lost. My efforts to help had no more effect than at the Palace Hotel. Blackened faces charged from building to doomed building, defeated in every effort they put their hands to. As nightfall arrived, only a quarter of the city remained. Ugly silhouettes blackened against the starlit sky. The Burns family, like so many others, had lost their home.

I stood there thinking; where were the titanic snowstorms that filled the streets to the horse's bridle? Where were the menacing thunderclouds that dump their glutted contents? Where was the mercy from heaven? Rather, the clear night revealed a thousand twinkling lights in merry disregard, with not a drop of moisture. While millions of gallons lay atop Pikes Peak, we in the basin below had access to none. And so, an enormous red glow filled the ancient volcano bed, presumably as in the days of Noah when the foundations of the deep were broken up. And in one day, a thriving gold camp of twenty-five thousand souls was reduced to an evening bonfire. Everything was gone.

Five thousand men, women, and children would spend the cold April night without a stick of shelter. I saw a mother collecting her children, all huddling next to a little fire without their daddy. It had been a brutal disaster, not easily explained to the inquiring young.

Isn't it a mystery? One morning you wake up in a warm straw bed, and the next you huddle under the stars in fear. And not a single clue preceded the cruel event. Perhaps we are only sojourners here, I thought as I studied the mother and her children, and not the sovereign masters of it.

"We've counted," said the head of a committee of aldermen coming up Bennett Avenue, holding a clipboard. A short pencil perched over his bloody ear.

I turned to focus on their faces in the darkness.

"Sixty-two saloons, brothels, and opium dens, twenty-one groceries and meat markets, thirty-two churches, sixteen hotels, fourteen newspapers, forty assay offices, and a dozen clothiers have succumbed to the careless actions of one lantern in the Loose Slipper dance hall. In all, it's a two million dollar loss, and six souls now stand before their Maker. No one at the Loose Slipper has confessed, so it must have been the lantern's fault. At least a hundred and fifty mining operations will have to suspend operations while the assays, rail offices, and homes are rebuilt."

"What?" I managed weakly.

"Clark, I hope we can recover. Are you going to make it okay?" the alderman asked.

I looked around, stunned by the question and unable to answer. In the destruction the only sound I heard was the delicate crackle of smoldering embers and the occasional whimper of survivors coping with their losses. Thousands of people picked through the rubble, scrounging valuables, while curls of white smoke rose softly around them. Naked brick chimneys stood visible against the moonlit sky, an eerie reminder of William Tecumseh Sherman's campaign in Georgia so many years ago.

Unable to answer the alderman, I stumbled toward the west end of town. My body was blackened from head to foot and I had sustained a thousand stinging splinters, cuts, and burns for my efforts. I hadn't slept or eaten in over a day and was too feeble to muster a cough to clear my crusty throat. I stood there alone, breathing in silent resign.

What had the alderman said? Would I make it?

I tried to remember my people in Missoura but could not recall their faces. Ma... Grandpa... Uncle Olin... my own sisters still living in Randall's Flats... not a single face came to mind. These poor folks of Cripple Creek were my kin now, and I mourned their losses with every dry tear within me. These were the ones who had lost hearth and home while my own possessions were safe up the mountain in Independence.

The president of the Cripple Creek Stock Exchange trotted up with a bucket of clean water and a few loaves of bread. He spoke with powerful optimism, dismissing the losses so evident around us.

"Jeremiah, a man's life does not consist in the abundance of the things he possesses. As crazy as it sounds, this fire is exactly what my stock exchange and this city needed," said the president, kicking the charred remains at his feet.

I looked down at the burned rubble. "What? I'm sorry; I'm just tired."

"We're one of the richest cities in America. That is a fact, and it is high time we showed the people of America what we're made of. I've consulted my partners, and we're going to rebuild the stock exchange with brick. We were trading sixty million shares a year from that cramped little call-room. I think we can afford a new building. And just this morning I talked with a dozen business owners about the same thing. Everyone agrees. You won't recognize this city when we're done."

I tried to focus on his face, but understood only half of what he said.

The stock exchange man waved his hand. "This isn't a tragedy. It isn't even a setback. Why, this is the blessing we needed to build this city in a manner befitting its hardy citizens. Give us six months, and you won't suspect a lick o' fire ever took hold here."

I looked around, trying to see his vision.

"Yes, I grieve for those unfortunate souls who lost their lives, but I am optimistic about our future. Let us lay their weary souls to sleep and press onward. We can overcome this."

The president offered a cup of cool water and a slice of bread, and then eagerly trotted off to dispense his next dose of optimism wherever he could. He was no light under a bushel, and evidently did his job well. The idea was so powerful, it took me by surprise. But, just as with the aldermen, I couldn't even say a word in reply.

But he was right.

Hopefulness lapped over the camp, even after the last remaining structures burned in another freak accident four days later. Even in the wake of tragedy, folks grew excited with the notion of rebuilding the city in brick. It was a fresh thought, one that everyone in Cripple Creek took hold of in a tangible way.

Winfield Stratton called a rare meeting the day after the second fire. They had set up a special podium in front of the old Imperial Hotel on 3rd Street. It was still a smoldering wreck. Stratton looked ill, but held up a white bank sack and spoke softly to the gathering crowd.

"Any man who needs help, I'm here to offer it. I'll give loans to carry you through. Or charity if you know you can't pay. See my agent at the stock exchange."

With that, he simply walked off. No explanation. No follow-up questions. But the crowd exploded with cheers and applause.

The tent cities of the homeless were empty as citizens laid brick to brick in a race to receive paying customers again. Men, women, and children contributed. Merchants seized the idea of beautiful new stores for their gold-rich customers. Citizens wanted new homes to impress their friends. Everything would be new again. All on account of one generous man and a little optimism.

Buildings rose like bamboo in China.

"This is amazing, Patricia," I said. "I thought this town was finished."

She smiled and pointed at the Midland Depot. "Have you seen the rail cars?"

A stream of ore cars loaded with food and goods arrived at the Midland Depot, sent from our Christian brethren of Colorado Springs. The lead cars, which were ordinarily black from the smoke of the engines, were brightly painted with images of flowers, rainbows, and happy people. Large block letters, on each car in line, spelled out the words, "WE … CARE … FOR … YOU!" The brotherly love spoke clearly to the citizens of Cripple Creek as we went about the business of clearing and rebuilding the city.

To my surprise, scores of enterprising children, Micah and Caleb included, picked through the silky ash of burned out buildings for one precious item.

Nails.

"Look Daddy!" Caleb cried out as he dashed up, hoisting a bucket of blackened nails from the fire. "Buy some of my nails for the new shed. I've already sold four buckets today, and if you buy one, it'll make five!"

I laughed and handed him a Morgan silver dollar for his hard work. He proudly waved it to his friends with blackened little fingers and scampered off to secure another load of the precious material for sale.

Used nails brought ten cents a pound. And those lads produced an astounding daily amount. Some boys earned fifteen dollars a day, three times the wage of a skilled powder man, which produced no small measure of pride in their fathers. I'd never seen so many dirty faces or perhaps so many scolding mothers with wet rags to scrub them in all my time. I bought fifty pounds of those old hand-wrought nails just for the opportunity to shake those little hands and send them off on their important business. I'm not sure I'll ever empty the many nail buckets now concealed high in the rafters at the Black Jack Mine. I saw this as just another sign of those amazing times.

1896 was the year we rebuilt Cripple Creek from the ground up.

Chapter Eight

IT SEEMED THE CITIZENS of Cripple Creek had a lucky providence that turned tribulation into treasure. By summer's end, Bennett Avenue was reborn with modern architecture towering over the city streets. The fire that had reduced the camp to ashes was history. Construction was finished, debts were paid, and business proceeded at the brisk pace of a gold camp producing a quarter-million dollars a month, and in the space of only six months. During the summer, giddy folks spoke of the fire as lightly as a schoolyard tale. It seemed their good luck and optimism could overcome anything.

"Hello, Clark," McGunthry greeted, as I stepped into his new store on Bennett Avenue. It had just opened the week before. "This two-story brick sure beats the old pineboard we had last year, don't it?"

Everything in the store was neatly arranged and modernized, and it even smelled new. McGunthry had a fine operation and he was justly proud of it.

"It sure does!" I eagerly agreed. "And have you seen the Palace Hotel? Three stories and modern electricity. That's a sight!"

The eyes of God watched over Cripple Creek, handily dismissing every evil deed aimed against it. In such a state of grace, a dentist could toss a hat into the wind and strike a million dollars where it hit the earth. A stable hand could stumble on a rock and come up with a fist full of high grade and a seat on the state legislature. Good fortune bubbled up from the ground like living water offering every citizen the opportunity for riches.

The president of the stock exchange walked up to McGunthry and me. "We have passed from rowdy gold camp to sophisticated metropolis," he said, beaming. "Our government facilities are the best in the state. Every block on Bennett is three stories. And the ladies look so fine in their fancy hats and parasols. Have you noticed?"

"Yessir," McGunthry agreed.

The president smiled. "The stock exchange now trades over a hundred Cripple Creek mining stocks and is attracting the finest businessmen in the country."

"How about in the Eastern exchanges?" I asked, happy for his excitement. "Are you selling anything there?"

"Oh, yes. In New York, Boston, Philadelphia and many other places I've never set foot in. These Cripple Creek mining operations have hit a healthy stride and we're here to help when you're ready to issue some stock."

I shook his hand vigorously. While he was just passing along the good news, I could tell he was also trolling for a little business. "I may take you up on that."

"Clark, the rough and tumble days of the frontier gold camp are slipping into the history books. We've turned the corner toward real growth and that little fire was the impetus to change. Didn't I tell you so?"

"Little fire?" I said, glancing at McGunthry. "Well, I guess you can say that in hindsight. You did offer a pretty promising outlook at the time. I guess that's why you head up the stock exchange. I'll let you know when I'm ready to offer some stock."

Things were going well; I had to agree. But with steady ore production and good employment also came the longing on the part of some to strike it rich on their own. Men had seen operations go from humble startup to prosperity, and wondered why they weren't entitled to their own bit of good fortune. But by 1897 every ore-producing scrap of land in the district was claimed and operating. With such limited space there were very few new mines starting up. And they were mostly out on Signal Hill near the cemetery where the ore was not as plentiful. I was lucky to get in when I did. The Black Jack Mine was still fighting for a profit and I would not yield until I had gotten what I came here for. No stock offerings for me just yet.

That's when handbills promoting the Alaskan gold rush began to multiply like rats. "Gold Discovered in Alaska!" the leaflets read. You saw them posted on telegraph poles, doors, windows, and even blowing along the beautiful new streets. Most were published by Seattle outfitters offering to supply the needs of the 100,000 stampeders now pouring into the Alaskan gold fields. Naturally my employees wanted in on the action. A few such fellows rallied packs of hungry men with the intention of heading into the northern wilds to strike it rich. I confronted Lenny Blake as he sought to plunder my fledgling workforce.

"Back off, Blake. These men aren't going anywhere," I said, determined to hold onto a few faithful employees.

"Clark, you're a danged fool for staying here in Colorado," Lenny and the men of my graveyard shift argued. "The #6 is nearly pinched off. We haven't hit paydirt in a hundred years, and you're wandering around down there like the blind leading the blind."

"I don't care; just take your message down the street," I said. I wished they had talked to the stock exchange man as I had.

"The real action is up in Dawson City, up in the Yukon," Blake continued, ignoring me. "They're pulling out a thousand dollars a day up there, while we're bustin' our bones for three dollars a shift. It just ain't fair."

"Blake—"

"Clark, we want in on the big action up on the Klondike. A group of us fellas figured we'd hitch up there and git some of that. Don't try to stop us. Our minds are made up." The men strutted around my office snapping their shoulder straps, already counting their riches in the gold fields of Alaska.

"Okay, okay, I understand, fellas. This hard rock mining is a heck of a way to make a living. But it's an honest living, and it's not as bad as some. Heck, you're making five times what they make in the slaughter houses of Chicago, or any other place. You've got it plenty good up here. What do you think the storekeep and stableman in Colorado Springs make? Not a quarter of what you bring in."

"We're talking about getting rich," Blake countered. "Not just making a living."

"Well, hang on, Lenny. We've got good schools, good food, and good entertainment up here."

Blake danced a little jig. "Shall we take in a melodrama at the Butte Opry House?"

"Well, if that don't suit your tastes, there's Johnny Nolan's bucket of blood. What more could you want? It doesn't get any better up in the Klondike territories. Betcha they don't have Dynamite Dick."

I could see the argument wasn't carrying sand with the men who had gotten a fresh dose of gold fever into their blood. I remembered Missoura and my own crazy ideas. Practically every toothless rat-eater in the state had picked up stakes and joined a wagon train headed west. No more than a small passel made it past Dodge City, but that never stopped the hordes from coming in the first place. They never got news of the ones that quit. They were mostly so ignorant they imagined that everyone had just gotten rich some place out west. Indeed, I was one of them, but I was one of the lucky few who had the grit to keep going or perhaps just lucky enough to land at the right place at the right time. Not every man heading west was that lucky. And certainly not every silly chap stampeding into Alaska was guaranteed a mansion with a view. These men had to understand that. Although in honesty, I knew I was chopping cotton in a chicory patch.

"And another thing," I said, facing Blake. "Those handbills don't tell the whole story. Do you fellas know what you're in for, just to get up into Dawson City? I've heard the Chilkoot trail out of Skagway goes up three thousand vertical feet over forty miles."

"We can do that," Blake spouted off. "We'll get some mules."

"No you won't. You can't get a pack animal up that trail. You must have heard that. Right?"

Blake looked hurt.

"And those Canadian Mounties won't let you into the territory without at least one ton of supplies. One full ton! Imagine hefting two thousand pounds up from Colorado City to Cripple Creek on solid ice. That's about what you're in for, Blake. You've got to cache the supplies every mile and make multiple trips to keep it moving. Oh, and don't git yourself stabbed or froze to death. They'll leave your bodies right where they fall. Are you boys ready for that? I came out of Colorado City two years ago under similar conditions and it would liked to have killed me. And I had two mules. I'll never do that again. Of course I didn't have the five-hundred-mile trip up the Yukon River to deal with afterward."

Creases formed on the men's foreheads. I tried to drive the point home while there was still a chance.

"Two-thirds of those stampeders get turned back or killed. It's sixty-below up there. That's why those Mounties require a year's supply. And they say the gold is buried under ten feet of permafrost. Are you sure you're ready to go off and freeze to death?"

Blake countered, "Aw, you're just a lazy old fool, Clark. Are you still taking the advice of the Cornish and Chinamen?"

The men laughed nervously.

"None o' that talk scares us, and half of it probably ain't true. Probably about as true as that Tommyknockers legend those Cornish keep repeating. We've heard stories of millionaires set for life. So don't put that load of crap on us."

Upon those words, the men brightened up.

"We've already made up our minds, and we're heading out this Sunday so have that lazy paymaster ready. Good luck in this dirty ol' hole in the ground, Clark. We're going to get rich!"

They hollered in wild excitement and headed out to the saloons to whoop it up.

And so half my workforce walked off their shifts for bolder aims up in the wild blue yonder. So it was all across the district. Men who were accustomed to drifting from strike to strike lit out for Alaska in stampeding herds, leaving me shorthanded and looking like a fool for staying.

But I was no fool.

We were sitting on the richest block of granite in the world. We had had one lucky strike and would have another. And another after that, and another after that. I was confident of that. No pig in a poke could persuade me otherwise. We would stay the course in Cripple Creek and be the better for it. And warmer too.

But being shorthanded left us pretty bad off. The men who stayed were working longer shifts and taking bigger risks to keep the operation solvent. Four to six men now did the work of eight. Shortcuts were taken to secure the next strike and keep the Black Jack Mine alive. It was true as the men complained, that we had exhausted the strike at the hundred-foot level and now needed another to keep the operation out of receivership.

That was always the case in Cripple Creek. We lived from strike to strike. It was all about the lucky strike, and the iron-will to press through tons of granite to reach the next one. Those who pressed onward were rewarded, while those who lost the will to the opium pipe never quite got the luck in sufficient supply. It was all about faith and believing the ore was there for the taking. Of course the Cornish attributed their good fortune to the work of their elfish little friends, the Tommyknockers, but I knew the true science behind our luck and knew we could count on it year after year.

I'd lived on molasses and cornbread in Missoura long enough to know I wasn't going back. This dirty little hole, as the stampeders put it, was where I'd make my mark.

Sam suggested we bring in split-check leasers to make up the shortfall. The shifters could help us financially as they leased the lower producing drifts, but I wasn't ready to split the fortune a hundred ways. This would be our stand, if we could only take the pressure.

"Patricia, I'm dang-near skinned out," I complained, dragging into bed at 2 AM. "Blake and his crew lit out a week ago. Williamson and two of his crews are leaving next week. That leaves me with only half my men."

She rolled over to kiss. "What does Sam say?"

"Split-check leasers. If we don't, he thinks we've got a month left before the banks move in."

Patricia sighed. "Are you going to do that?"

"No. But we're going to have to cut shifts, and if nothing turns up, maybe quit or join the shifters myself. I had hoped to build you a nice house up on the north side of Cripple Creek, but that isn't going to happen. Maybe I can get work in Colorado City. What do you think? Would you be happier down there where I can make a living?"

"You're just pouting. I think we've got a fine home right here," she said, looking around the two-room miner's shack we now occupied. "And I think you already know what I believe. We'll make it just fine. Something will turn up... another strike maybe... a new vein... some high-grade... something. Now get some sleep before you worry yourself sick. You always do this."

I guess she was right.

The next day Sam had another idea to replace the Alaskan stampeders. "Just let yer men walk off with a little of that danged high-grade."

I practically fell down. "What? That's our meat and potatoes."

"Think on her. You'll get every man from here to heaven applyin' for work. The bloomin' ore's right there, you jes need the muscle."

"Well, maybe you've got a point. It'll drive the men as if the mine belonged to them. Another strike, and they'll take home some good money, and we'll be in the clear."

"And, you'll be different than them other operations where the profits only go to the shareholders. When word of this gets out, you'll be floggin' 'em back with a leather strap."

We decided to give it a try.

With the new plan in place, the men scratched like badgers to hit the motherlode and be partakers in the next bonanza. And, I think they wanted to show the stampeders that Cripple Creek was as good as any other mining camp. But under that kind of pressure accidents happened, and it was only a crap-shoot until one did. I had wagered on those lucky dice so many times I had forgotten it was the lives of my men that were at stake. Unfortunately for my crew on the #6 drift, those old ivory bones would eventually come up snake-eyes.

Maybe Moyer was right. Maybe I was taking too many risks and endangering the lives of "his" men. Maybe the Black Jack Mine was an unsafe place to work. But no mine in Cripple Creek could be called safe. Men could die a hundred possible ways, and Moyer knew that. But safe or not, tragedy would strike the Black Jack Mine, and there was nothing I could do to prevent it.

Chapter Nine

A MONTH AFTER THE stampeders left for Dawson City, I was mucking ore with one of the crews down on the #6 Drift. Every drift measured a clean six feet by six. That let everyone work standing up in relative comfort. Not so in all the outfits in the district. But I figured we worked faster and moved more rock because of it.

It was all about moving rock.

Just as I moved in to muck out a four-ton load from a set we'd just blown, my feet went out from under me. I was knocked down before I even knew it. My cap blew off and a pile of dust and rock swept over me. Every candle in the entire drift went out.

The compression of a huge explosion rocked my chest. And I couldn't hear a thing.

Was it a stick of nitro that hadn't gone off from the last set? I tried to remember the count. No. Every stick had gone off. We counted those. 1... 2... 3... 4... 5... 6... 7... and finally number 8. Every stick had gone off. So what was this?

The compression had been enough to flatten me. And enough to extinguish every candle in the mine. The Cornish had a saying "when the flame goes out, you get out."

Darkness lingered for another fifteen minutes while a wind swooped out the #6 and up the vertical shafts. Hordes of rats, which the men had caught and painted white for sport, ran squeaking for safety, scratching up the manways and cracks to higher levels.

Hacking, wheezing, and clanging tools rang out in the darkness. Men cried out. But most just coughed and sucked in more of the noxious air. Every man on the #6 was in peril, including me. We'd just have to stay calm and wait for fresh air.

"Chief... you all right," I heard in the darkness. A match lit up in the distance, and then flickered out.

"I'm okay." I picked myself up and dusted off my diggers. "Can you get down to the end of #6?"

No sound.

A minute passed. More wheezing and a groan, but no response.

"My leg's broke," the voice finally said.

As the smoke cleared and fresh air filtered in, I stumbled down to the end of the #6 and found a new wall of rock where the men had been working. I lit up three new candles. All went out. I waited and lit them again. Out again.

Bad air.

Asa Baker limped up coughing. "That moron. Now my leg's busted," he complained as we inspected the rubble. "That new powdermonkey didn't separate the nitro cache from the fuse cords. I told him a dozen times, but he likes to save a few steps. Lazy slug. Forty feet, I told him. No less than forty feet apart."

Three more men joined us, cleared their throats, rubbed their eyes, dusted off, and studied the new rock. There must have been a whole crew behind it – eight men. As far as I could figure.

"Look. The canaries are dead," a man said. He pointed to a cage with five yellow birds – all at the bottom of the cage. We used them to know if the air was still good, but the compression had killed them. Or the bad air. Or both.

"You ever seen one of them big brick powder magazines blow?" Another man put in. "I seen it out in Anaconda. Thirty foot hole in the ground. Dangest thing you ever saw."

"Well, once I–" another began, hoping to top the story.

73

"All right, all right, enough of that," I said. "Let's get 'em out of there. And Baker... go get your leg looked at. On your way out, have Sam send down some help. Good muckers."

At least two hundred tons of rock blocked off the blast site. Every many except Baker with the broken leg worked as muckers and trammers to clear it. Calloused miners worked their hands bloody until they were physically forced to leave the work so fresh hands could spell them.

"Yield, you big red Irishman!" I demanded, ten hours into the rescue effort. "Yield that muck stick so another man can spell you. We're trying to move this rock fast." But Big Doc McCoy would not yield. He was the biggest man on the crew, and dumb as an anvil. He'd been fighting down at the Portland Mine each night. But after ten hours of mucking was a useless wreck. He was slowing the rescue operation down.

"Jump on his back fellas!" I said. "Bring him down. He wants to help so bad, but his hands are as bloody as a prizefighter's. He won't be fighting tonight. Bring him down and get his shovel."

"They're all dead by now," one man said.

"But we don't know that, so keep tramming," I yelled. "We'll muck until we find out."

Doc McCoy was an inspiration, even as he bellowed for another spot at the mound of rock. Hours later we finally broke through the blockade to get our first sight of the relieved miners.

"Whoa... look at that," a man said, eyeing the blast site.

"Ohhhh," another marveled.

"Unbelievable," I said.

The blast had opened a ten-foot hole into the granite floor. And there sat a vein of the richest gold ore we had ever seen. The seam looked a foot wide and worth a fortune. Gold flake had been blasted in all directions, covering the men's hair, diggers, and cavern walls – a sparkling wonderland.

"A vug," the men began repeating. "A danged old vug right here in Cripple Creek."

I snapped my cloth cap across my thigh. "Didn't believe they even existed."

The trapped men could not have seen it in the darkness, but you could wipe a glove across the rock wall and come up with a fistful of gold dust. Three thousand tons of this stuff would fetch a million dollars.

Big Doc McCoy stepped up, lifting his cap. "Chief… you'll be a m-m-million… a million man tomorrow," he said in his measured tone. "If-if-if… if you don't spend… spend it all on liquor and fancy hats."

I stationed four hired Pinkerton guards at the strike site and gave everyone a day off. We could use the rest. Winfield Stratton walked up the hill to congratulate us.

"I'm glad no one was killed," Stratton said. "You know this could have been bad. But good for you, Clark, on a nice strike! I'm glad to see you made it through those hard times. That was a long haul for you. I was afraid I'd see a new owner soon."

"Yessir, it was. And I'm glad to have you as a friend. I wouldn't have made it without you. Remember the old mule and the motorcar? I've been through some rough patches. But this ought to satisfy the union boys. They've been after me for working the men so hard."

"Is Moyer still beating the tar out of you? A lot of small operators are dodging him. He knows enough to stay out of the Independence Mine. Have you heard the talk?"

"His dreams? Yep, I've heard plenty. They say he's going mad. I just wish he'd do it some other place. He's getting hard to satisfy."

"One day he's your best friend, and the next he'll take a mattock to your skull. You'd better watch him, Clark. Well, if you need any help, let me know. I've done all right up here, and I try to help the little guy."

I shook his hand. "Thank you, sir."

"They all think they'll get rich out here. None of 'em ever thinks they'll chew their saddle strings for a little grub, but it happens. Old Womack got liquored up and sold his strike for five hundred dollars and a bottle of whiskey," Stratton said, shaking his head.

With the biggest operation in the district, I knew Stratton could help, and would be happy to. I just didn't expect to need any.

But the very next week we found ourselves in the El Paso County courthouse defending the new bonanza. It seemed our lucky strike was interesting to a few others, and they were not as benevolent as Winfield Stratton.

"Here Ye! Hear Ye! Hear Ye! In the matter of Lucky Dollar Mining Corporation verses Black Jack Mine Incorporated, the Honorable Judge Horace E. W. Mackenzie of El Paso County presiding, all rise," cried the uniformed bailiff who opened the court to the public.

After the fire Cripple Creek had spared no expense in the new mahogany, brass, and ivory chambers. Any man finding himself in this court was reminded to sit up and mind his manners. Sam Whitman leaned in to enlighten me on the situation we now faced.

"Jeremiah, you ol' Missoura possum eater, they got you dead to rights this time. Yer belly-cut, you miserable beggar," Sam whispered roughly in his Texas drawl, meaning no offense but helping me understand the weight of the charges leveled against us. "You can forget them other two dozen suits. This one's got ya fer sure."

"But it was our strike!"

"You heard of Colorado Apex law? If you strike a lode, and that vein apexes under another man's claim, you don't own it. That man does. Get it?"

"No, I don't. That's a law?"

"Dern right. You got to stay under yer own claim, or give up the gold ya find. Don't ever think o' cuttin' a drift under the Portland or Theresa. They'll take yer whole operation and leave you with a black eye."

"But I did," I complained. "I stayed under the Black Jack."

"Get a surveyor out there. Bet that vein comes right up under the Lucky Dollar. I seen it myself. You got no wiggle room, Jeremiah. You hear me, son?"

Sam was probably right. If this was true, it meant our bonanza in the #6 rightfully belonged to the Lucky Dollar. We had done the backbreaking work of discovering it, but by law it belonged to them. Maybe that was only fair, but frivolous Apex lawsuits had cluttered the courts as vultures swooped in hoping to cash in on our hard luck.

The Lucky Dollar had even erected an iron barrier to seal us out of our own drift. They claimed to have the right.

I threw off my cap. "Alright Sam, I may be belly-cut but I am still standing, and I aim to find a way out of this mess. The Lucky Dollar has not broke a lick o' sweat over that gold. That drift is five hundred feet of honest toil, and I will not give it up to a bunch of lazy squatters. Where's their five-hundred-foot drift they gave up their last dollar for? Have you seen their operation? They've got nothing but a twisted little hole you've got to lower yourself into with a rope."

"No haulage skip?" Sam laughed and picked his teeth with a folding knife. "Just a danged old rope?"

"That's right. A rope. It's pathetic. Every operation has the same twenty-four hours but they spend theirs drinking and sparking the ladies on Myers Avenue. This is our strike and I aim to secure it, if for nothing else but those who suffered to uncover it. That's only fair, I expect."

"Well, Jumpin' Jehosaphat!" Sam cried out with a raw shriek roughly approximating the Rebel Yell. The outburst drew the attention of solemn attendees. "I know'd you had grit the day I put eyes on you. You'll send them chickens flyin' fer the henhouse. You go after 'm you ornery ol' wildcat!"

But the lawsuit dragged on for weeks and stalled our operation. I had run out of options and was forced to let most of the men go. Our little operation would be finished without this strike but I finally resigned to let the Lucky Dollar sluggards take the million dollar strike and call it a day. They'd burn it up in a year's time drinking and gambling, but I was tired of the worry. The sleepless nights and exhausted finances had taken their toll.

The Lucky Dollar boys boasted of their good fortunes in the saloons. They bought drinks and made grand appearances like millionaires. If they had only kept their mouths shut things might have gone okay for them.

It was that kind of talk Winfield Stratton and I heard as we entered the Crystal City Saloon and Café. Tommy and his gang hadn't noticed us come through the door, and ran their mouths as recklessly as ever. Stratton was used to the idle gossip surrounding his millionaire status, but it took the air out of me.

"Yeah, old Clark sure got hisself into a mess up there in our claim," Tommy bragged at the card table, completely unaware of our presence. "What addle-brained moron lays a six foot tunnel under another man's claim?" he said, laughing wildly at the blunder. "And they dang near blew themselves up. I wouldn't trust them dopes with a stick of nitro at the North Pole. Give me two more cards!"

His brother edged in. "He's jes like that old hermit, Stratton. They're both holed up in them mines seven days a week. You never see 'em out. That makes 'em both about as a crazy as apes."

Tommy hooted and loaded five rounds into his Navy revolver. He spun the cylinder and made as though he'd fire them through the café ceiling. "They'd probably blow themselves up under water."

"I don't reckon neither of them could play a hand o' cards," his brother said. "I'll see your hundred dollars, and raise you two hundred more. This here's a game for high-stakes gentlemen!"

The men whooped and hollered with the other players at the table. The Navy revolver went off three times in quick succession. Everyone ducked for cover. Dust and debris fell from the ceiling.

The million dollar claim was as good as theirs. There wasn't any point in working it anymore. The claim would just sit idle as the court case wore on. Why work? They would be millionaires soon, and poker suited them better than blasting granite in a dark hole. Tommy and his brother would just bring in some New York financiers and live off the cream. That was the life they came here for. Not blasting rock.

But Stratton wouldn't tolerate the wild talk.

"The way I heard it, a man lost three fingers and an eye in that incident," said Stratton, walking up behind Tommy.

The tone was one of silky monotone. "And you boys just sit here drinking and mocking? You don't seem like gentlemen to me. You're not only a pair of saddle tramps but a couple of cowards to boot," he said with contempt, peering down at Tommy's hand. Tommy still hadn't noticed me so I kept my mouth shut and walked around the corner.

Tommy's face boiled at the words. He wasn't about to take that off anyone. With two slugs still in the revolver and a belly full of whiskey, he figured he'd just spin around and ask who was doing the talking. That was his first mistake.

Tommy choked. "Oh, Mister Stratton. I didn't know that was you. I meant no offense. I just never seen nobody as dumb as that Black Jack crew. Why, they didn't even know where they was. They dug right into our vein like we wasn't even there. A man that stupid don't deserve a lucky strike. You know... they say he wasn't nothing but a mule skinner before he came up here. You know'd that? I guess he don't know no better."

I almost laughed.

Tommy had tried his best to back out of the unfriendly words, but was getting tangled up all the more. He was plenty good at saloon talk but wilted in the face of Winfield Scott Stratton. I'm just glad he hadn't seen me. He might have shot me with that big Navy pistol.

"Well, I'd rethink that assumption if I were you. Clark is no fool. But yes, you are right about my reclusive nature. It is rare that I can make public appearances. I am so frequently mobbed by those asking for handouts and grubstakes that I must remain at home most of the time. I do not enjoy the luxuries that you and your brother so plainly display."

"Yessir," Tommy said, swallowing hard and setting the pistol down.

"But, it is quite a coincidence that I should arrive here today in this pub and hear these words. I was here only to deliver a gift to a dear friend, and in doing so I have confirmed the ugly rumors with my own ears. Half the town is repeating them. Given what I have heard today I recommend a more prudent course of action regarding your dealings with Mr. Clark and his unfortunate dilemma. I hope you will take that under consideration. Good day, Gentlemen," Stratton said, in his dry soft voice as he turned to leave.

Tommy and his brother knew better than to challenge Stratton. He may have been a frail man but his resources were endless. He could tie this case up in bureaucracy for a century. Everyone knew it. If they now believed they could get anything from it, they would be wise to keep shut.

Still, things couldn't have been blacker for me. Within a week, we were expected to walk away from the Lucky Dollar strike. Tommy and his brother would leave with practically our whole operation. And never lift a hand. The case had exhausted our cash reserves so the judge would have no other option than to award the bonanza to them. But as that dreaded morning arrived, Stratton also arrived.

I was glad to see him in the courtroom before the ruling came down. At least there would be an ally by my side. Stratton and I shared a kinship. While I was a mule skinner, as Tommy put it, Stratton had been a carpenter before his strike at the Independence Mine. I could always go down and work for him. He stepped forward before the bailiff stood up, with words that changed my life.

"Clark, I want you to purchase that whole outfit and dispatch that pack of mongrels back to where they came from. I'll put up the capital."

My arm slipped off the desk. "What?"

"This whole town has seen the Lucky Dollar antics and heard their bravado. It doesn't sit with me. You're smarter than them, so work the deal until you've bought them out, lock, stock, and barrel. We don't want their kind here. Consider this a loan between friends. Pay me when you can. Just run those vomit-eating curs off this territory."

I swallowed a plug of tobacco and retched like a cat on a hairball. Stratton must have thought I'd lost my mind. He said he could take back the offer if that might please me better.

"Thank you, sir. Nosir. Yessir, I accept." I managed to get the words out while spitting loose tobacco into the courtroom spittoon.

Stratton smiled at the episode and offered a frail hand. I wiped tobacco juice from my chin and accepted his handshake to close the deal.

"Do you need a writ of agreement? You know… to pay you back?"

He just smiled again. "Anything more than a handshake cannot be trusted. You should know that by now." He wiped traces of tobacco juice from his hand and gently turned to leave. I had just been handed a blank check.

As it turned out, $10,000 settled the million dollar lawsuit. I only needed to show Tommy a stack of crisp hundred dollar bills, and he took the money like I knew he would. We completely bought out the Lucky Dollar Mine. Tommy and his brother went off on a bender in San Francisco and lost the entire fortune within a few months, just as I had predicted. But at least they no longer lingered idly up on Battle Mountain where Stratton could see them.

After his death in 1902, I learned that Stratton had made numerous "loans" to working-class men after the fire, and had never made accounting of them. He had worked so hard to offset the vicious rumors of his wealth, but it never really helped. People just loved to talk. Stratton was just a humble workingman's man who wished he could pull only enough gold from the ground to sustain his operations. Any more, he said, was a waste. He had even wished he'd never become rich. That was the kind of man he was.

Chapter Ten

April, 1898

"I WANT YOU ON my side, Clark," Charles Moyer said. "I'm willing to offer you an executive position in the miner's union, if you'll consider it. You'll be working with Bill Haywood and George Pettibone."

I nearly fell off the door step.

I had just stepped out of the new Cripple Creek Stock Exchange building on Bennett Avenue with hopes of issuing a round of capital for the Black Jack Mine. Moyer was right there to meet me.

"Thank you, Tom," I said to the man inside. "I'll have a box of stock certificates to you by Monday. I hope we can sell some in New York and Boston."

"You're determined to double-down on that new Lucky Dollar acquisition aren't you? Who says you're not a gambler?" Tom said with a smile. "We'll do ten times the business now. Good day to you, Clark. I'll watch for the package."

I turned to Moyer who had pitched his offer before I was prepared to hear it. It seemed he'd been waiting for me and popped the question before we even shook hands. Even Haywood and Pettibone looked surprised, as if they'd also heard it for the first time.

"Well, good morning to you too, Charles," I answered with feigned surprise, stepping off the threshold onto the sunny sidewalk.

New sandstone curbs installed after the fire in '96, accented the redbrick stock exchange building I had just emerged from. The nice touch captured my attention almost as much as Moyer's offer. "What? Join the union? Why would I do that? And what would I do there?"

"Well, I haven't thought that through yet," he said with a wide smile hoping I might be persuaded. "The thought only occurred to me this morning. I've got acquaintances in Coeur d'Alene willing to buy your shares in the Black Jack Mine. Free of that sweat hole, you'd be mixing in real society. Why don't you join me in Altman to talk about it?"

Even with his mechanical smile and hearty handshake, Moyer looked worn out. His unbuttoned suit coat exposed an unkempt shirt and trousers. Unpolished shoes and mussed hair completed the picture of a badly stressed man – very different than the man I'd met right here on Bennett Avenue three years ago. Something was wrong and I couldn't quite figure it.

"I really don't have time for that. But let's have lunch some time. Are your union bosses getting what they need? The Black Jack Mine is doing well, and I want to make sure things are square between us before we capitalize the new Lucky Dollar operation. And I want to make sure my men are happy." I smiled. "Your men, I mean. No more hoist accidents, right?"

We did have lunch – and four more times after that. Each time, Moyer pressed for an answer. He wanted something from me but I couldn't get a bead on it. Every time we met, Moyer looked worse, like he might have a nervous breakdown any time. But he still pressed for some kind of alliance, mostly favoring the notion that I abandon the Black Jack Mine and join him at the Western Federation of Miners.

"I do not know what he's after," I told Patricia. "And I'm afraid to answer him straight out. I'm afraid of what he'll do if I refuse."

"What do you mean?" she asked.

"Well, is he just trying to get the Black Jack Mine like he did a few years back? Or is he after a capitalist defector he can use against the other mine owners? It feels awkward and I'm afraid to answer him."

Patricia turned back to her work. "Maybe he just needs a friend. Everyone knows he's getting desperate with mine owners. And I think he's working himself to death."

"But what does he want from me? You know he's got his finger on the heads of those union bosses and could cause some real trouble if I turned him down cold. I don't want to blow this Lucky Dollar deal with union trouble."

"I guess you're going to have to find that out. It can't hurt to talk. And be his friend, at least."

I finally agreed to a few union meetings in the late spring of 1898, but had no plans to join Moyer or sell my shares at the Black Jack Mine. Things were going too well for that. The new shares would set us up for some big things. I just wanted to see an end to Moyer's awkward romancing in a gracious way.

He set a date for the first meeting.

"Monday morning. Three weeks from today at 8 AM," Moyer said, evidently still hoping I would come around to his thinking. "The board meets on the first Monday of every month. I'll see you there. You'll see how a real organization operates." He looked so eager.

I could hardly wait. Maybe I could sidestep his offers if I attended his meetings and made a show of enjoying them. My apprehension heightened over the three week period, and then the day finally arrived.

"Listen up, men," Moyer opened the Monday meeting. "We have Jeremiah Clark here. He represents the Black Jack Mine and is considering switching allegiances. He's an ally, so please offer him a warm welcome, and speak freely in his presence. Let's show him how the Socialists do things," he said with a flourish. "Capitalism is a rotting disease. Fortunately we've got the cure!"

I suppose I hid my shock well enough because Moyer asked me back again and again. He wasn't giving up until I either accepted the exalted tenets of unionism or slapped him in the head with a coal shovel. After two more meetings I wanted to do just that. The weeks wore on and I saw little value in Moyer's proposition. Maybe he sensed that, because he gradually gave up the niceties of romance and reverted back to his old self – the self I had seen after Black Jack's sudden demise. The next meeting was a disaster.

"I'll tell you what bothers me," Moyer began, shifting impatiently at the monthly board meeting in July.

Big Bill Haywood, George Pettibone, Harry Orchard, and ten other stakeholders had assembled in the bright new Altman offices. All leaned in around a mahogany conference table. Why I was still there? I'll never know. I tried to be his friend like Patricia asked. Maybe that was it.

Moyer looked bedraggled from worry, as though he hadn't slept since the last board meeting. Small beads of perspiration dotted his forehead and his eyes fought to focus. Tufts of uncombed hair jutted at odd angles and a creased collar sprung out a few inches from last week's wrinkled white shirt. It was hard to focus on his words with his physical appearance so haggard looking. Maybe the nervous breakdown had already happened.

Moyer came out hot. "They don't need us any... more." And then cooled. His eyes floated up to a point on the intricate tin ceiling. He had evidently spotted a fly on the detailed design and studied it as it inched across.

Fifteen seconds passed.

We all looked up and then back again at Moyer. And then another fifteen. Moyer began to mutter partial phrases as if struggling with a half dozen other voices that seemed to be winning the argument. Completely self-absorbed with the insect, he ignored me, Haywood, Pettibone and the other attendees who waited to hear his issue. They had all seen the fat spring fly too, but failed to connect it with the scant words from Moyer. The awkward silence was too much.

"Who? Who doesn't need us?" Haywood finally broke the silence. The others wondered the same. "You said they don't need us. Who?"

"The miners, you simple idiot," Moyer screamed, emerging from his inner struggle. "The miners say they don't need us anymore. They mock us behind our backs. And they see Altman as a diseased old scab hanging off an otherwise healthy body. They're going to pick that scab even if it oozes puss for a month. Can't you laggards see that? Clark's the only intelligent one in this group."

The men were stunned. The outburst didn't make sense and they couldn't see where Moyer was going with the argument. The incoherent words seemed to fit his disheveled appearance, which had become common in recent weeks.

"I have no idea what you are talking about," Haywood said. His eyes flew open and he snapped his head wildly. Pettibone and the other ten members of the executive council all seemed equally confused.

Haywood leveled his eyes. "What are you saying? Are you saying the miners are all going to quit the union? That's what it sounds like you're saying. It's completely absurd."

Others nodded, glancing between Haywood and Moyer.

Haywood drew a long breath. "Clark, I know you're on the other side but please back me up on this. They love us, or at least the old-timers do. I can understand some disloyalty in the New Boots, but overall, we're in good shape."

I nodded.

The others seemed to agree. Of course they all hoped to soothe Moyer's nerves. But I had no interest in backing up Haywood any more than a simple nod of agreement. I just wanted to satisfy Moyer with my presence. But I didn't expect talk like this.

Moyer gnashed his teeth. "Haywood, you are as dumb as a shovel. I don't even know why I keep you on. Why don't you go down to the nearest drainage pond and drown yourself? Keep acting like that and I'll replace you with Clark."

I blinked in surprise.

"Don't you get it, Haywood? The mine owners are taking over! Get your head out of the opium dens and you'd know that. There are men in those mines making five, ten, and even twelve dollars a day. You heard me right. I have information that a young man named Ben Rastall down at the Cresson Mine makes twelve dollars a day. Get your slate boards out; that's almost four thousand dollars a year! With wages like that, who needs the union? That's exactly the sort of thing that will ruin us. The miners are making so much money they don't know we exist."

"Well, why would the mine owners pay like that?" Pettibone argued. "If we don't exist, those capitalists would enslave them like darkies if they could – present company excluded," he said, turning to me. "You know that. They're no better than slavers. Why would they pay miners like that?" he added, sheepishly agreeing with Haywood, but hoping to escape Moyer's wrath.

Moyer tore out a tuft of hair. "Because they are taking in money hand over fist, that's why. Stratton's worth eleven-million dollars, and with that Lucky Dollar strike, Clark here is worth at least two. They've got so much money they don't know what to do with it. They can pay any wages they like and it doesn't affect them. What miner needs three dollars a day when they're already getting twelve?"

"Well... that's not exactly true," I argued. The whole discussion felt awkward, but I couldn't just sit there and take it, regardless of where Moyer thought my allegiances lay. I think Moyer's self-delusion had extended to the point where he thought I could tolerate such statements.

"The mine owners struggle to make profits just like everybody else. A few missteps, and a healthy mine is out of business. It's not as simple as you make it out to be. Last year–"

"Well, it burns me up," Moyer interrupted as though he hadn't even heard. "How can an ex-carpenter be worth eleven million dollars? That just doesn't make sense. There are half-starved miners coughing up blood from the consumption, and one man sits on top like a king. Where is the justice in that? I guarantee Stratton isn't producing that much ore."

"Charles, the wages are not directly connected to the ore we produce," I said. "There are investors."

Moyer's hand shot up. "That's exactly what I was thinking. Gold ingots are still trading for $25 an ounce just like they always have. But mine owners are paying like they're $50. The numbers just don't add up." Moyer returned to the fly on the green and gold ceiling to consider the new information.

But the point went completely over the attendee's heads. They looked as confused as ever. Having just begun the capitalization for new expansion, I knew exactly where Moyer was going with the argument.

"Those New York investors will pull down Pikes Peak for a stock certificate from the Independence Mine, or Portland, or Vindicator for that matter. Those stocks are the hottest ticket on the market, and the mine owners can't take the silly investor's cash fast enough. The revenue those mine owners are pulling down has nothing to do with the price of gold ore. It has everything to do with the over-inflated stocks they pawn to unsuspecting Easterners. Any citizen on the street can buy one, and there are thousands of idiots with a twenty-dollar gold piece to squander on them. The mine owners could pay monkeys to muck ore if they wanted to. With money like that, why should they care what it costs to extract it?"

I tried to stay cool. "You're right about the recent swell in mining stocks. But those operations are more fragile than they look. Everyone's fighting for a piece of the pie. They are all leveraged. Every mine out there is ninety days from bankruptcy." I pointed up to Battle Mountain.

"Well, the Independence Mine pays twice the normal cost to pull that ore out. Twice!" Moyer complained. "Does that sound fragile?"

"Don't you understand?" I started to get hot. "Nobody is getting rich. It's all on paper. All the wealth is theoretical. That is, until you cash in your stock. And nobody's doing that. So there's no realized wealth. Stock money comes in… and it goes right out again. No cash. Sure… you might be a millionaire today… but tomorrow you're a stable hand again. It's just numbers on paper. That's all."

The explanation didn't help. At any minute, I expected Moyer to start bouncing off the walls. The situation was completely out of his control, and in his mind the union was headed for obscurity if something wasn't done about it. It had driven him to a state of distraction. This meeting was evidently the breaking point.

"Okay, that may be true, Clark. But the union has become a pack of gawking bystanders. We have nothing to bring to bear on the new economy in Cripple Creek. No pressure for higher wages. No teeth to bare for better working conditions. They're laughing at us."

Moyer turned to Haywood and Pettibone. "We don't hold the cards anymore, and you idiots haven't discovered that yet. And that's precisely the reason I'm bringing Clark in."

"Well, you just give me the nod," Pettibone said, tired of the insults. "And I'll have this city in such a state of anarchy they won't know which way is east. Remember that little fire in '96?" he said with a smirk.

"No, you flaming pyromaniac! Is that all you can come up with?" The veins in Moyer's temple nearly burst at the stupidity of the answer. "I swear; you are as brainless as a chimp. Do you want to get thrown out of Colorado like we did from Idaho? That was your doing up there, Pettibone. So don't be so thickheaded. My only regret is that we didn't finish our business with ol' Frank Steunenberg when we had the chance. Maybe we'll meet him again some day. But this problem requires another solution."

The meeting ended only after Moyer ran dry of ideas and a dozen other docket items were written into the meeting minutes.

Moyer sat facing the corner and glared.

"I'm sorry you had to witness that, Clark," He apologized afterward. "Sometimes, it takes a steam shovel to get through to those lunkheads. But you can see why you're so important to our struggle. We need a man who understands things."

"No apology necessary." I shook his hand and smiling as best I could. But I wanted to bolt. Moyer's desire for my defection was so misplaced it was sad. He still didn't get it. I only wanted to extract myself politely and avoid a backlash.

But Moyer was definitely onto something in the meeting. The Black Jack operation was as healthy as any in the district, producing like a pump. The daily high-grade into Colorado City now approached eighty tons a day. The Lucky Dollar strike had saved us from disaster and at the same time launched us into incredible prosperity. And, it was the new investment dollars that boosted the mining operations beyond anyone's imagination. Not the ore. Not the gold bars. Investments. Cash flowed in from every corner of the nation in an unstoppable torrent. From nothing but stock certificates. Everyone hoped to get a piece of the operation in some tangible way. Sam was even forced to hire an accounting firm to handle the stock mailings alone.

For every ton of high-grade sent down for processing, we stashed twenty tons of waste rock and low-grade ore outside the shaft heads.

Mountains of red, gray, and white mine tailings towered around the shafts, which was true of all the high-producing mines in the district. And the constant roar of steam engines, ore cars, and stamp mills offered a comforting feeling to anyone doing business in the district. It was the reassuring sounds of commerce.

The sounds of big money.

Seventy-five tons of ore a day fetched a million dollars a year. And with investment dollars pouring in we could hire anyone at any price. Just like Moyer had said, the Black Jack Mine was now worth several million dollars on paper. And maybe under the surface, that was Moyer's real beef. But he didn't understand how delicate finances were. My friend 'Johnnie the Miner' did.

Johnnie had warned me. "Pay no mind to Mammon. Or them riches 'll make themselves wings and fly away to heaven, as sure as I'm standing here today."

Moyer's awful appearance only got worse. He had been plagued by nightmares in which he was belittled and humiliated. The dreams seemed so real that he began repeating them to me during lunch meetings, hoping for any relief he could find. I decided I just wanted out of his distorted world. But he went right on repeating his woes.

In the same awful dream night after night, the miners of Cripple Creek strapped him into a baby carriage, cuffed his hands and feet, and strapped a baby's bottle into his mouth to muffle his cries. He struggled to free himself but no measure of tossing and turning could accomplish the simple task. The dream just went on and on.

Along the avenues were herds of swine. They squealed and bit his flesh. The swine hated him and snapped at him with dirty snouts, dripping with hog slop. Some were busy feeding at the numerous troughs along the streets, but many of the glutted beasts glared at him with menacing eyes, just waiting for a choice bite of his tender baby flesh. He could feel the bites in his dream and tried to lash out, but was bound hand and foot in the little carriage. There was nothing he could do but wail.

It was the type of dream that seemed to last all night. Moyer could not get any sleep. He could sit up in his bed, look around, and adjust his nightcap, but returned to the same torment as soon as he lay back down.

I could tell his actions in the boardroom were a direct result of this nightly affliction. I felt sorry for him. He claimed the dreams were so vivid that he became unsure which parts were real and which were not. Whenever he saw swine in Cripple Creek they were avoided. He gnashed his teeth at mothers with buggies. Crossed the street when certain groups of miners strolled up Bennett Avenue. But even he knew those were crazy notions and desperately tried to dismiss them.

I laid a hand on his shoulder. "Why don't you just see a doctor? I've heard there are good ones in Denver with the latest remedies for head sickness. Maybe they've got a cure."

After hearing the story a dozen times, I wanted to tear my teeth out with pliers. Moyer seemed to stick to me like a rare earth magnet. Maybe Patricia was right; maybe he just needed a friend. He evidently felt there was something to gain by my defection to the union, but I didn't see things his way. That didn't stop him from inviting me to his meetings every week.

"That's a good idea. Let's go to Denver. We could stop by my good friend, Mr. Charles Spalding Thomas while we're there."

We... I thought, and resigned to either tag along or suffer the persistent offers. I owed Moyer an honest answer.

Chapter Eleven

CHARLES THOMAS HAD PRACTICED law in Creede, Leadville, Aspen, and Cripple Creek. He had become quite an influential circuit litigator. They said he knew mining law like the insides of his pockets. Moyer and I met him in Denver on a Tuesday morning.

"Well, I appreciate you stopping by and sharing these things Chuck," Thomas said. "It's good to catch up on news and such. I think you'll find Doctor Anderson's remedies a real relief. Those new cocaine derivatives do work. And in moderation don't leave you with The Cravings like morphine and laudanum. I expect all the druggists in Denver will be peddling the new remedies soon. They'll even have it in the soda fountains for a little extra pep."

Moyer smiled and stuffed the glass bottle into his pocket.

Thomas continued. "Now, I did have a thought concerning your dilemma up in Cripple Creek. I'll share that in a minute, but I never knew things were so bad. From here in Denver, everything up there looks so rosy. The economy is the best in the state, and Cripple Creek seems to be leading in a lot of areas. You must be doing something right. But I guess you see more since you live there."

Moyer tightened up. "Like I said, it's the millionaire mine owners." His couldn't stop scratching his arms.

Thomas sniffed and cleared his nose. "I've never understood millionaires myself. I don't trust them. It's the common man that bears the brunt, so how do they get so rich? How do you stand on that, Clark?"

"Well, it's the capitalist that creates jobs," I said blankly, forgetting the company I was in.

Moyer's eyes flicked open.

"Well, I suppose if they didn't, someone else would," Thomas retorted. "They'll be the ruination of our country, if not the state of Colorado first.

"But actually, there's a simple solution to your problem with mine owners, Chuck. Just draw a line around them and isolate them," Thomas explained, looking to Moyer for his reaction, not wishing to tangle with me any further. That was good because I wasn't in the mood to argue the merits of free-market capitalism. I just wanted to dig a little ore and make money.

Moyer stopped scratching. "I don't understand. Draw a line around them?"

"Just provision a new county in the state of Colorado and leave the millionaires in El Paso. All the mine owners are living down in Colorado Springs where it's warm, true? So, leave them there in their own county and start a new one up in Cripple Creek. It's really that simple. Just draw up a new county!"

"You can do that? You make it sound so simple."

"Aah, it won't work anyway," I butted in. "A little thing like county lines isn't enough to separate mine owners in Colorado Springs from their interests in Cripple Creek. And remember, some of us still live in Cripple Creek. Denver is a hundred miles away and some live there too. Don't forget that. It's a crazy idea that'll never work."

"Yes it will," Thomas replied without eye contact, still addressing Moyer. "I could do it in a couple of months. And then we'll find out who's right. New county, new rules." He tilted his head in confident reflection. "The best politics always separate one class of citizen from another. Works every time. Draw a class distinction and your problem is solved."

"Wow!" Moyer exclaimed, his attention now fastened to every word Thomas uttered. "Tell me more."

"Well, there's not much more to tell. We'll just 'calve it off' west of Pikes Peak. Let El Paso keep their precious Peak. Try to take it and you'll lose the vote. You can sneak a sliver of Fremont County down near Victor, but leave the Peak to the millionaires. Millionaires on one side. Workingmen on the other. Two classes. Like I said, it works every time."

The itching ended.

"I'll do all the leg-work up here in Denver," Thomas continued, seeing that Moyer liked the idea and might want to proceed with it. "We've got a sympathetic House and Senate here in the state of Colorado, and when I'm Governor in a few months I'll just make it happen. It's not that hard. I can call in a few favors and collect the votes you'll need."

"Yes!" Moyer let out.

"Of course when this flips, it'll restructure everything along the Front Range. The new county will become the recipient of all those mining revenues. I expect El Paso County will shrink into obscurity."

"So… so, that means the new county will become the biggest revenue-producing sector of the state. Bigger than Denver?"

"Yes. In a hundred years, few people will have ever heard of El Paso County, or Colorado Springs for that matter. Anyone with real estate investments in either county will need time to reverse them. Some will be sold and others bought. I'll need time to realign mine, and in order to secure the votes we'll need, the other legislators will too. Just give me some time to make that happen. That will look awfully juicy. The real estate alone will get you all the votes you need."

Moyer's eyes gleamed as if he'd popped a half-dozen of Doctor Anderson's cocaine tablets. I could only imagine what he was thinking. The Colorado Springs mine owners would be isolated in a shrinking economy and his union workers would finally have the equality they deserved. Sure, some didn't deserve much, being opium addicts on Myers Avenue, but they deserved more than they were getting.

"Yeah, why should a few high-horse millionaires get it all?" Moyer said. "Why not share the wealth?"

"Exactly. Separate the classes and redistribute the wealth. Before long there will be no more classes. But there are a few things you'll need to do," Thomas continued, tempering the excitement. "I can arrange the vote but you'll need to assemble the political staff up in Cripple Creek."

"Okay. What'll we do?"

"First off, find four county commissioners you can trust. Have them waiting in the wings. When this pops, they'll be elected. Next, you'll need a police commissioner, sheriff, and some reliable judges, along with an army of lawyers. If you can put those details into place you'll have your own county. The other things will fall into place naturally. Constables and policemen will be hired. Everything will realign to your new policies."

"I can do that," Moyer agreed with a smile.

"Make sure they know who to vote for. If you can call in your own favors with them you'll get enough names to make it happen. Of course, I'll expect their vote for governor. If I'm not elected, the whole deal is off. But I suppose that goes without saying."

"Anything else?"

"Keep an eye peeled for General Palmer in Colorado Springs. William Jackson Palmer. He'll be one of your primary opponents. He's an old Quaker who thinks he owns the whole county on account of a few rail lines he installed. You know he worked with that monster, Carnegie? If you can keep him in the dark, you'll get the majority. And that's all that counts. Simple enough?"

"Oh, one more thing!" Thomas remembered. "Got a name for it?"

"I hadn't given it any thought. Any suggestions?"

"Sure. Why not name it in honor of old Henry Teller, the Silver Republican? That will dress it up a little and both sides of the aisle will push it though."

"Teller County... I like that."

"When it's all ready, we'll just slap it on the docket, and two months later you'll own the whole shebang. I figure we can do it all by March of '99," Thomas finished.

Moyer chuckled and tossed his head about. He liked the notion of owning the whole shebang.

But it didn't even sound possible to me. How could a new county affect relations between mine owners and the union? It felt like a contrivance so I shrugged it off. But Moyer couldn't contain his excitement on the trip back to Cripple Creek.

By October, 1898, the next scheduled board meeting of the Western Federation of Miners was about to commence. This was to be my last. Maybe Moyer did need a friend, but I wasn't going to be it. I would attend one more meeting to be polite, but planned to decline Moyer's offer at its conclusion.

The same troupe of union executives trundled in for their regular tongue-lashing from President Moyer. They all braced for his usual verbal abuses. But Moyer was unexpectedly gracious, with a zip in his step. He even smiled.

"Thank you gentlemen for your attendance. I have arrived at a solution to our dilemma of the last meeting."

Haywood tilted his head. "So... no drainage pond for me?" Moyer ignored him.

"As you recall, I raised the issue of declining union relevance in the Cripple Creek district. And of course, down in Colorado City. As hard as we've tried, we cannot gain a foothold in the processing mills down there. We've had a little success at the Portland, Telluride, and Colorado Reduction, but almost nothing at the Standard Mill."

"Yeah, that's Charlie MacNeill's mill," Haywood said, grimacing.

"Well, I have a solution!" Moyer beamed. Everyone perked up. They had expected another beating but felt something had changed. Moyer was happy for a change.

"Let's swap decks with those mine owners. Clark will be joining us, and the rest will never see it coming. Let's create a completely new county, just for the union!" He wagged his head in boyish excitement, repeating the contrivance of his friend, Charles Thomas in Denver.

"That's right! We'll divide the mine owners from the miners by drawing a line right between them."

Moyer scrambled to remember every word Thomas had said. He was trying to present the material with the same degree of simplicity.

"Most of the mine owners now live in Colorado Springs, right? There are a few hold-outs like Stratton up in Independence, but most are living down where it's warm," again repeating more of Thomas' ideas and accepting the credit for himself.

I just shook my head and looked out the window, mostly because the idea was so stupid.

"But, most of the miners live up here close to the mines, either in Victor, Goldfield, Independence, or Altman. Let's just draw a line between them and The Springs.

"After all, shouldn't the Cripple Creek miners have a county of their own, with their own representation and their own tax structure?

"And, if we control the county, we control the labor in it. The mine owners will find themselves on the outside for once. We'll see how they like that. It should be the will of the people that rule, not just a few royalty down in Colorado Springs, don't you agree?"

The attendees loved the idea while I silently planned my exit from Moyer's caustic world. The whole silly scheme seemed based on the notion that rich mine owners hurt the industry, and that they should be isolated like a cholera epidemic. It didn't make sense and I just didn't think the idea had any merit. But at least I got to see things from Moyer's perspective.

Moyer practically giggled. "There are a few things we'll need to do. I want this done by March of next year so we'll need to work hard. We're not going into 1900 without this."

George Pettibone slid forward. "What can we do?"

"First, we'll need to put together a new county government before we approach our friends in Denver. I want everyone from the top down named and on board. Provide me with a list of candidates, and I will interview them personally. I want this all wrapped up in a nice tidy bundle. Nothing left to chance. Everything will be in place, just as smooth as silk underwear. Do you understand? Haywood, I want you on that. Can you handle it?"

Haywood scratched a few notes on his legal pad. "I can do that."

"Barksdale, I want you to rally the men. They should know exactly who to vote for, and why. Get a cheat-sheet in every hand, and have them memorize it. And then memorize it again. No dissent. Either they vote right, or it's your skin.

"And for heaven's sake, get your men down to those Colorado City mills. I don't understand why they have refused the union. Maybe they need a little more persuasion – the right kind of persuasion. Understand? The defiance at the Standard Mill is eating my liver alive. I swear I'll go down there myself if I have to. Now get the job done."

"Yessir," Barksdale replied. He wrote only a single word on his legal pad: MacNeill. Then circled it.

"Pettibone, I'll save your ideas for later. If this doesn't work, then we'll talk, but let's give democracy a chance. These capitalists really set me off. Eleven million dollars is too much for any ex-carpenter to spend in ten lifetimes. He doesn't deserve it any more than the next man on the street. Labor produces all wealth, and wealth belongs to the producer thereof," Moyer finished, having laid out the plan and set his men in motion.

"Join us then?" Moyer asked expectantly at the end of the meeting. That was just the time I intended to break off the love affair, but still didn't have the courage.

Chapter Twelve

Christmas, 1899

B Y MARCH, 1899, THE deed was done. Thomas and Moyer had pulled it off. Teller County was born. Cripple Creek was named the County Seat. And just like Thomas had said, Moyer owned the whole shebang. Every elected official and every policy maker in Teller County had been installed. By Christmas, staffing had trickled down to sheriffs, police chiefs, and officers just like Thomas said it would. And new policy was likely to flow from it. We could only wait to see how the new utopia would treat mine owners.

"You look a little nervous," Patricia commented, as we traveled the one-mile road down Battle Mountain to Victor. The black horse-drawn buggy bounced down the steep slope, with not a flurry of snow in sight.

"There's a lot on my mind. A passel of rich people will be there tonight, you know. I guess I'm a little uncomfortable about that. The Gold Coin Club has such an incredible story, and I don't feel at ease with so many newly minted socialites."

"Maybe Winfield will be there. I think you are his best friend; he doesn't have many. Maybe we can sit together."

"Not likely. He doesn't travel in those circles. He's more uncomfortable at these events than me. People mob him every time he leaves that cabin. I don't blame him for staying in."

99

"Well, you'll be all right. You can always talk about your mine."

I popped the reins. "There's a Christmas party at the Lonely Lode Saloon. All my men will be there. But they don't allow women."

Patricia smiled and rolled her eyes. "Well, I guess you're stuck with me, then. No cock fights and bloody brawls tonight."

"Well, maybe in a different way. You heard... the Gold Coin was originally a hotel idea. But when gold was discovered at the footers, the lucky investors jumped into the gold mining business instead. Isn't that bizarre? This little City of Mines is so rich they pave the streets with gold."

"What? Pave the streets?" Patricia pointed out the lights in the distance.

"You knew that, right? The Gold Coin Mine supplies low-grade waste ore for street maintenance. Been grading it into the streets for six months now. Look closely; you'll see a sparkle from time to time. It's low-grade stuff, but there's still a lot of gold in it."

Patricia's eyebrows lifted.

"All the highest producing mines operate in this little triangle from Victor to Altman to Cripple Creek. And all those mine owners are going to be at the Gold Coin Club tonight. Somebody told me there are now a hundred millionaires in the state of Colorado. Thirty of those were minted in Cripple Creek. Doesn't that intimidate you a little?"

"Not in the least. Because you are one of them, so get used to it."

That was easy for her to say, but she didn't have to deal with the social positioning that occurred at these events. At least at the Lonely Lode, the cock fights would be civil. At the Gold Coin Club, everything from coattails to cravats, and top hats to transportation would be scrutinized as men fought for social position in the rich climate. This was no box social. Sure, you didn't lose an eye at the bucket of blood, but what about your reputation?

"Maybe I'd feel more comfortable back in that row of bachelor shacks we started out in," I wondered aloud, drawing closer to the club, and eyeing the new motorcars sputtering up.

It had become fashionable for society men to arrive at the Gold Coin Club sporting new gasoline-powered Ford Quadricycles. This may have become one of the richest six-square miles in the world. And Johnny's prophesy of riches making themselves wings and flying off was simply not possible. He couldn't be right about everything.

The new machines were so grand. I recalled a conversation several months earlier.

"Have you seen the new gas buggies? They'll replace the horse and carriage in twenty years," an eager salesman in Cañon City had informed me earlier in the summer. "Yessir, this is the newest thing for a man of your means. They're snatching them up like contraband."

The man had been selling as hard as he could, and had worked himself into a sweat.

"Well, I reckon a good mule suits me, but how would I get one?" I asked, hoping not to encourage the man too much.

"This fine specimen of Yankee engineering comes in from Detroit, through Denver. I'd let you have it for $380, gold. Five months, and you'll have it! These Fords are hand-built, you know. Every man of means just has to have one. I'll throw in two bottles of mineral water from Manitou Springs! A natural curative, they say."

"Really," I said.

"Where do you work, Mr. Clark?"

"I shovel ore up in Cripple Creek. Make about a dollar a day."

Patricia slapped my shoulder and frowned. "He makes a lot more than that!"

The gas buggy peddler brightened up.

"As you can see, there's a solid chassis on four bicycle wheels. No more harnesses for you. It's got leather seats, chain drive, and stick steering. There's even an electric bell and lantern for night driving, should one attempt it. It's a scandalous extravagance to be sure. Want one? I'll take your order today."

"Yes, we want one!" Patricia let out with a big smile, ignoring my scowl.

Maybe I could change the subject. "What's the top speed?"

"Nine miles per hour... ah... but they're getting faster." He smiled expectantly.

"Nine? Well, that's not exactly a fitting match for a thoroughbred horse at a quarter the cost, now is it? I'll think about it." I didn't let on, but inwardly I wanted one worse than all the newly minted socialites in Cripple Creek.

At least two hundred of those socialites would attend the party this evening at the Gold Coin Club. Yearly fees rung in at $650, limiting it to millionaires, executives, and men of social standing. The Gold Coin was a rare sanctuary for such gentlemen, offering a quiet tone for dining and business without the nuisance of hollering, gunshots, and brawling miners. Men could craft deals in a secure environment free of harassment. I felt out of step with the flagrantly rich – those who had already snatched up their Fords like contraband. The tension increased as we approached the extravagant accommodations, still unfamiliar to my tastes. Nevertheless, I sat content beside Patricia who enjoyed the higher class my endeavors had now afforded us.

"Just hold your chin up," she reminded me as we parked the buggy. "You're as good as any man in there, and we're as good a family as any in Cripple Creek. Just remember that."

Patricia had single-handedly marshaled our fledgling clan from white-canvas to rented room, and then to grand manor on the hill, adding lavishness to luxury. Yes, we were as good as any in Cripple Creek. She once spent a hundred dollars on white-lace window curtains. They were intricately detailed and shipped in from Paris. Those curtains entangled us in controversy for a month. And God Bless her for it. She had earned the right to a little luxury, and doted on our new home with the enthusiasm of a honeybee. But was obliged to silence a few old spinsters from time to time.

"Oh, just mind your own P's and Q's, ladies," she had boldly told the gossiping members of the Cripple Creek Women's Society. "We've earned every penny of it, and more for what we've been through." But that hadn't quelled the hot rumors surrounding the hundred-dollar curtains.

They hung in our new mansion with two thousand feet of living space, built at the sum of $6,480. Hand-scrolled wood trim graced the white structure. And of course there was matching picket. A grand entertaining parlour had red velvet curtains, cedar panel, and large fireplaces. Surprised visitors were greeted to an imposing cantilever staircase rising three stories.

Patricia insisted on faux marble and printed wallpaper, and no longer allowed me to slap newspaper on the walls for protection from the bitter winter wind. "I will never look at another advertisement of brooms and bustles on my parlour walls," she argued.

We dismounted the buggy and headed for the club. I braced for the worst.

A waiter escorted us to a large circular table in the center of the room. With my first glance, worry escalated to a new level. Our dining company would be worse than jockeying socialites – Charles Moyer and his men.

"Merry Christmas, gentlemen!" I said. "You know my wife, Patricia. How do you do this evening?"

The man closest to us introduced himself as the proprietor of the Victor Hardware Emporium. The hardware man appeared stiff and unhappy with his seating next to Moyer. Moyer had evidently had a few drinks and ignored the man, talking more loudly than the atmosphere comfortably allowed.

"Hello Clark!" Moyer announced. He turned to Patricia. "Mrs. Clark, this is George Pettibone and Bill Haywood. Nice to finally meet you. I'm Chuck Moyer. We're the union representatives up in Altman."

He added emphasis, "And I'm the president."

Patricia extended a hand. "Nice to finally meet you all, too. Jeremiah has talked so much about you."

And not all good.

"How's your operation, Clark? Still busting rocks up in Independence? Have you given any more thought to joining us?"

Bill Haywood wagged his head. "No, ol' Clark won't join us. He's too proud. Big man now! Ain't ya, Clark?" I ignored him and kept an eye on Moyer. He was still holding my wife's hand and gawking at her evening gown.

"Well, business is good!" I answered cheerfully. I led Patricia around to the other side of the table, away from Moyer. "And it's going to be good again next year. I expect it will be our best yet."

Moyer had released Patricia's hand reluctantly, but his eyes remained fixed.

"Ain't this a wonderful place to live? I love the mountains and fresh air up here. I would even tolerate a little snow for the holidays. How about you boys? Didn't the Farmer's Almanac predict snow next week? How do they know that?" I had hoped to shift the conversation away from the Black Jack Mine and the progress we had made. It was none of Moyer's business.

"Okay! Well, you're a big man then," Moyer said, sporting for some action in the conversation. He was clearly not satisfied discussing the Farmer's Almanac. "Are you and Stratton still working together? Stratton sure has stepped on the backs of a lot of good men to get where he is today. I reckon you've done your share of the same, haven't you, son?"

No longer friends, I guessed. Or maybe it was the alcohol.

I felt no desire to quarrel. I just looked down at my thick calloused hands and formerly broken knuckles, and knew I had stepped on the backs of no one. Unbeknownst to Moyer, I would be working in the Black Jack Mine tomorrow on Christmas Day as I had every day for the past four years. And as far as I knew, Stratton had done the same. We were both workingmen just like those we employed. And we had exploited no one but ourselves in our bid for success. The remark was an unjustified offense.

I leaned in and spoke, "Have I wronged you in some way, Charles? I told you the first day we met that I make my own way. Winfield Stratton and I are friends. That's all, and I reckon Mr. Stratton has made his own way too."

"Whoa! Draw them reins, son. Don't get your blood up. You sure are quick to temper."

"Well, you—"

"It just seems you mine owners are getting rich off the hard work of these three-dollar miners. That's all. You know how I feel about that.

Don't you suppose they deserve some of the prosperity? After all, labor produces all wealth, isn't that true?"

"I don't see it that way, sir. And we've been through this before. Every man has the same opportunities. I came into camp with a grubstake and a half-dead mule, and I'm sitting here today. Any man out there could do the same. I am not obliged to feed the idlers and drunks. Let them make their own way as I have done."

"Well, ain't he a wildcat! I told you he was proud," Haywood blurted out with a big laugh. "Clark pulled a gun on us once. Remember that!" He laughed so hard he sprayed spittle and food particles onto the others at the table.

The three men found the incident so amusing they cackled erratically and turned again to banter amongst themselves. They ignored Patricia and me as they had the hardware man earlier. We endured the rest of the evening with the hardware man's obsession for shovels and screws and the varied hardware needs of the district. But it was better than being buffaloed over the prosperity of the Black Jack Mine. Moyer didn't speak to us again at the party.

I guess he got the answer I owed him.

Fortunately, the holiday spirit made the evening light enough to endure. We dined on roast Christmas duck in relative pleasure. I vowed to not let this get me down. At least until we left the club.

Outside, I threw down my hat in disgust. "Gosh, Patricia. Did you hear that? I sounded like a country cowboy in there. They don't respect me. Did you see how they treated us? I swear, I will learn to talk right when in company like that."

My hat rolled away in the wind as if mocking me for my poor showing in the club. I stumbled after it, finally snatching it up, determined to show it who would prevail in the end.

"Jeremiah, you did all right in there. Don't let them get to you. Plus, I have a Christmas surprise to cheer you up. I have arranged for a vacation! And I won't hear excuses to the contrary."

"We can't afford that." That was my standard answer to almost every expenditure.

"Yes we can, and you know it. Your precious little ledgers show you've worked 1275 consecutive days without a day of rest. So I have arranged with Sam Whitman to take your responsibilities for a week, and Mrs. Burns to watch the boys, starting tomorrow."

"Tomorrow? What about–"

"Don't fret yourself; your little hole up on the hill will still be there when we return. Get your mind straight on this, Jeremiah. You're not working tomorrow, as you told Moyer. We are going to Colorado Springs for Christmas!"

"Well, I–"

"Wait until you see what's sitting at home in the shed!"

Patricia tolerated my excesses but knew when to assert her own authority. Early the next morning she swung open the shed door to reveal my new Christmas gift: a shiny new Ford motorcar!

After the rude conversation with Moyer and his men, I was ready for a vacation, especially with a sleek new motorcar.

"Now, you boys don't give Mrs. Burns any grief," Patricia warned before we left. "We'll be back in one week."

"Yes, Ma," Micah said. "I'll make sure Caleb behaves. He teases the Burns girls with salamanders."

Caleb glowered.

The rough dirt road to Colorado Springs shadowed the Midland rail line through Divide and Woodland Park, down the old Ute Pass driveway into Manitou Springs, Colorado City, and finally Colorado Springs. The forty-five mile route would take about ten hours. Of course one could take the Midland railway in two. But we planned to enjoy the scenery of Pikes Peak and then kiss in the meadows of Cascade Lake.

I liked the kissing part.

I had packed the four-horsepower Quadricycle with six corded tires and tubes, block-and-tackle, five gallons of gasoline, five gallons of water, and three puzzling pink bags of lotions and ointments for which I could not readily supply a purpose.

The rutted wagon road posed a terrible challenge to the ill-equipped Quadricycle. Rock ledges, washouts, and deep water made the route nearly impassible. We winched over obstacles that a team of mules would pass without notice. I hoped the Farmer's Almanac was wrong about the predicted snowfall. I feared our return trip up the steep pitches would not be without incident, but instead gave myself to the anticipation of the adventure ahead.

Old memories rose up as we emerged from the rocky heights of the Garden of the Gods and entered the bustling streets of Colorado City. Dozens of smelting operations and stamp mills now filled the valley with a thick brown smoke and a deafening roar. Tents, shanties, and mills packed the valley floor. Gold ore came in by rail every hour, forming a complex network of tracks and spurs to negotiate.

But the little auto did fine.

In the mills, Cripple Creek ore was stamped into powder and sifted onto shaker tables for extraction. A mercury amalgamation separated gold from powdered rock. The tiny gold flakes were collected and smelted into bars, leaving vast amounts of waste rock to be discarded.

"Patricia, there sits a hundred million dollars of gold! Did you know that the shaker tables have recovered only half the gold from that ore? The rest is out of reach of the amalgamation process. That's a mountain of gold," I explained, raising my voice in quirky excitement at the dozen iron mules grooming the huge mounds.

Patricia perked up. "Yeah, and with all that mercury, a blade of grass won't grow on that hill for a hundred years."

We sat quietly as the little motorcar puffed slowly by the masses of crushed waste, still containing a thousand fortunes.

We drove east along the rock mounds, over Fountain Creek, and into the open space between Colorado City and Colorado Springs. The city lay just ahead.

"We're here!" I said. "It looks so different than when we came through in '95. It's only been four years."

Patricia edged in. "Know who lives here?"

"No idea."

"William Jackson Palmer. The Northern general that knew your uncle Olin, back in Missoura."

"Civil War hero, right? And Quaker. He founded this town in '72. I know that much." The little Ford clattered along the wide streets, each with a view of Pikes Peak. It felt like a resort. "Palmer sure did this town up fine. Must be a good fellow."

"That's what I heard. And I want you to meet him!"

Chapter Thirteen

GENERAL PALMER'S NEW RAILHEADS next to older towns like Colorado City created high land premiums, just like they had at the Pennsylvania Railroad. Colorado Springs was one of those towns, and we stepped off the motorcar, amazed at the modern city.

"We're here!" Patricia squealed in excitement. "And there's our hotel, the Alta Vista. Six floors! Can you believe it? Let's go all the way to the top! I wired them to expect us. I hope there's hot running water and maid service. And no children. I won't have to do a thing!"

The Alta Vista Hotel was the perfect resort. Everything was provided, even hot running water. A newspaperman in the lobby offered to take our photograph and publish a special Christmas piece about our visit. Exactly why, I was not sure. You could see the whole city from our window. We felt like gods. After all, Cripple Creek had no buildings this tall. We had never seen such a sight.

The next evening we thought we'd try dining at the El Paso Club. It was right down the street from the Alta Vista, so we walked. Patricia and I stepped up to the large mahogany door. And it magically opened before us.

A well-dressed doorman appeared. "This is a private club, sir. If you wish to join, it will be $118 upon entry sir." The doorman spoke in a high-spirited but gentle tone. I was rapidly becoming acquainted with the social cultures of the well-to-do, and the cost to mingle with them.

"Will you accept my personal check and assurance for the amount, sir? I own the Black Jack Mine in Cripple Creek."

"Most certainly, sir." To this man, I was not a Missoura plowhand with eighth-grade English. I was a gentleman of leisure. A mine owner. "Please see the executive administrator on the third floor, and enjoy the pleasure of our electric elevator to your destination. Welcome to the El Paso Club!"

What a place! We stood arrested in what felt like the entrance to heaven itself. Even the contrast to the Gold Coin Club was obvious. Hushed tones of service personnel, soft illumination, and flawless execution hummed like wheels in a grand machine. I was on my best behavior.

The El Paso Club attracted the wealthiest men of Denver and Colorado Springs. It had become the center of financial activity and a sanctuary for the area's richest businessmen. A million dollars could pass from man to man in the space of a handshake. Unlike Cripple Creek, Colorado Springs forbad the consumption of alcohol. It had been founded on the temperance principles of the Quaker faith – General Palmer's Quaker faith. They allowed nothing that might dilute the blood, taint the wits, or hinder the ability of wealthy men to make countless sums of money.

The newspaper article submitted by the cub reporter at the Alta Vista the night before became our calling card. Influential men who managed the processing mills of Colorado City approached with handshakes. I could only guess… to get the Black Jack ore business.

Charlie MacNeill and his wife dined with us. He managed the Standard Mill. I had met Charlie a few years earlier when Spencer Penrose, the founder of the C.O.D. Mine became his business partner. We made pleasant company and the evening soon filled with rich conversation. A big contrast to the ugly exchange with Moyer and Haywood. I was happy for the change.

MacNeill turned to me with a wide smile. "I don't know the mining business up there in Cripple Creek, but Penrose does. He's always had some bizarre tales of what goes on up there, and he's never bashful about repeating them. There's one tale that sticks in my gullet like a chicken loaf," he said, pausing for my reaction.

"Well, go on," I said, indulging him with a laugh. "What does Spencer Penrose say now?"

"You really have to hear him tell it; he's got a cockamamie story of little creatures they call Tommyknockers. He claims they're elves or some such thing. I guess they cause all manner of mischief up there, at least to hear him tell it. Have you heard that one?"

I chuckled. "Oh yes, the Cornish repeat it often. But I've been told Penrose is a little on the wild side. I've only been up there four years, but I can tell you some pretty good stories."

Since I'd never actually met a Tommyknocker face to face, I skipped that story and recounted my exploits as a Missoura sharecropper-turned-gold-magnate, to the amusement of the MacNeill's and three other couples who had joined in to listen. The story was just as good. They roared at the utter nonsense of entering the gold business with nothing but a worn out plow mule, hammer, and bit. Within the space of two hours, a good share of the membership had joined the circle, and had raised quite a commotion.

The club executive leaned in to our table. "Gentlemen, this is not a place for braggarts and brawlers. We are not Leadville. We are not Cripple Creek. Loud banter will not be tolerated."

When we'd had finally quieted down, and groups of men had splintered off to close business deals or discuss new ones, General Palmer approached our table to introduce himself.

"My name's William Palmer. Those were some wild tales, son! How much is true?"

"Jeremiah Clark, sir. And they're all true," I replied, happy to shake the General's hand and finally meet him. He had been a legend for founding Colorado Springs and developing the Denver and Rio Grand Railway. I never expected to actually meet him in person.

Palmer smiled. "I'm glad to see some new blood in here. Sometimes this place gets pretty stuffy, with old money and such. I guess you riled things up around here. Good for you! Don't listen to the executives here. Everyone else enjoyed the stories. Some of these stodgy bluebloods have never faced such trials and tribulations. I suppose they found your raw grit and good fortune fresh entertainment for the evening. They got their money's worth."

"I don't have much time or talent for fanciful tales," I said. "Most of the time, I have an eight-pound hammer in one hand and a clipboard in the other, riding herd over a gang of rough miners. Mostly, I just muck ore."

Palmer laughed. "A millionaire ore mucker. I guess that makes you plenty busy! Hey, I saw the newspaper piece on your stay at the Alta Vista."

"Yes!" I said. Patricia leaned in to listen.

"I sure wish the Antlers Hotel hadn't burned down. We'd have you stay there. But the Alta Vista is nice."

Patricia beamed. "Oh, we just love it."

"Why don't we plan to meet tomorrow? I'll show you the town. I'd like to hear more about your operation, and maybe get to know you two a little better. I'll have a carriage pick you up. Good evening to you both. I really must be getting on."

We looked forward to spending some time with General Palmer. We had an immediate kinship that I knew would last beyond the week we planned to spend in his city. Plus, I wanted to know how he knew my Uncle Olin.

We returned to the Alta Vista for a pleasant night's sleep in a decadent feather bed. What a night! And like a child on a schoolyard slide I wanted to do it all over again. And again. And again.

Patricia didn't argue. "Dear, if you wish to squander a workingman's yearly wages this week, you are entitled. This is your vacation and you may spend your time and money as you like."

How vane and demanding I felt.

Evening after evening, the El Paso Club bore out the reality of the dream. I struck lifelong friendships and came to terms with new ideas. That alone was worth the money. Of course, the newly formed Teller County was the sizzling topic every night. Since the redistricting in March, El Paso county businessmen no longer held direct political control over their own mining interests in Cripple Creek. That concerned them, and the debate raged every night.

"Smith, you newspapermen bore me," Charlie MacNeill said. "You are a blamed fool if you think the Western Federation of Miners won't bring Teller County down on us like a hammer."

"A hammer?" The newspaper man practically laughed.

MacNeill tightened his fist. "Did you know—"

The newspaperman waved his hand. "Bahh."

"Just hear me out. I understand that the miners and mill workers need a vigorous defense of their livelihoods, but this is going too far. A whole new county just for them? That just doesn't make sense. I just wonder who was asleep at the switch when this passed the House and Senate. I guess we all were."

"Well, it was certainly a stroke of genius, that's for sure," Spencer Penrose put in. "We've all been hoodwinked this time. I just don't see what will stop them, now that the political engine in Denver is behind them. What's to stop them from ruining the whole system?"

MacNeill edged in. "You watch. The price of gold ore will be out of sight, and profits as thin as a razor. All because of an overaggressive union with its own county to control."

His neck muscles tightened. "I despise those vermin, I swear."

"Remember the silver bust?" Penrose added.

MacNeill nodded. "In '93. Yep. That was another political maneuver."

"Betcha we see the same results from this one."

"And will they ever take the responsibility when it's all over?"

"Oh, you two are blowing this completely out of proportion!" the news editor jumped in. "Can't you just let them have their day? They're not going to ruin anything. It's high time the workingman got a little support. You mine and millmen bore me too. That's all I've got to say."

And so went the debate, night after night. The WFM had either pulled a big black gunny sack over our eyes and would seek our demise in the worst way, or were simply defending the working class with good politics. There was no clear answer, at least not at the El Paso Club.

But I preferred the time spent with General Palmer over wrangling politics. We spoke for hours of business and family, wife and children, and tarried over memories of home in Jackson County and my decision to leave after the death of my mother.

"So what got into you, back in Missouri?" Palmer asked. "It's a big thing to toss off the plow reins and head for the wilds of Colorado. I reckon your clan occupied most of Randall's Flats after the war, didn't they? That's a barren territory for sure but you were holding down some good work there weren't you? So where did the idea of Colorado come from?"

"There were a lot of families heading west. I couldn't make a living in Randall's Flats."

"Yeah, I remember how bad it was in '93. And I know a little about Missouri," Palmer ventured. "I guess when that cholera epidemic hit, half those clans moved on. Randall's Flats got pretty empty. That's what I heard."

Palmer's knowledge of Missoura amazed me.

"I expect most of the work dried up, what with the Panic and all," Palmer said. I just sat and wondered how he knew it all. He must have been a man of the world.

"I do believe I know a relative of yours," he finally said.

I sat back and smiled. "I don't see how. But Patricia—"

"Didn't you have a cousin named Buford Cantrell still living in or around Randall's Flats? I met him in the summer of '66."

"What? You met Buford Cantrell?"

He paused to think. "Hang on now, while I get this story straight…"

"Wait… 1866? That would make me two years old at the time. Born in '64."

He raised his finger. "Alright, I remember now. I met Buford and his Pa down at the crossroads of Randall's Flats and Big Hollow. There's a big stand of oaks there, right? I was just passing through at the time. It was only a year after the war had ended. And that territory was devastated. Absolutely ruined. Farms burned. No work. Devastated.

Well, Olin and me had some words on that summer day I'll never forget."

"You spoke with Olin Cantrell? My uncle?"

"Yes, I remember him well. Young Buford was wearing only one boot as I recall, and I couldn't figure where the other one might be, or why anyone would go hobbling around like that. Funniest thing I ever saw. The fact is, Olin took me for a carpetbagger and threatened to tar and feather. Or hang me. You know... Yankee accent and all. From Pennsylvania."

"And how did you get out of that scrape? Olin is no one to mess with."

"Little Buford saved me." He laughed. "Chunked rocks at his own pa until he left off harassing me. And I was able to skedaddle out of there."

"Buford was a bit tetched. Still is," I explained. "And, he was born with a crooked foot, so he didn't like the one boot. Uncle Olin toted him around everywhere, but they never had a stick of sense between them. Olin Cantrell was my mother's brother. I liked him plenty." I smiled and looked into the sky. "He always made me laugh, and once bought me a drop of hard candy which he could not afford. I never forgot that. Funny how you remember things like that."

"Sounds like a good man."

"I don't know how you know them, but you've got the right clan. You sure do venture into some strange places, Mr. Palmer."

And so, with many such conversations of the hardships in Missoura, and Randall's Flats, and Big Hollow, and drops of hard candy, our friendship grew deeper every day.

We visited the Glen Eyrie Castle in the Garden of the Gods. It was the pride of Palmer's life, where he entertained city officials, Colorado state dignitaries, and on occasion world leaders. I learned he despised the automobile because it was too impersonal, and that he had ridden with his daughters on the Glen Eyrie estate nearly every day for the last twenty years. Patricia and I were now privy to those private family rides.

115

"These are the old Ute Indian trails," he pointed out as we rode along. "The army drove them all out after the White River massacre in western Colorado. Eleven men killed… That was a sad story, but I'll tell you a funny one that occurred a little earlier."

He looked into the hills to gather his thoughts.

"One day, a group of curious Indians came into Glen Eyrie uninvited. My house! They were foraging for food when the wait-staff encountered them in the kitchen pantry. I'm not sure which party was more alarmed. They both fled in opposite directions hollering in their native tongues! I'm not an Indian lover, but I kept good relations with the savages when they were here. It was a hard day when the Rangers finally rounded them all up."

We all laughed at the funny story.

On the last night of our vacation there was a grand New Year's celebration at the El Paso Club. As the stroke of midnight approached, we all prepared for the unknowns of a new century.

"Ten… nine… eight… seven… six… five… four… three… two… one… Happy New Year, 1900!" We all shouted. What a glorious time to be alive.

The vacation was coming to a satisfying close. Too short, of course. In a few days I'd be shoveling ore again. But satisfying and profitable. The coming of the new century had arrived in style. Expectations were high. Business was booming and temperance and good nature was at last a reality, or at least in Colorado Springs. This would be the greatest century man had ever known – a century of goodwill and understanding.

Palmer escorted us out to our motorcar after the celebration. Even in January, an overcoat was all we needed. Every star in the universe mustered for our viewing pleasure. I saw genuine care in Palmer's eyes. I had never dreamed of making the acquaintance of such a man, and never expected his generous acceptance into his family. It was hard to leave.

We stood there for several minutes exchanging pleasantries and wishing well for the New Year. With a trace of sadness in his eyes, he took me aside as if to impart one final bit of fatherly advice. We stood face to face.

I opened my soul to his words.

Palmer glanced up at the stars. His hands shook in the cool air, and he looked as though he might cry. I stepped back as he regained composure. It must have been hard for him too.

Hi voice trembled. "Son, I knew your…"

Another pause.

He had trembled like this on the ranges of Glen Eyrie, and supposed it had something to do with the old Utes. After a long silence, he continued again.

"You know I fought in the war…" He stopped and hung his head. I just stood there, waiting for him to regain his poise. Quavering. Shifting about.

"There's just no good way to say this, so I'm going to just say it," he explained, swallowing hard. With a final pause and a crack in his voice, he spoke.

"Son, you probably wondered how I knew your kin in Missouri. I am deeply sorry for what I am about to say, but… Jeremiah… I killed your daddy at the Battle of Chattanooga."

Chapter Fourteen

"I WILL KILL HIM. I will hunt him down and kill him," I growled.

It was a quarter past noon the next day, and I had only just woken up. Images of murder and revenge had invaded my sleep. I decided to avenge my daddy's death that very day.

"Oh just get dressed," Patricia demanded. She had been up for four hours, and was bored sitting in the hotel room. "You're not going to do any such thing. We're going home today. You'll get over it."

"My mother never recovered from my daddy's death. We had nothing. And then she lost our home on account of that Yankee murderer."

Patricia faced the mirror and dabbed on some eye powder. "General Palmer?"

"Yes, you know that. He took everything from her. I will not allow him to draw breath another day. After the war, those Yankee carpetbaggers took everything we owned," I said, rolling over to face the wall. "Uncle Olin was right to hate them."

I grumbled and stared at the ceiling

"They swarmed the South like locusts. Those rich Northern bankers took every farm and home left standing, and for pennies on the dollar, or outright theft. They took everything Sherman's army didn't set ablaze. Five hundred thousand homes and farms burned. With three younguns and a farm to feed, my mama lost everything to those thieving Yankees. And he's one of them."

Patricia left the mirror and stood over me. I expected her to slap me. "Stop that hateful talk. Mr. Palmer is your friend and I will not have you speak of him in that wicked manner. Just remember who you're talking to. My daddy died of typhoid in that hellhole they called a prison in Elmira. And my mama lost everything, same as yours."

I rolled away. "Yes, we did. Everything."

"Well, we all did. But the war has been over for a good spell, so get over it. Now you go find that man and ask for his forgiveness for your rude behavior last night. You will not get rest from this root of bitterness until you do. I will not have you lying about like a wounded dog."

She threw the blankets from the bed and flung open the heavy green velvet drapes to the early rays of afternoon.

But she was wrong. Yes... I would find him, but I would also cut him to pieces for my mama's sake. She lost two decades of her life on account of that Yankee war. Should her early death of a tired heart go unpunished? I aimed to kill that murdering Yankee at the next opportunity. There was no question of that now.

I dragged myself from the bed and dressed shabbily without shaving. We left the Alta Vista Hotel still quarreling.

Two more volleys of cruel words followed. I started the Quadricycle and sped north on Cascade Street looking to hunt him down. The little auto bounced over four-inch curbs and tore across green lawns. Patricia nearly fell out.

"Stop it!" she said. "You're scaring me, and if you're going to drive like that, I don't want to go."

I didn't listen.

I cut through Acacia Park and bounced onto Nevada Street, determined to find him. I knew Palmer visited the shops and businesses every day to give aid and advice, stopping to share a story or swap spit. He picnicked in the park every day under the oak trees and took life with simplicity. If I could have found him there, I would have cut his heart out with a knife.

119

Nevada Street was home to a growing number of tuberculosis lungers. The poor souls spent their days in the Colorado Springs sunshine and their nights in the warm air. A quarter of the citizens had sought out the city to either get well or live out their days in what pleasure the western climates afforded. We passed rows of lungers resting on their open porches reclining on convalescent beds, with quarts of milk by their sides and thick comforters draped over their tired legs. All as thin and fragile as ribbon candy. All watching the curious Quadricycle speed by.

Nine miles an hour can be a holy terror.

The lungers claimed the western air was light and easy to inhale. They said you could wave your arms and feel the lightness on your skin. The thick air in the east weighed too heavily on their lungs. And, entire eastern towns were sometimes covered with low-hanging clouds of brown smoke. No such ugly smoke lingered at the base of Pikes Peak.

Rows of convalescent huts also sat on the slopes of Manitou Springs. They had been placed at the base of the peak where the air was said to be the best. But oddly, most of the lungers still preferred the resort atmosphere of Colorado Springs even if the air was not considered as good.

Several hollered from their porches as I sped by, obviously irritated at my lack of care for the safety of others. The Quadricycle was at full throttle.

It must have been a terrible sight of mechanical madness.

One leaped from his steamer chair. "Stop, you reckless lunatic! Watch where you're going. You're going to kill someone!"

With my eyes still fixed on the row of convalescent beds, I felt the spiteful urge to shout, "Mind your own business, and I hope the exercise did you good." But eying my stiff wife, I chose to hold my tongue. Patricia had had almost enough.

Just as my eyes returned to the road, a slow herd of milk cows crossed before the little Quadricycle. I heaved the hand-brake with all my strength. The bicycle tires skidded on freshly scattered cow droppings and we slammed broadside into one of the large animals.

The cow mooed loudly and bolted for the pasture. I sat in the middle of the road with a bent fender and broken headlamp. The delicate vehicle stalled upon impact.

The lungers leaped to their feet, aghast at the freak accident. Thirty milk cows just crossed in front of the stalled carriage in quiet disregard while I endured the humiliation of leering eyes.

"We told you to look, you blind man," added one of the lungers, as if his witness had not been humiliating enough.

The damage to my new motorcar only added fury to the violent mission. I finally got the thing started and jumped back into the seat. Patricia looked up. "Okay, Mr. Rib-Bender, let's go kill somebody."

Fifteen minutes passed with no luck. I could not dispel the sight of that large spotted cow from my mind, and even I had to laugh a little. I had to admit the comedy of it all and how it had disrupted my evil plans. Maybe God has a sense of humor.

Softening occurred street by street. Of course I tried to renew my anger with unkind words but it didn't really work. Mostly because Patricia kept bringing up the cow and laughing at me. I wanted to hold it long enough to justify the violent acts I had planned for Palmer, although I was unsure what I would do when I actually confronted the man.

As we rumbled along still at full throttle, I could plainly see the thoughtfulness Palmer had put into his community. Perhaps the cow had opened my eyes in some small way. His utopian experiment was an obvious success. It was his mission field, and it was fulfilling its mission.

I thought back to an earlier conversation.

"Ever wonder why we don't allow alcohol?" Palmer had asked before the New Year's party.

I remember shaking my head. "That did cross my mind."

"Alcohol contributes to pauperism and ill-mannered behavior. They can drink it here... but not buy it. See the difference from Colorado City? One small thing like that makes a big difference."

Indeed, the contrasts were numerous. More than just the effects of alcohol abuse. The constant roar of stamp mills and ore processing in Colorado City made this feel like a resort in comparison. It was quiet and peaceful – a place where gentlemen tipped their hats and ladies curtsied to passing parties. Ill-mannered men did not spit tobacco on the walkways, or stumble from saloon to rowdy saloon. And they didn't tear up and down the streets in motorcars. Cripple Creek had even begun calling the city "Little London." It was such a place of high society.

Or maybe it was just because General Palmer and his wife Queen kept going back there for retreats and kept bringing the high society back with them.

Surely this was not the work of a common murderer, the likes of which I had encountered in the rowdy gold camps around Cripple Creek. Yet, he took my daddy away. And that sole act had killed my mama in the doing. Could I let that stand? Could I abide my own daddy's killer and not lift a finger?

A silent voice spoke. "Vengeance is mine saith the Lord, I will repay."

Of course the racket of lungers and my erratic driving attracted the attention of a cop on the beat. A whistle blast summoned the vehicle to stop.

"Have you lost your mind, man? We still permit women and children to walk these streets, even with madmen like you about," the arresting officer harshly reprimanded in a thick Irish accent. "And if you were to strike one? Would you be so brazen then? I've a mind to lock ya up if you persist in such a reckless manner. You know we've got laws here, and they're here to protect these fine citizens. The speed limit is five miles per hour."

"Yes sir," I said, ashamed before Patricia. "I understand. Five miles per hour."

He got even madder. "Well, you were doubl'n that, or I'm the Prince of Wales. Get out. I'm takin' ya in."

"Oh no. I'll slow down. I promise."

"Can ya proceed in a safer manner? Or would you prefer a night in the pokey to slap some sense into ya? I'll kindly accept only a yes or nah answer to that question, mister."

I chose to comply upon demand. Patricia just frowned, like a child who had just received a good spanking. No further words were needed.

After restarting the vehicle with a stroke of the crank, we were off again, this time, in a more civilized way. The merry little auto-car clattered over neatly graded streets. By this time I had lost my aim but continued the mission out of stubborn pride. White picket fences and marble carriage steps buzzed past without notice as I drove in fixed gaze and empty thought. Five miles per hour. No faster.

Who was this man I pursued with all my being? Did I know him at all? Conflicting information tortured my already senseless mind. And at this point, I was unsure what I would do if we actually located Palmer, for in our heated flight from the hotel I had not thought to pack a weapon.

While mindlessly guiding the little buggy up and down the streets, the engine abruptly quit, offering no obvious reason for the loss of service. This was the third time. It was easy enough to restart with a quick crank, but it had begun to annoy me. I wondered if the incident with the cow had led to its erratic operation.

I jumped out to pop the crumpled hood for a closer look, and came face to face with General William Jackson Palmer.

I reeled back against the auto, grasping for some words in an awkward moment. The purpose of my mission was now gone, leaving me in dumb silence. But Palmer salvaged the situation gracefully.

"Why… Jeremiah, my boy! I am certainly pleased to see you about on this pleasant afternoon. You're just the man I've been looking for. Don't you find the sight of Pikes Peak magnificent in the winter?"

"Yessir," I said nervously, closing the hood.

"Do you suppose a fella like me could muster the grit to climb such a peak? Its namesake, Lieutenant Zeb Pike never did reach the summit. Did you know that?"

"No sir. I didn't." And I still wondered why he was looking for me. Didn't he know we were heading home?

"Only a passel have done it under their own power. I've often thought of leading an expedition up that little knoll myself. It's only 14,110 feet elevation. Almost as tall as the European Alps, you know? By George, I'll do that before I die!"

He looked up at the snowcapped mountain and rambled on about the little carriage road that Spencer Penrose built ten years ago. It went all the way to the top, he said. Be he would not consider such a leisurely trip equal to the vigorous efforts of climbing the mountain under one's own power.

"No sir! That would be the true challenge, I expect."

"Yessir, I expect so," I said, still trying to hide my strong feelings, but not knowing exactly what to make of them.

"Son, do you suppose you might spare another week in your vacation schedule? I know you are a busy man. You've got the mine and all. But I should like to have you ride circuit with me to visit my railheads." Palmer ignored what might be left of our conflict.

By this time, Palmer had connected the entire state of Colorado by rail and owned a fair piece of it himself. Those railheads turned into cities. And cities meant vast real estate holdings. I stood in the presence of one of the wealthiest men in America. And just minutes ago, was fixin' to kill him.

"Well, sir... I suppose... Let me ask my wife."

Palmer had somehow been able to talk me down. Perhaps just the sight of his friendly face had done it. Or the cow. Or the bobby who threatened to take me in. In any case, my senses had been calmed to the point where I could reasonably entertain his offer. After stepping back and discussing the proposal with Patricia, we decided Sam could manage another week without me if I could hold my salt against Palmer. We decided to take him up on the offer.

"But no more mean-spirited talk," Patricia warned.

Without another word, we stowed the motorcar and boarded the Denver and Rio Grande passenger train to Denver. Without a ticket! Palmer traveled in his own private sleeping car and made arrangements for a private car for Patricia and me, plus a meeting car for the entire party.

"You'll see some of the most magnificent scenery in the United States," Palmer said, beaming in excitement. "This will be a fun trip."

Palmer pointed out his riding haunts north of Glen Eyrie and the Garden of the Gods. The train stopped in the little settlement of

Monument. He said someday pretty little homes would cover this entire wilderness and that men would travel from Denver to Colorado Springs in the twinkling of an eye. Eyeing the wide-open scenes of rock outcroppings and scrub oak, I could not envision so many people, but listened intently and accepted his every word on the matter.

Curious rock formations formed by the cataclysm of Noah's flood played delightfully about us, ignoring our intruding presence. We saw the Kissing Camels and Elephant Rock, which mystified us all. From the train, Palmer pointed out Mount Herman in Monument and the namesake, Monument Rock.

"Jeremiah, are you enjoying the Colorado Front Range? I expect you saw a fair piece of these foothills on your way in from Missouri to Colorado City. But wait until we get into the big mountains. Nine thousand feet is nothing next to those leviathans! And we've laid iron right through them."

"Really!"

"Well, around them I should say, but when necessary, right through the heart of them. My men have blasted thirty-eight tunnels from here to Aspen and back."

"Isn't Aspen on the other side of the big mountains?" Patricia asked. "Can we get over there?"

"Yep. I've picked up a fair piece of Colorado territory just running rail into Aspen. I've been in this line of work since I was a little older than your sons. Except for a few years during the war, I've been doing it ever since. It's what I really enjoy. Every month I ride rail to visit my employees just like we're doing today. But I have something special planned this time."

The slowly passing scenery made a refreshing diversion from the torture of evil surmising. My passion to avenge my father's killer had been tabled until I could make sense of my emotions. Perhaps the incident in Chattanooga was just another ugly aspect of war that was foreign to me. Although we suffered in Missoura, war was not part of my upbringing and I knew little of its actual horror. So for now, I would sit and enjoy the Colorado scenery and give my frazzled mind a rest.

Palmer pointed up the tracks. "We'll be in Denver shortly. You should meet my banker. I'll set up a dinner meeting."

"What's his name?" I asked.

"James Peabody. You'll like him. Pay attention while we're there. He'll connect you to the investors and bankers you'll need to take your operation to the next level. Just like the men you met at the El Paso, this man can help your career. But I'll warn you. He's a smooth talker from down Cañon City way, near your neck of the woods. So I'm not sure he can be trusted." Palmer laughed. "Actually, he's a good man to know."

After disembarking at the Denver station Palmer telegraphed the banker's office and arranged for dinner. I also took the opportunity to dash off a quick note to Sam explaining our extended vacation. He would ask Mrs. Burns to watch the boys for another week. We freshened up and met Peabody within a few hours. Those pink ointment bags take time.

"James, I'm pleased to introduce my friend, Jeremiah Clark and his ravishing bride, Patricia. Jeremiah, meet my banker, Mr. James Peabody. You two will have plenty to discuss over dinner, I expect," Palmer said, smiling, pleased to make the introduction.

James Peabody was a smartly dressed, energetic man, with confidence at every turn. He was the kind of man you just liked to listen to, and with strong business and political positions. He never allowed a conversation to stall and always reinforced my own ideas with new ones. I suppose those were admirable and necessary qualities for a banker.

Kind of like Charles Thomas, but thinner.

"Son, how is it that you know old Private Palmer here?" Peabody asked with a wide smile. "I was a little too young to fight the Rebs, but I understand Palmer wormed his way into the 15th Pennsylvania Volunteers. Even managed to sneak off with one of those Congressional Medal of Honor ribbons from the War Department. Go figure! And whoever convinced the army brass to elevate a crook like Palmer to Brigadier General? I will never know the answer to that. All kidding aside, he's a good man. How did you come to know him?"

"Well, Mr. Peabody, I operate a little gold mine up in Cripple Creek. My wife and I went to The Springs for a few days out of the hole."

"What's a pretty little wife like that doing in a hole?" he joked.

"Oh no! She doesn't work in the mine," I said, feeling a little dumb. "We came to The Springs and met Mr. Palmer there, sir. How do you know him?" I asked, still unsure what to say.

The question was a stupid mistake. He was the General's banker, of course. I scolded myself for asking such a question, but Peabody graciously obliged.

"Palmer and I do some business from time to time. He's got a few rail operations west of Denver we financed. And we worked with him down in Cañon City at the Royal Gorge. That's all."

I smiled, but couldn't keep the conversation afloat.

"So, let me ask you, Clark, what are your thoughts on the new Teller County up there in Cripple Creek? Are you expecting any trouble from that Federation of Miners bunch now that they've got a whole county to themselves?"

"I don't know, sir. I stay plenty busy in the mine. What do you mean?"

"Palmer doesn't know this yet, but I expect to start campaigning for governor next year. I expect to take the election in '02 like a thief in the night. Governor Thomas isn't doing a good job, and he's about to lose the office. He might even step down and return to his law practice."

I eased up a little. "Yessir, I've heard that. I've actually met Mr. Thomas, here in Denver."

"I've been watching this Teller County thing, and I don't like what I see. It looks just like a political empire in the making. Charles Moyer has got himself quite a bunch up there. Now that they've got their own county, I'm not sure where they'll stop. If ever. It's not every day a local miner's union convinces the state legislature to provision a new county just for them, now is it? What'll happen one morning when they come calling on you mine owners saying, play ball with us or we'll run you out of business?"

"I don't think they'll do that, sir."

Peabody's eyebrows lifted. "No?"

"The city fathers would never allow it."

"You know, that's another thing," he said. "Every elected official… every appointed position… and every government employee in Teller County is affiliated with a single political party. Did you know that?"

"Humm, I guess you are right. I hadn't considered that. Is that a problem?"

"Well think about it. There is absolutely no balance of power up there. I mean every man from the dogcatcher on up belongs to a single party. Doesn't that strike you as odd? Smacks of cronyism to me, and I cannot figure how a new county in Colorado could be structured that way. Unless it was designed that way from the start. But I can't be sure who the mastermind was. Charles Moyer maybe, but I'm not sure. It's just not natural. The next thing you know, they'll be printing their own money up there!"

He paused to clear his throat, and realized he'd been rambling. But Teller County was clearly a problem for Peabody.

"Oh, I suppose I've dramatized this enough, but we'll see what comes of it."

While ore processing rates, labor relations, and incidents of miner's consumption kept me up at night, political maneuvers like Teller County were the pressure points that occupied Peabody's mind. If he was to be the next governor of Colorado he would certainly wrestle with such matters on a daily basis.

The conversation moved on before I could tell Peabody what little I knew about the new county, and the meeting with Charles Thomas, and Moyer and Haywood. But I still didn't see it as a big threat. Of course the men at the El Paso Club did. And now Peabody had. So maybe there was something to it. But it still felt like a contrivance to me.

Patricia excused herself early and returned to the sleeping car, while the three of us jawed into the morning hours. Mr. Peabody was a pleasant man. I hoped we would meet again soon, and that our friendship would last. Maybe I could lure him up to Cripple Creek for a tour of the Black Jack Mine.

Chapter Fifteen

THE NEXT MORNING WITH a hot fire in the box we steamed
west from Denver into the big mountains. These were iron rails
Palmer laid twenty years ago. We stopped at the rough mining towns of
Idaho Springs, Georgetown, Silver Plume, Breckinridge, and Leadville.
Doc Holliday had shot a man in Mannie Hyman's saloon in Leadville.
His local lore from Tombstone was still enormous even fifteen years
later. Continuing on, we disembarked at Glenwood Springs where
Holliday was finally laid to rest, having died of the consumption. Many of
the colorful characters of the Old West had died off or were killed. The
dime novel accounts of their exploits still fascinated me. At least Wyatt
Earp was still alive.

I noticed one oddity while hopping from depot to depot. At each
stop Palmer rallied the rail men and dispensed envelopes to each. And
every time there were shouts and gunshots. Surely, this was not his
standard method of dispensing wages, or their normal reaction to
receiving them. I was curious.

"What are those envelopes?" I asked. "Those men seem awfully
happy to get them."

General Palmer explained, "Those are gifts. I will dispense a
million dollars to my loyal employees during our little trip. I told you I
had something special planned."

"A million dollars!"

"Yes, there are nearly twelve hundred families that depend on this rail line for their livelihood. They have faithfully helped me build an empire and I have not forgotten their humble service. None of them are wealthy persons, and they have nothing to offer but their faithfulness and hard work. Some of these checks are over ten thousand dollars. This will set these men up for businesses of their own. I have no need of excessive wealth, which I will never spend. So I'm offering it here before I grow too old to make these trips. God Bless them in their labors."

I stood there dumfounded. Palmer went out and pitched bundles, stowed steps, and offered generous greetings to patrons on their way to parts unknown. If only the world were filled with the likes of such men.

Continuing down the line, we visited Aspen and Crested Butte in our traversal of the great Rocky Mountains. The same scene repeated itself at every depot. And I enjoyed it every time, but also enjoyed the wonderful scenery between them.

Mountain peaks over 14,000 feet in elevation passed before our large cabin windows. Little log cabins dotted the mountain slopes where hearty souls had prospected for gold and silver in the rugged mountains. Trails of red and gray tailings spilled down the steep crags – waste rock emitted from horizontal adits cut into the near-vertical granite. Just like in Cripple Creek.

"Are murderers living out in those old cabins?" Patricia asked. "They look so inhospitable."

"Christian murderers, maybe. I know the folks in that one." He pointed to a shack hanging off the side of a mountain. "Just prospectors trying to make a living. Living their dreams. Cripple Creek was the same before Stratton and Womack came in. Rugged and inhospitable."

During one tight maneuver, the little train passed through fifteen feet of heavy snow recently cleared by a crew of German plowmen. The twenty-man crew with shovels in hand waved us onward with a cheer and a hearty "heave-ho."

"Hoffentlich haben Sie lange Unterwäsche!" they joked as we passed through the big snowdrift.

We watched the men disappear into the distance as the little train slowly trundled up the mountain. They waved broad shovels, signaling their appreciation for the man they loved.

"What did that mean, Under vassher?" Patricia asked innocently.

Palmer smiled. "Do you really want to know? It means, 'I hope you have long underwear!'"

"Oh!" Patricia shrieked and snapped her head down. "I'll just keep my mouth shut now!"

Everyone laughed.

We crawled up the enormous Monarch Pass, the pinnacle of the Continental Divide. The modest steam engine on its narrow-gauge track clicked along at two miles per hour up the narrow mountain ledges. Patricia hid her eyes from the large open windows when cliffs were so sheer you could not see the roadbed. One loose iron rail could derail the train, sending us to the valley floor to meet our Maker. She shrieked and covered her head as Palmer and I teased with such plausible scenarios.

"Look down there!" Palmer urged. "There's an old railcar a thousand feet down."

"Stop it!" she yelled. And hid her eyes.

From the top of Monarch Pass we could see a hundred mountaintops. At this crease of the Continental Divide, I learned that waters to the east flowed into the Atlantic Ocean while waters to the west eventually emptied into the Pacific. We were at the very top of the great United States. We disembarked at the summit for a breathless view of the terrain below.

Snowcapped peaks stretched for a hundred miles.

"Take a look," Palmer said, handing me his field glasses and compass. "Even with the mountain peaks and slight curvature of the earth, you can see Cripple Creek from this mountain pass. It's 63 degrees magnetic north."

"Yes! I see the smoke." It was right where he said it would be. I couldn't see well, but strained through the glasses for a glimpse of the Black Jack headframe situated at the top of Battle Mountain. It was too far.

"Cripple Creek is only sixty-five miles east of us. And the Black Canyon of Gunnison is equal distance to the west," Palmer said.

The sensation of standing on the top of the world was practically unexplainable, inviting me as before to leap from mountaintop to mountaintop. I felt I could reach out and touch them all, and jump from tip to tip. It was the stuff of dreams, or perhaps of heaven itself.

As if the views from Monarch Pass were not enough, Palmer pulled another ace from his sleeve. A coal-blackened workman slid open the door of a special boxcar to reveal a monstrous steam-powered contraption. The boiler had been stoked for two hours and now had a full head of steam. The workman jerked a cord and a loud whistle blast echoed over the mountain peaks.

"It's not another engine to power the train," Palmer explained. "It's a hoist. Just like yours in Cripple Creek. We'll use it to get back up."

Patricia's mouth curled up. "Get back up? Back up what?"

The workmen swung out a long steel boom from the boxcar. They began reeling the cable over the rocky ledge on which we stood. The cable stretched a dizzying thousand feet down the southern-facing slope. Palmer and some of the workmen strapped long Norwegian skis onto their boots and said, "All right, let's go!"

"Down there?" Patricia cried. "Oh, no! I'm staying right here."

"Yep, the men will help you," Palmer said, and scooted away, over the steep cliff on his skis.

Patricia and I strapped on the same long wooden skis and managed our way down the slope to a large frozen lake. The fresh powder made the new experience very enjoyable, although a little frightening and a bit awkward. But with time we floated on pillows of snow all the way. At the bottom we stood in the center of a huge mountainous bowl. By this time, a freshly built bonfire awaited us. Ice skates were supplied, and for two hours, we skated against the backdrop of steep mountains and heavy snowfall. We felt like miniature figurines in a tiny winter scene sailing effortlessly across glassy surfaces.

All around were walls of snow-covered granite with hearty evergreen clinging to their slopes. A family of bighorn sheep picked their way down narrow passages toward the low country. The little train could be seen far at the top of Monarch Pass. From time to time its whistle echoed across the huge mountain bowl. It seemed like a miniature wooden toy up there. On distant slopes avalanche chutes erupted, throwing aside evergreens like little tumbling matchsticks. The power of God was at work in exotic places I had never known existed.

As the sun settled over the mountain ridgeline, the long steel tow-cable powered by the boxcar hoist drew the entire troupe to the top. After reaching the summit we all turned for a last look at the little mountain lake below. It now looked as small as a tin nickel but had offered an experience to last a lifetime.

We boarded the passenger cars after a quick meal with rail employees. Patricia solemnly warned me not to repeat the same performances of the previous leg of the trip. No more scary talk! I offered my most sincere assurances with a devilish little smile.

The eastern slope of the Continental Divide descended into the warmer climates of Poncha Springs, Salida, Buena Vista, and Cañon City. Palmer had won the railway rights through the dramatic Royal Gorge just west of Cañon City in a bitter contest against the Santa Fe Railroad. This southern route through the Rockies was now the principle rail line for silver ore into Pueblo and Colorado City.

As we exited eastward out of the dramatic walls of the canyon, I suddenly realized we were near home. The treacherous Shelf Road to Cripple Creek spanned a mere thirty miles from Cañon City. I was only a day's ride from home. My summer employees lived here so I decided to follow the General's lead and pay a quick visit to some of them as they plied their winter occupations in the warmer climates of Cañon City. It was no place to spend a baking summer but the winters were mild enough.

We waved goodbye to Cañon City and Palmer pulled me aside to talk. He had been uneasy with the way things were left between us on New Year's Day. It was his nature to not leave things unsaid. Life was too short. You might go into eternity with something like that on your conscience.

Palmer explained my father's death.

"Jeremiah, I knew your daddy as a fine officer and soldier. It was not uncommon for the men of the North and South to converse on occasion. As such, I came to know him as a friend. On rare occasions during cessations of hostilities, we swapped a little tobacco, coffee, and salt pork, and found our conversation pleasant. We even played a game of bat ball on one occasion. You won't believe this, but we even stole a chicken and cooked it together. We had a fine friendship, even while on opposite sides of the war. Strange, but true.

"Your father had just been brevetted to Colonel and led the charge at Chattanooga. I can see a lot of him in you. He was a brave young man who would not shirk the dreadful charge laid before him – although in truth it was suicide. Those men charged ten-pound Napoleon's with the convictions of saints. But those who passed the Minnie balls and grapeshot were dispatched with sword and bayonet. The field lay red with the blood of thousands, shocking the sensibilities of the most callous observers. That was the way it was back then. Even Bobby Lee said it is well that war is so terrible, lest we grow too fond of it. Those cannons parted men like the Red Sea, but they kept coming ever fierce. Regretfully, I was there to meet your daddy at the end. It was either him or me, and I chose the practical part of valor. I have never forgotten that terrible day as your daddy fell before me, dying for the cause, and looking into the eyes of a friend."

Tears formed. I had never been told this in Missoura.

"After the war I sought out your family in Randall's Flats to make amends for an act I have regretted ever since. That is how I knew your uncle Olin and cousin Buford. But the South was a hostile territory for Northern generals after the war. I found your daddy's kin, but was unable to linger in the region long enough to make amends. Your uncle would have strung me up. So I wish to extend my sympathies to you now. Please accept my apologies for an unfortunate act that I will take to my grave in sorrow. I am your servant from this day forward, and will protect you with my life. Please accept this as the truth."

He looked up with tears for his acts of duty, which were hard to resolve against his Quaker faith but necessary nonetheless. I had already forgiven him long ago. His explanation was enough, and we had reached an understanding that satisfied my pain. There had been no personal malice.

We shook hands and hugged, both in tears.

Our final leg lead down to the settlements of Walsenburg, Pueblo, and finally back to sunny Colorado Springs. We had just seen the greater part of the state of Colorado in just one week. I was now eager to emulate Palmer's kindness and generosity and would never forget my dear friend. I resolved to be rid of those tormenting thoughts of revenge.

"Oh… Colorado Springs!" Palmer said. He lifted his arms for a satisfying stretch. "It's nice to be back, and I sure enjoyed the time we spent together. I hope you have a safe trip back up the mountain. Will we see you soon?"

"Yessir," I said, shaking his hand vigorously. "Very soon!"

After unstowing the motorcar, I emptied a gallon of gasoline into the little brass tank. A nearby mercantile sold it by the bucket. It was beyond my understanding how a contraption of this kind operated on such a foul mixture – a waste product of kerosene, nor why Mr. Ford had chosen it as the primary fuel source. I guess he knew a thing or two.

Nevertheless after retarding the spark, closing the air intake, checking the oil level, resetting the spark gap, adjusting the fuel flow, we cranked the engine and the little wonder sprang to life. This small event produced smiles all around causing us to marvel at the technology available to those living in this remarkable new century. We started up the mountain to Cripple Creek within the hour.

Chapter Sixteen

April, 1901

"THIS IS THE TRIP that bankrupts the English language!" said
Vice President Roosevelt as he stuck his head out the passenger
car window and waved to the crowd.

A throng of seven thousand pressed the railway depot to get a
look at Teddy Roosevelt, the hero of San Juan Hill. It was April 21st,
1901, and the Colorado Springs & Cripple Creek District Railway, or
Short Line, had just been completed and opened for traffic. The new line
shortened the trip from Colorado Springs to Cripple Creek by half. For a
nickel and a boxed lunch, adventure seekers could finally see the heart of
the Rocky Mountains and be back in civilization in time for supper.
Weekend pioneers wanted a glimpse of the rough and tumble mining
operations of Cripple Creek. They came in the hundreds. A band played
"The Battle Hymn of the Republic" just as the conductor opened the car
doors, ushering Theodore Roosevelt onto the red carpet walkway to an
avalanche of cheers, whistles, and great anticipation.

Quieting the enthusiastic multitude, he said, "What a trip! I have
never seen the likes of such territory in my entire life. Out on the Short
Line you can actually see Kansas. They tell me you've got fifty thousand
people living up here now. My only question is, how in blue blazes did
y'all git up here? When I said this trip bankrupted the English language, I
wasn't just speaking of the natural beauty. I'll explain. They gave me the

Medal of Honor for charging up San Juan Hill. That was a pretty rough hill. Well, I can't wait to see what I'll receive for gittin' all the way up here. Bully!"

Applause and laughter erupted from the crowd.

"Honestly, my hat is off to you fine folks. President McKinley thanks you for your service. America thanks you for your service. And indeed, the world thanks you. The men and women who built this fine city deserve a hearty measure of recognition, and I'm here to deliver it in fine style!"

By this time the crowd was so whipped up by their love for the man that they could not contain their cheers and whistles. They barely let the Vice President speak. He just stood there with a big humble smile trying to hush the crowd. A good man has that effect. It was they who wanted to speak, and the abundance of applause was their way of doing it. Only after a long while did the torrent of accolades subside, allowing Teddy Roosevelt to continue his short speech.

"Thank you everyone. Thank you from my heart. You are a fine audience for such an inconsequential man as me. I'll say, in my brief days with the Rough Riders, and certainly not to upstage those fine 10th Cavalry Buffalo Soldiers I served with, I have yet to witness the fortitude displayed by the frontiersmen who scratched out a living in this forbidding territory. In Cuba, we just killed people. Bad people, yes... But up here, you pulled life from your own guts. There wouldn't be fifty thousand people out on the back side of Pikes Peak if it weren't for you few mavericks. You've wrestled the elements to their knees, and took what was due. Entrepreneurs like you are the backbone of this great nation, and it is your spirit that makes it great. I take a humble bow to you and offer President McKinley's congratulations on a great year of gold production. Hip Hip Hurray!"

For the space of three minutes, men, women, and children cheered and hollered in unison, "Hip, Hip, Hurray! Hip Hip, Hurray for Cripple Creek!"

Sam looked over at me. "That's for you, boy. You done good out here."

"Well, you too," I said.

137

T.R. let out a big Texas grin and finally calmed the multitude with his gestures.

"I understand you pulled nine hundred thousand troy ounces of gold out of five hundred mines last year. Some of you visitors in the crowd may not appreciate what that means. That's about twenty million dollars of revenue in one year, and it means our country will continue to expand economically while holding to the Gold Standard. Our currency must be backed by gold or it becomes worthless. And you are the ones producing it. As you know, the U.S. Treasury is your biggest customer. Up at the Denver Mint, they're stamping out ninety-percent pure Double Eagles from the gold you produce. President McKinley and I look forward to many years of healthy production, and we'll do anything we can to help. I swear, if you ever encounter any trouble up here, you call on us. I'll even bring in the Rough Riders! You have our full support, and you can be proud of what you have accomplished."

Ladies threw flowers onto the depot platform. Patricia wished she had one to throw. Roosevelt picked one up and continued his speech.

"On another note, I would like to introduce a man who shares your enduring spirit of faith and optimism. This man standing to my right has faithfully served your banking needs for the last twenty years. But he's told me he now wants a different job. Can you guess what it is? Ladies and Gentlemen, please welcome Mr. James Hamilton Peabody, the next governor of the State of Colorado!"

I jumped up and down. "Look, Honey! It's Peabody!"

The crowd seemed to welcome Peabody as they had Roosevelt, with more generous applause. He had been a local boy from down in Cañon City and most folks already knew him to be an upstanding banker and statesmen. He'd be sure to get their vote.

"As you know, Mr. Peabody is running for governor on the Republican ticket, so we share a fair degree of political ground. I'd like to invite y'all out to Butte Hall tonight, and every night this week. I hear they've got a mean melodrama. The entrance fee has been waived. You are all welcome. There'll be free refreshments, and I'll tell a few tall tales about my part in the Cuban conflict in '98. Mr. Peabody and your friend

General Palmer will share the stage with me. Please welcome them as you would me. Y'all come out and we'll have a grand ol' time! God Bless y'all now! Bully for Cripple Creek! And God Bless America!"

Once again, the crowd exploded in praise for Roosevelt and the other men on the platform.

This was a great day for Cripple Creek and I felt a deep sense of pride in our achievements. Large numbers of citizens were still cheering and waving little American flags to show their acceptance of the speech. Men were smiling broadly, pounding fellow citizens on the back, and shaking hands. A group of boys threw off fireworks, which popped and banged, encouraging the crowd to release their overflowing emotion. It was a grand occasion that every citizen enjoyed to no obvious end.

"Come on, Sam. Let's shake some hands," I said.

Patricia smiled. "Go on! You boys love to talk about your mine."

Visitors from Colorado Springs and Denver sought out those citizens of Cripple Creek to congratulate them. There were handshakes and thanks for a great year of production. It felt good to be honored in such a way.

Roosevelt leaped off the depot platform into the crowd and began pumping hands, slapping backs, and kissing babies. He was a natural-born leader everyone loved.

But just as the words warmed our hearts, I noticed a growing congress on the fringe of the throng, clearly irritated by the Vice President's address. I wondered how any man could take exception to such positive words. Intrigued, Sam and I wove through the crowd to catch a word of their conversation.

"Look at that hypocrisy," one outspoken man with a big hat said. "Those big-business bankers and Robber Baron politicians are fleecing the people of Cripple Creek and slapping them on the back at the same time."

"I swear I don't trust a word they say," another put in. "If you believe half the lies they spew, you're as much a lapdog as that Peabody."

"And Palmer worked side by side with Andrew Carnegie," another said. "Where do you think he got all that money? Thieves in silk cravats."

The first man adjusted his stiff white hat, waiting to get another word in.

"Roosevelt wasn't nothin' but a cutthroat terrorist down there in Cuba," Big Hat said. "He's certainly no hero. That's for darn sure. And the miners down in Victor knew that. Did you see the thrashing they nearly gave him when he stepped off the train over there? We'll show these swindlers a thing or two. You mark it down. We will gut those greedy mine owners within the year. Watch what we've got planned."

The group of men each added more fierce words to the growing congress, forming a pact they could not readily extract themselves from, even if they sought it diligently. They noticed Sam and me standing there.

"What are you lookin' at, you old grease spot," Big Hat said.

"Well, I guess a pack of monkeys," Sam scoffed. "Ta look at ya. You got somethin' against mine owners? Gonna gut us, are ya?"

"Want to find out?" Big Hat walked right up to Sam's face and stared him nose to nose.

"Awright, you little cream cup. I ain't horsewhipped a brat like you in ages. It'll be my gratification."

Sam reached down and upended the man with a swift yank of his pant leg. Big Hat fell to the ground in a cloud of dust. The others scattered like crows.

"Now what was that about guttin' mine owners?"

I grabbed Sam by the shirt, dragging him back. "They ain't worth seeing Judge Hawkins over, Sam. Let them believe what they want. You know it ain't true. It's all talk."

"Ain't got the sand, old man?" Big Hat taunted, scrambling to his feet again.

Sam struggled for the men but I coaxed him back to the festivities where picnic tables were being set up, and folks sat down to mingle. The men were obvious malcontents, not worth getting riled over.

Sam soon forgot the incident and rejoined the fun. I found Patricia and the boys next to McLeary's Assay with lemonades.

"Can we?" Micah and Caleb begged, standing on their tip-toes with fireworks in their hands.

"Let 'm fly, boys!"

Roosevelt, Peabody, and General Palmer spent the week stumping for votes at the Butte Opera House and other venues around town. The Imperial. Palace Hotel. Even Johnnie Nolan's bucket of blood. I helped where I could, mostly staging meetings with mill and mine owners. The week turned out a great success, where the citizens of Cripple Creek met the Vice President and Peabody, shook their hands and made known their hopes for the coming year.

After a great week of meetings we attended the Whosoever Wills Church which was still meeting in a large tent at the south end of town. We planned a motorcar trip to the Florissant fossil beds afterwards.

"We're doing a fair bit of the marryin', buryin', and baptizin'," the preacher said. "And we got nothin' but this here bleached canvas tent. Praise the Lord!"

The preacher put his hand over his heart. "Actually, that's a good lesson for you and me, ain't it? Don't come to Jesus with a big fancy façade expecting to impress Him. You won't. Just seek Him with your whole heart and you will be saved. Amen?"

Roosevelt enjoyed the lively meeting. Afterward he insisted on heading out to the petrified trees and fossil remains in Florissant which had become a national interest. Visitors came from every state of the union to see the spectacle, and Roosevelt would not be put off. He wanted to see them as much as the next man, and it sure beat the Wizard Oil Musical Medicine Show, although that venue promised cures of rheumatism, whooping cough, lazy eye, and a host of other ailments we might find ourselves plagued with.

The rowdy miners in Victor were probably another reason to escape the political pressures of public life for an afternoon. Roosevelt's rude welcome in Victor had been harrowing at best, and Florissant was a pleasant retreat from it all. I never mentioned the angry men at the Short Line depot.

I hoped to horse-collar Roosevelt and Peabody into offering some advice with my investors who had begun to raise difficult questions about the Black Jack operation. For me, the day's trip would be as much business as pleasure. I coveted their advice in matters that seemed beyond my understanding.

As we were leaving the house, Patricia, who had been cooking yogurt and sorting dirty socks and overalls, perked up to see us off. Her quiet contentment with socks and underdrawers still amazed me, even with so many options open to her now.

"You all boys have a nice little picnic now," she said, returning to her work.

I cast an eye to my comrades, and then back to Patricia. Trying to disguise my corrective words, I whispered, "Now dear, this is not a little picnic. This is important business. I'm a busy and important man now. You know that." Even as the words fell out, I knew Patricia would spot the gaffe and exploit it for her own pleasure.

Wiping errant hairs from her eyes, she realized the opportunity to dive in for the kill. "Why is it when the ladies go to see the fossils it's a nice little picnic, but when the men go, it's important business?" she teased with a tone loud enough for the other men to overhear.

And as I stepped away, she added a little louder, "Yeah, you boys go on your little picnic now."

She paused and smiled.

"And oh, the laundry lady says, don't bother bringing those holey red underwear in anymore. The blacksmith keeps finding them in his rag bag!"

I knew I'd been had when I looked out the door and saw the Vice President of the United States, a Brigadier General of the United States Army, and the next gubernatorial hopeful urging my wife on in her devious work, snickering and gesturing behind me. Clearly outnumbered, I simply raised my hands acknowledging defeat and smiled in surrender. What a gang of backstabbers!

Palmer jabbed me in the ribs. "Don't look at me! It was those other two devils that got you in deeper. But still, you might be too busy and important for the likes of us!"

They all laughed as he cranked the little motorcar to life.

The Florissant fossil beds were incredible. A hundred petrified tree stumps dotted the little valley, each ten feet in diameter and as tall as a well-bred horse. Tourists ambled among them, silent in the presence of God's creation. Millions of fossils littered the gently sloping valley floor.

Eager tourists chipped loads of petrified wood from the massive stumps and carted them off. There was an incredible abundance, yet I wondered if it could last forever. But just as the others, we gathered interesting specimens for our own private collections and carted them off to the auto-car for safekeeping.

After a few hours of strolling among the sleeping giants, I found a good time to breach the subject of my investor woes, finally blurted out, "Fellas, I'm getting trouble from my backers."

They all looked up from the fossils, surprised at the sudden change of tone. I felt embarrassed.

"I get the sense my investors are dissatisfied with the operation. Last year we produced more gold than ever, and more dividends. And yet there's an undercurrent of discontent. I don't know where it's coming from. It seems the excitement we've had is being swallowed up. The investors are no longer content with ten percent returns. They send letters and telegrams demanding more. Mr. Roosevelt, what do you suppose I've done wrong?"

"Well, son," T.R. began. "I guess you've heard of the scandals at the railroads and steel mills in the East? The workingmen claim they can hardly make a living. Is that happening out here? If it is, you best correct it."

"Not that I'm aware. My men are enjoying the boom like the rest of us."

"Are they making a good living?"

"Yes. Many have opened new mines or started businesses of their own. They've gotten richer than the ones who came up here first. It's good for everyone. Of course there are always a few idlers down on Myers Avenue, but generally the miners are well-off."

"I think it's the Western Federation of Miners," Peabody interjected. "That Teller County business still bothers me. You've heard of that, Mr. Roosevelt?"

"Oh, yes. The newspapers back East love them."

"The union's getting aggressive. They're bullying the mines and stirring up trouble. In my opinion, Teller County is turning into a Socialist hotbed."

T.R. considered the idea, but said nothing.

"Did you hear the latest? The miners are told to visit only union doctors. Support only union-run businesses. And read only their sponsored literature. That's all coming out of Teller County."

Palmer stepped up. "I see where you're going with this, James; but what does Teller County have to do with his investors? Unless those investors live near enough to understand what the union has been up to."

I shook my head. "No, most of the investors raising questions are from the East. The local folks know about the union badgering, and are used to it. They're not easily fooled."

"I think you're going to have to ask a few more questions and get to the bottom of things," T.R. said. "Without a little more information, it's hard to say where your problem lies. You don't want to lose your investors. That's your future."

"Yes, they are a fickle crew," Peabody agreed. "Lose them, and you're finished."

With the question still nagging me, the day ended with Roosevelt departing for Canada, Palmer returning to Colorado Springs, and Peabody heading off to Julesburg for more stump speeches on his way to the governor's mansion. I enjoyed the time we spent together, and I would never forget that pleasant April day when the world was still in balance and everything in relative harmony.

Chapter Seventeen

EARLY THE NEXT MORNING, as divine providence painfully allowed, the arrows of the enemy flew. My investor troubles escalated to new levels of frustration. It began with a simple telephone call, just as I sat down to a plate of eggs and grits.

"Clark, you there?" the caller said, gruffly. I recognized his voice – one of my Eastern backers. What a welcome on my first day with the new device.

I had installed telephones in the executive office, superintendent's offices, and my home in Cripple Creek. Operations were now running twenty-four hours per day, with three eight-hour shifts. I was routinely called up to make decisions at all hours of the day and night. It could be a cross to bear, but perhaps the equipment would simplify matters, I thought.

The caller opened with a combative tone. "Clark, what is this I'm reading?"

"Go on," I said.

"The Boston Monitor writes, 'Cripple Creek gold values are dropping from last year's levels, even while a few greedy millionaires rake up profits and practically starve loyal employees. If this continues, the workingmen of Cripple Creek will succumb to financial exhaustion within the decade. Some estimate this labor inequity cannot, and will not continue. They speculate that the Cripple Creek gold boom will soon end, leaving investors holding empty assay sheets and a bucket of rocks to chew on. Investors are advised to seek alternative portfolios to sure up flagging gold stocks. Cripple Creek gold securities are no longer recommended.'

"Clark, I don't like the sound of that! What are you country-club millionaires doing out there? Have you lost your minds?"

"No. Where did they get such—"

"Can't you treat your employees with a little decency? You're going to ruin everything with that kind of mismanagement. You know I've been a faithful investor even while you dug the nuggets yourself. Have you forgotten that?"

"No, I haven't forgotten. But—"

"Well, you've got to see the big picture. Without investors like us, you're just a wildcatter with a coupla' prospect holes. Keep that in mind, will you? Good bye, Clark."

Still reeling from that gut-punch, a repeat performance occurred only three days later. And this one really hurt.

"Jeremiah? W. E. Walker from New York City."

"Hello Welford," I said, trying to be cheerful, but suspecting the worst.

"Have you seen what the New York Bulletin just printed about your operation? Let me read it. I am not happy."

"Don't bother, Welford. I know what's going on. Those stories simply aren't true."

"Just let me read it. Wait till you hear this. 'Cripple Creek mine owners continue to mismanage the labor force. One such operation, the Black Jack Mine may lead the pack. Employees are forced to comply with a dizzying array of safety policies brought on by near-fatal explosions at the mine, which bring swift and onerous punishment for noncompliance. Some employees, like slaves are even beaten for acts of forgetfulness. And some are forced to resign the outfit in search of more suitable employment. Millionaire mine owners like Jeremiah Clark of the Black Jack Mine are evidently driving well-heeled labor from their ranks for their own profits. Is this the steel mill scandals all over again?'"

146

"Walker, that is simply not true. You have to–"

"Let me continue, Clark."

I just clamped my eyes shut and clenched my teeth.

"It continues. 'This rude behavior may even be rubbing off on the processing mills of nearby Colorado City. Mr. Charles MacNeill of the Standard Mill is reported to have fired good men for nothing but union affiliation. Is lawful assembly no longer permitted in Colorado?'"

"Welford–"

"Clark, what is going on out there?" Walker shrieked. "This sounds like bad business. I don't want to be associated with another millionaire-scandal."

"Well, you won't be. Mining operations in Cripple–"

"Well, it sounds like I am. Listen, this long-distance call is costing me a fortune. Either you get things straightened out or we're pulling out. Do you hear me?"

Click. Teeth grinding. Telephone flying.

I could see an awful storm coming, and I had the feeling those news reports would be a pleasant spring shower compared to what was coming over the mountain from the East.

As Peabody had surmised, I too suspected the Western Federation of Miners. Only they and their newspaper cronies could emit this kind of nonsense. No honest citizen in Denver, Colorado Springs, or Cripple Creek could have come up with such fantasies. There simply was no truth in them.

Jimmy Burns at the Portland, E.A. Colburn at the Ajax, and Charles Tutt had all gotten similar calls. Something was in the air. Something new.

If trouble was brewing, I would need more information to understand what I was up against so I called the only man I knew who could educate me in such matters: General Palmer.

Palmer knodded. "I'm thinking Charles Moyer. This feels like a way to soften up mine owners for something new. But let's go see Dr. William Slocum. He has been president of the Colorado College since '88, and knows labor in Cripple Creek better than anyone."

I was a relative newcomer to the territory, and Cripple Creek had been booming since Bob Womack's strike in '86. I wanted to understand the union dealings leading up to my arrival in '95.

Dr. Slocum received us the next day in his modest but efficient office in Colorado Springs. He was a man of knowledge and intense passion.

"Clark, I understand you need a quick rundown of the Western Federation of Miners."

"Yessir."

"Well, I haven't much time, but I will lay out a quick synopsis of the last few years. That should let you know what you are up against. I can tell you now, they're a militant organization fierce enough to destroy any opposition. Think Molly Maguires, and you'll have an idea. If you're thinking of messing with them you'd better have a war chest; here's what I know."

I lifted a finger. "Dr. Slocum, I want to know about the Bull Hill strike in Altman before I came here. Back in '94."

"I can start there. I think the '94 strike gave Altman their first taste of power. That's when things really got started. When did you come?"

"Spring of '95. Around May, I believe."

"Oh. Well you missed the big show," he said, rolling his eyes. "I won't even go into the Coeur d'Alene affair in Idaho before that. That was bloody business, so we'll stick to Colorado for now. Here's what happened up on Bull Hill."

I glanced at Palmer, and Slocum started in.

"Mining labor up there was mostly just hordes of desperate men tramping west in search of work. As you know, by '93, the country was in the midst of a depression, especially the South, which is one reason they came out here in droves. Men sold their labor for room and board, or in some cases indentured servitude."

"I know those days well," I said.

"With so much cheap labor, the mine owners in '94 made a bid to increase working hours from eight to ten hours a day. But they kept the daily wage the same, you see? Miners were required to work an extra two hours for the same pay. That really made them mad."

"I understand. It's been an eight-hour day since I came."

"Yes, well some of the mines in Cripple Creek were already operating on a ten-hour schedule, which enticed the others to follow. It was only a matter of time before all the mines moved to the new schedule. The enraged miners moved to organize."

"Was Charles Moyer in Cripple Creek then?" I asked.

"Oh, yes. His crew came in from Idaho after the Coeur d'Alene bombing spree. The Free Coinage No. 125 labor union started in Altman, and then got swallowed up by the Western Federation of Miners – the organization Moyer was running."

"I see."

"With so much tension over the ten-hour shift, union picketmen and local deputies faced off, and an insurrection erupted. The old Governor Waite and his militia eventually dealt with that. There was quite a skirmish up on Bull Hill for about six months."

"I'll bet. How did it end?"

"Things cooled down, mine owners assented to common sense, and the work schedule went back to eight hours for all mines. The fault clearly lay with mine owners who tried to capitalize on desperate men, and they failed. Following me so far?"

I leaned back, crossing my legs, and Slocum continued.

"I think the mine owners knew they'd made a mistake, and finally gave up on the ten-hour shift on their own."

Palmer touched Slocum's shoulder. "Of course, the state militia and a few Gatling guns helped. It was messy, but in the end they did the right thing."

Slocum nodded.

"The strike worked so well that the Free Coinage exploded with power. I guess they felt they had won a huge victory and proceeded to run with it. They didn't even consider the possibility that the mine owners simply gave up. They could never sustain the 10-hour day in the face of such public opposition."

"Would they have given up without the militia?"

Slocum looked up. "Probably not."

"That's what I thought."

"By now, Moyer could do no evil. He had made a good show of protecting the workingman from so-called 'oppressive powers.' Although that is not exactly what had happened, the rhetoric has been building ever since."

I smiled at the remark. "Moyer mentioned this the very day I arrived, back in '95. It stuck with me."

"How so?"

"He said they put mine owners back into their places."

"Humm. Well, you have to understand that the victory in '94 vilified the mine owners and made saints of the union. After all, where would the men be if the union hadn't stepped in and saved them all?"

Palmer nodded. "These guys walk on water."

"Okay. Tell me about Teller County," I said. "I was in the room when Charles Thomas proposed the idea to Moyer."

Slocum's eyes widened. "You were there? So, you know all this."

"No. Not really. It sounded silly to me at the time, but not to everyone else I talk to."

"Okay. Well, Moyer's political standing has increased a hundredfold since the creation of Teller County. I suspect he sees it as an opportunity to keep his thumb on the Cripple Creek mines and local politics in one fell-swoop. All he has to do is install his own men, and he runs the whole county."

"And he's been doing that," Palmer added.

"So... What's wrong with that?" I asked. "One politician is the same as the next, right?"

Slocum smiled and glanced at Palmer with a knowing look. "Moyer and Bill Haywood openly espouse the Socialist doctrine. George Pettibone is an outspoken anarchist who would like nothing better than to overthrow the Republic. Yes, the whole United States."

I coughed at the wild assertion.

"You heard me right. I'm not casting baseless aspersions. These are well-documented facts from their history in Idaho. Look them up."

Palmer broke in. "To hear them tell it, they are the friends of the working class and the enemies of their oppressors. This plays well for their political position in Teller County. Name a miner west of Pikes Peak who doesn't want a group of pit bulls like them on their team. The same is true of every elected official in Teller County. They can't lose with Moyer gunning for mine owners. He's a powerhouse, and he won't stop."

Slocum roughly illustrated the organizational hierarchy of the WFM on his black slate board. Moyer on top, Haywood, Pettibone, and the lessor minions.

"Now listen, Clark. You need to understand this next point. This is very important, and could affect you."

"Okay," I said, nervously.

"Recently these three men – Moyer, Haywood, and Pettibone – were successful in passing a union resolution that removed strike authority from the general vote and moved it up to the management cabinet. Do you understand this? Take a minute and think about what it means."

"Well, I'm not dumb, but I don't," I said, feeling like a schoolboy with a new McGuffey Reader. "What do you mean by strike authority?"

"If the union wanted to strike today, it would no longer require votes from the miners. It puts all strike power into the hands of three men, and out of the miners themselves. The board could move unilaterally, with or without the men's consent. You watch; this single act will have disastrous effects for mine owners, and for the miners themselves who may not have understood the value of their votes. Unfortunately, things get even worse, so try to stay with me."

I was trying, but wrestling with this strike-vote thing. Clearly, the miners of Cripple Creek had pulled out the palm branches and given their allegiance to a false messiah.

Slocum felt my pain, but continued piling on.

"The newspaper offices of Cripple Creek, and as it would seem, the Eastern presses have become willing partners with Moyer. With a little help from the steel and railroad scandals, the whole country is jumping all over this new anti-capitalism wave. It's the latest thing."

151

"And the newspapers are making hay," Palmer added. "The socialists are just good-natured folks looking out for the common laborer, while the capitalists want nothing but their blood. That's your basic news story. Get it?"

I perked up with a smile. "That, I understand. Sam explained it to me early on, and I saw it firsthand a few years back. Muckraking journalism."

"That's right. Your own Victor Record newspaper is leading the way for Moyer, regularly maligning mine owners and their operations in editorials and news. It sure sells papers, doesn't it? People lap it up like milk from a saucer. Since you make your living up there, I am sure you understand."

"Yes, I do."

"But you must understand that controversy, whether real or fabricated, is a steady paycheck for them. It's unfortunate, but they have a vested interest in conflict and human suffering. The more they can gin up, the more newspapers sell. They're not going to admit to any such skullduggery, but it's obvious it exists."

Things were a lot uglier than I had first imagined, and the telephone calls I had gotten earlier clearly seemed connected to this anti-management movement. With my head still swamped, I thanked Palmer and Slocum for their time, touched my hat, and hopped the Short Line up the mountain to Cripple Creek. This would take some time to soak in.

The Boston Monitor and New York Bulletin editorials seemed to strengthen Slocum's theory. It also explained the connection between the labor union and my investors. The Eastern railroad and steel millionaires had sure done some dirty work, and it was now spilling over onto us. It was guilt by association, and I now saw the thread of alliance between the union and the newspapers. I also saw the position Moyer had engineered for himself, and while I respected his prowess, I feared his history and motives.

Why hadn't I seen this coming?

I decided to learn the source of the thinly-veiled lies. My investors were reciting half-truths and naked lies that must have originated somewhere.

Where to start?

The Free Coinage No. 125 was the obvious place. In Altman. It was headquartered in a three-story redbrick building on Double Eagle Street. The building was walking distance up the hill from the Black Jack Mine in Independence. I had met with Moyer there in the summer of '98 – back when he tried to convince me to join him. I wasn't certain of the exact source of the lies but had a hunch it came from the infamous hive I was about to enter.

Best not to bring Sam.

Double Eagle was the main street in Altman, and practically the only one in town. Even while in the highest-elevation incorporated city in the United States, it was nothing to look at. The city boasted two thousand citizens who apparently all occupied unpainted miner's shacks along the main street. Evidently, Altman miners would snatch up an ounce of sour mash faster than a gallon of paint. Even at the rugged pitches of 10,800 feet, the union headquarters was the only building worth mentioning. It stuck out like red rouge on a wild boar.

I entered the building and wiped my boots in the foyer. Swanky. The offices had recently been remodeled and looked nothing like before. Glassy African teakwood with silver inlays, gold fixtures, a sculpted marble stairway, electric elevator, and red velvet carpeting. Finer than the El Paso Club. Fine as gold bullion. The rich scents of cedar and teak drifted by. The building seemed to flaunt all the amenities labor money could buy. I took several minutes to orient myself.

I finally approached a pasty-looking clerk with rimless glasses on the second floor and stated my business. I simply wanted to know if they had any connections with the Boston Monitor or New York Bulletin, or any comments on the dubious editorials. It was a simple request.

The clerk avoided eye contact and spewed rehearsed phases at me, clearly not engaging in true conversation.

"Have you ever stepped foot into an actual mine in this district?" I asked.

"Labor produces all wealth, and wealth belongs to the producer thereof," the staffer repeated. Evidently, he was trying to make the point that all the wealth produced by the Black Jack Mine should go to the miners themselves since there were doing the actual work, and not the shareholders. He could not grasp the concept that entrepreneurs had fought to build their organizations, and that wealth was their reward.

"Okay, but what about the news articles?"

Our stymied conversation increased in volume, attracting nearby clerks and paper handlers to partake in the entertainment. A capitalist was taking a good licking.

After a period of frustrated dialogue the clerk abruptly ceased his mantras, peered over his spectacles with a wide smile and said, "Now I recognize you! You're that little gopher for Roosevelt and Peabody. McKinley and Roosevelt are running this country into the ground. Can't you see that? Somebody ought to put those two crooks out of our misery."

The other clerks all cheered.

"Wait just a—"

"And what's with that old Civil War pest, Palmer, who's always buzzing about like a fly on brown sugar? Doesn't he have anything of value to contribute? He doesn't seem to produce a thing. It's about time somebody put him out of our misery too, and about time this country had some fresh blood. Peabody can run for office in the North Pole for all we care. We don't want another one like Roosevelt in this state. He won't get a vote in Teller County."

Getting a taste of blood, the horde of ideologues all joined in.

"Tell that old Whitman character that if he lays another hand on our union men, he's a dead man," added one of the thugs from behind the crowd.

"I'll drop the old mule myself," the frail clerk put in, emboldened by the security of his home territory.

That line sucked the last drop of my patience dry, sending me over the railing at him.

I may have been an oppressive mine owner, but I was also a Missoura plow hand who could heft an eight-pound hammer at seventy-eight blows a minute. I could knock this little weevil into next week before he had time to recite another of his collectivist mantras. And, just as I cocked my arm to do so, the thugs pounced.

154

Four ruffians came to the little man's aid. Each threatened with burning eyes. I debated whether to take the band of five single-handedly, or endure ejection from the building. I chose wisely, resulting in a forced flight down the marble steps and into the black muddy street. With the hot stares of onlookers, it would be a humiliating walk home.

A bit soiled but no worse for the wear, I had learned the source of the printed folly and my investor's growing anxiety.

Chapter Eighteen

July, 1902

"THESE MEN ARE GOING to be all right," the doctor concluded. "They may look bad, but their wounds are not as serious as they appear. I've wrapped their ribs. As long as they remain still they'll recover," said Doctor Burns as we walked past the beds at the Sisters of Mercy Hospital in Cripple Creek.

One man's eye drooped with a large gash extending over his right eye and upper cheek. Another man's face was black and blue and half his beard was pulled out. All their ribs were taped.

I suddenly realized something. "These are all Charlie MacNeill's men. I recognize them. They process ore for the Black Jack Mine. How long will they be up here?"

"They'll need a month's rest before they can even think of resuming their duties at the mill."

"A month? Are they that bad off?"

"Yes they are. We'll need to keep them up here in Cripple Creek for a while before they can go back down to Colorado City. I hope they have found the men responsible. This is getting ugly. My colleagues in Colorado City have seen others just as bad, and I'm getting concerned. What is happening with these millmen?"

"Haven't they told you?"

"No, I suspect it's union related, but they're not talking."

"These are the first I've seen like this, but they say things are heating up down in Colorado City."

He stopped walking. "Heating up?"

"Skirmishes with men who refuse to join the union," I said, looking at a man. I honestly didn't know any more than the good doctor, but was becoming alarmed just the same.

"Well, they had better find the men responsible. Things can't go on like this. The union should take a role in stopping this violence."

"I think the opposite may be true."

Relations with the Western Federation of Miners looked worse than ever. And it wasn't just in Colorado City.

"Patricia," I complained, late that night before bed. "Have mine owners done something to offend the union?"

"Of course not. Why do you ask?" she said.

"I feel like something has changed. They won't even meet with us regularly. I've left messages. They won't return my calls."

"Moyer would have told you, wouldn't he? Doesn't he confide in you?"

"Not any more. He knows I have no interest in his cause. Especially after that little incident last month up in Altman. You know… when I threatened to beat up his clerk. But the mills in Colorado City are what bother me. You should have seen those millmen at the hospital. That was ugly."

"Go see Charlie MacNeill. He'll know what's going on. I'm going to bed now. It's late."

"Maybe you're right. I'll call him in the morning."

Fortunately, there were also plenty of good things happening without worrying about a few bruised-up millmen. Teddy Roosevelt had become President, although under unfortunate circumstances, and Peabody had won the governor's race in Denver by a landslide. They were powerful allies who offered us access to more investors who could see the operations to new levels of production. The Cripple Creek mining business had grown up, and was finally recognized by the nation's biggest moneymen. Ordinary men who had mucked stalls, measured kitchen cabinets, or pushed plows, now kept company with the highest men in the land. So why worry?

Patricia finished changing for bed. "Jeremiah, has Charlie seen those men up at–"

Before she could finish, the clanging wooden telephone box interrupted, and I instantly knew who it was.

Strange timing.

"Jeremiah? MacNeill here, from the Standard. Are you available? I need your advice, and I think you'll need to see some new developments down here."

"Certainly, what's the problem? We were just talking about you."

"Well…" Charlie paused. "It's late. I'll let you know when you get here, but it's about those men at the Sisters of Mercy. Can I expect you Monday morning?"

MacNeill's words struck a nerve. He obviously had something boiling in the pot, but was unwilling to release the details over the wire. Charlie ran a good service at the Standard Mill. Spencer Penrose and Charles Tutt had sold the C.O.D. Mine and joined MacNeill about the time I had arrived in Cripple Creek. I trusted men who had been in the business themselves.

"Of course. I'll see you in the morning."

The next morning at 4 AM I was on the Short Line to Colorado City. I knew Charlie would be in by six, and I promptly trotted into his office at five minutes 'til. He was already at work, shuffling contracts, ore receipts, and paperwork, preparing for another busy day. Charlie forced his eyes from the desk, clearly having burned a dozen wicks. He was a mess, but brightened up to greet me.

"Nice to see you, Jeremiah. You're always a welcomed sight for the weary. Have a seat," he said, returning to dispatch the avalanche of paper.

Fifty bright yellow bricks lay stacked on the cement floor of his office – the final product of the mill and smelting operations. The neat little stack of bullion would fetch a half-million dollars. I became fascinated with the polished bricks, having never seen so many in one place. "Aren't you afraid somebody will steal them?"

"Oh, who would do such a thing? Don't worry about those right now; I've got a crew coming to pick them up. They're going to the new Miner's Exchange, over on Nevada Ave. We've got bigger issues. Here's the situation," Charlie said, diverting my attention from the pleasing attractions and pulling me into the fray.

"You know that the Western Federation of Miners is working to get a headlock on the Colorado City mills just like they did with the Cripple Creek mines. Every employee at the Black Jack Mine is a union man."

"That's right. All the mines are union. Have been since '94."

"Not so down here at the mills, but they're working hard to change that. They're trying to duplicate their success down here. Every day, they've got a union man in here spreading discord, stirring up the men."

I glanced back at the gold bricks. "So? That won't get them anywhere. It's just talk."

"But something has changed. It's no longer just talk. They've added some nasty intimidation to their rhetoric, as you saw at the hospital up in Cripple Creek. Millmen in Colorado City now have a choice: either join the union or lay in traction for a month."

I picked up a brick to inspect its weight and quality. "Maybe that was an isolated incident."

Nice heft.

"No. And put that down. It's been happening for a month. But it's not just their coercion to join the union that's in play. There's a lot to explain, but one issue is wages. It's a small thing but causing some big trouble."

I set the brick down and edged in. "Okay, you've got my attention."

"The millman wage is $2.25 a day, right?"

"Yeah."

"These snakes are promising $3 if the non-union holdouts will join the Smeltermen's Union, and at the same time threatening with consequences if they don't. Which would you choose? Any honest man knows they'll never get that, but they're pointing their crooked fingers up the mountain to Cripple Creek and saying the miners are getting it up there so why not down here."

I waved him off. "Miners and millmen are completely different. Mill workers can't expect $3. That's absurd."

"Exactly. But that's what they are promising. It's an underhanded tactic to promise a man one thing, and deliver another," MacNeill said, growing more irritated as the words tumbled out.

"The union reps at the Portland and Telluride mills just called a strike yesterday for those wages," Charlie said. "They don't have a majority in those mills, but there were enough to bring the operations to a standstill. It doesn't take a majority to shut down an operation, just a few key employees. If you can intimidate them into striking, others will follow. Remember what you saw up at the Sisters of Mercy. That's going on down here every week."

"I didn't know that. That's news to me."

Charlie rubbed his eyes. "The big Portland Mill only processes ore for the Portland Mine, right? But the Telluride affects a lot of Cripple Creek mines. And since the strike, the mines have been forced to use the smaller processing mills. Even the Colorado Reduction and Refining Mill has voluntarily shut down to make improvements and avoid the nasty union confrontations altogether. They don't want any part of this."

"So, which mills are still open?" I asked.

"Out of the big-four, only the Standard Mill is open. There are no other big mills to process ore, and that's causing a lot of trouble. And I'll tell you flat out, Moyer is fixin' to shut us down too."

"No way. How can he do that?"

"Only a quarter of my men are union. But if they strike it may be enough to close the doors. Those are skilled men and I can't just replace them in a week. Do you understand?"

"I think so. It sounds like their plan is to shut down all the mills until they get one-hundred percent union membership, just like the Cripple Creek mines. But what do your men think? Are they going along with this? It's not what we think that matters."

"As far as I know they're happy with the $2.25 wage. After all, it's twice the average wage in Colorado Springs. There's a waiting list to get into the Standard Mill."

"Popular place."

"But Moyer claims the new rate in all the mills will be $3 by January." He looked at a calendar. "It's July now. The men are saying, why stay at $2.25 when everybody else is getting $3."

"Don't worry, Charlie. That will never happen."

"Listen, Jeremiah. I'm afraid this could get ugly for both of us. With trouble like this we won't last a month, so I've arranged a meeting with Governor Peabody. He'll be in The Springs at ten this morning. That's why I needed you today."

"Oh!"

"He's coming down from Denver right now to discuss this very issue. I know you two are friends and I need your support at that meeting. Can you stay for it?" Charlie pleaded, with weary eyes from the previous night's worry.

How could I refuse?

Spec and MacNeill planned to attend, but Charles Tutt could not. He had been detained in Colorado Springs for organizing a pigeon-shooting tournament. The duty officer claimed the party had killed eleven hand-released pigeons in the off-color event Tutt had promoted. Charles persisted in referring to the pests as flying rats and would not post the seventy-cent bail bond for his own release. I suppose he was making a statement of principle, but the incident didn't make a lot of sense to me. After all, Tutt and Penrose were raking in $200,000 a month in mill business and Utah copper interests. Perhaps this was the sort of thing the wild men of Black Forest, Colorado were apt to do. Nevertheless, we would have to do without him.

We met Peabody at the Colorado College at a quarter to ten. Charlie drove his new motorcar, a 1902 Stanley Runabout. Steam powered automobiles were the future, he claimed. It was hard to disagree. Penrose and the managers of the Portland and Telluride mills had all arrived before us. Our meeting began with Charlie's assessment of the situation.

"Governor and gentlemen, thank you for joining us this morning. I hope your travel was pleasant and uneventful. I enjoy an occasional motorcar outing on the streets of Colorado Springs, looking up at those beautiful mountains. We live in a fine city and a fine state, wouldn't you say? Well unfortunately, trouble is brewing for our neighbors to the west. I'm talking about Colorado City."

"Go on, Charlie," Peabody said. "Your telegram was rather urgent."

"Mr. Governor, labor conditions are reaching critical concern. The Western Federation of Miners, apparently without a scrap of misgiving, intends to force their way into every mill in Colorado City. It is not the wellbeing of the workers that drives their agenda, but rather a naked lust for power."

Peabody's eye's narrowed. "That's a powerful accusation. I hope you can back it up. Got proof?"

"Yes sir, I do. As I stand here now, militant picketmen surround every mill regardless of its strike status. The men are harassed and bullied into union membership even if they don't agree with its terms. Clark got a look at a few of their latest victims yesterday. Ask him if they were picking daisies in Acacia Park. Sheriff Gilbert has raised sixty-five deputies, but has been unable to contain the threats and violence. They are determined to force their hand on the mills of Colorado City."

Heads nodded around the table, and Peabody waved Charlie on.

"Secondly, the men are being told the union will raise wages to three dollars per day once the oppressive mill managers are forced out. Those are obvious lies."

Penrose broke in. "I'll be the first to admit that lying is no crime. But we appear to have both a ruthless and dishonest organization on the attack."

The Portland, Telluride, and Colorado Reduction mill managers argued the point for at least another half-hour.

"Beatings... intimidation... and midnight visits to worker's homes have been effective in bringing no small number into line. That's what sparked the strikes," Penrose summarized.

"And I don't think this is just a worker's revolt," I added. "The men processing my ore don't seem dissatisfied."

Peabody beckoned. "To understand any strike, you have to view it from the men's perspective. Are they happy? Can they feed their families? Have a good life? If not, they have the right to strike. And probably will. It falls on you to make sure they are happy. Not the union. If you don't, you can expect trouble like this. So, I'm a little suspicious. You claim no guilt, but men are walking out on you? They sound unhappy to me."

"Nope. Not the case," Charlie argued. "We talked about that right before this meeting."

"Exactly," I said. "The Standard Mill has a waiting list to get in."

Charlie picked up. "The mills in Colorado City and mines in Cripple Creek have been fair. We're not running sweat shops. And men are waiting to get in. Clark, you've had more than one run-in with union picketmen. What say you?"

I paused and looked at Peabody. "One question bothers me... What business does the Western Federation of Miners have in mill work? They are a miner's union. Not millworkers. But they're clearly making a bid to absorb the Smelterman's Union in Colorado City."

Peabody nodded. "Point taken."

"And they are not a peace-loving lot, as their newspaper allies claim. When you boil the cabbage, they're socialists, anarchists, and about as ambitious as Lucifer. There's just no nice way to say that. But I don't think they make any attempt to hide it. You can search the public records to learn that much from their activities in Idaho."

"Governor, I think they'll make a mess of this as fast as you can flip a nickel," Charlie said, taking his seat again.

I reflected on the meeting's tone. Had it been too harsh? Too quick to judgment? Having thought it through, it felt fair and accurate, although condemning to say the least. Charlie and I had both seen the brutality firsthand.

The Governor sat quietly before replying. "Men, I appreciate you bringing this to my attention. I'm still a little suspicious, but you can be assured I have heard your hearts. I will not permit a militant organization to gain a foothold in the state of Colorado. I will investigate these allegations and make a fair judgment."

"Thank you," Charlie said.

"But, I will tell you right now that the state of Colorado will not impose its will on the citizenry. I will not be a puppet to crush the fair demands of the workingmen of Colorado. Nor will I prevent the lawful assembly of citizens who wish to improve their conditions through forceful means. This is the rule of law, and I will uphold it with every ounce of strength I possess."

Charlie edged up impatiently. "Yes, but—"

"Don't argue with me. I've heard your case."

"Fair enough."

"Government is instituted to sustain the wellbeing of its citizens, and not to impose an oppressive framework over them. We are a republic, but it is the people we serve, and not our own interests, whether political, financial, or otherwise. My office will see to these claims in due time. Until then, please try to maintain a civil state of affairs in Colorado City. I will communicate my findings shortly."

Everyone looked relieved, especially Charlie. We were confident James Peabody was a fair man and that he would perform a fair investigation. And investigate he did. His telegraph arrived in Charlie's office a week later.

> To Charlie MacNeill. Stop.
> Have learned picketmen own foot traffic. Stop.
> Mills blocked. Stop.
> No local authority. Stop.
> Intimidation and brutality. Stop.
> Will send militia. Stop.

A month after the military men arrived things still hadn't gotten much better. Fortunately, the Standard Mill was still open and processing ore.

But Charlie wasn't satisfied. "Evidently, two Gatling guns and 125 militiamen are not enough. They were able to disperse the union picketmen and restore order, but Moyer only switched tactics."

"What do you mean," I asked. "Aren't your men able to come and go without harassment? That's all you wanted."

"The strike at the Portland and Telluride mills is still on, and there's still a picket line. I'm fine with that, as long as it's civil. But it's not, and here's why. Colorado City courts now have ten frivolous lawsuits for every militiaman in the field."

"They're suing the militiamen for carrying out the law? They can't do that!"

"Oh, yes they can. Those military boys are so busy in court, they can't patrol. So, the violence is just picking up again. We're no better off than before."

"That's low. What are you going to do?" I asked.

"I'm not sure. Peabody knows about the situation, and I think he is going to call another meeting. So I'm waiting for that. That's about all I can do. But I'm afraid the Standard Mill is next."

Chapter Nineteen

PEABODY CALLED ANOTHER MEETING in Denver, just like
Charlie said. The same mill managers attended. Even Charles Moyer
and Big Bill Haywood showed up. The Mine Owners Association
represented our interests in Cripple Creek, which meant I had to be
there.

The WFM union reps were brought in to answer for the frivolous
lawsuits against militiamen, aggressive picketmen, and outrageous wage
promises. This meeting promised to resolve the issues once and for all. I
was glad for that.

Finally, this would be over.

Governor Peabody opened with a word of prayer and these
words, "Men of this great state, we are in attendance here today to
resolve the grievances between the Colorado City mills and its unions. I
urge all parties to act in temperance and compromise. Please bear in
mind that these strikes affect the livelihoods of 482 men and their
families. I expect to resolve these differences and send those men back to
work. The lawsuits against those militiamen are a shameful practice, and I
will see that it stops."

Moyer and Haywood looked wounded.

"I remind you that I will not tolerate posturing. Present your
honest terms of compromise, and we will resolve the issues today. I

166

expect a complete resolution on my desk tonight or you will learn the full reach of my impatience. And, I want those attack dogs called off. Men cannot work under those conditions."

Peabody glanced over and noticed he had offended the union boys and then turned his eyes on Charlie and the mill managers.

"Millmen, can you live with any of the union demands? Let's start with you," Peabody said, motioning.

The Portland and Telluride managers compared notes and began with this compromise, "If aggressive union men will back off, we will agree to a wage increase for millmen to $2.45 per day, a wage increase to smeltermen to $2.30 per day, and enforcement of an eight-hour work day. We're very close to that already, and we just want the violence to end."

Obviously pleased with what he was hearing, Moyer added, "And to acceptance of ore from union mines only, do you accede? No non-union ore?"

"Yes, to this we accede," the mill managers said, feeling the pressure to compromise, but knowing that the Cripple Creek district was already under complete union control, and that they would not likely receive ore from non-union mines. It was a small point.

Moyer kept right on. "And to the preference of hiring union men?"

"Yes, to this we also agree," the managers stated reluctantly, one by one. Clearly they were weary of battle and wished to pacify the powers at hand. At this point, they probably would have agreed to public scourging – anything to please Moyer.

He smiled and leaned back.

With these points secured, the union would have total control of both the mines and mills, putting Moyer at the top of the dung heap. But the Standard Mill had not yet begun to negotiate.

Charlie MacNeill had sat quietly. He could see that the WFM was pushing for total control. We had talked about that earlier. Given the opportunity, they would crush the capitalistic spirit that built the industry in the first place. More was at stake than the paltry raises and working hours.

The use of aggressive picketmen to coerce membership and union demands was a foul act, nothing short of bullying. I'm sure if Charlie could guarantee the end of violence, he would gladly agree to a few small wage increases. But that was not the issue.

Moyer beamed at his former enemies, the mill managers. I half-expected him to spring from his chair and embrace them. Then he leaned over to Bill Haywood, cupped his hand, and whispered, "That was easier than I thought. Your boys really softened 'em up."

That changed everything.

Peabody perked up as if woken from sleep. "What?"

I wondered if I had been daydreaming too. But the others had all heard it too. Confusion turned to disgust. Haywood paled. But Moyer just kept right on smiling. He turned to Charlie like they were old pals.

After a quizzical look, Charlie rose to speak. "I accede to all points agreed to by the Portland and Telluride mills..."

Moyer brightened in anticipation. Within minutes he would control all labor in both the mines and mills. It would be his life's greatest achievement. He would certainly go on to become one of the nation's greatest labor organizers of all time. Praised in the history books. Everyone would know him. Moyer could feel it, and he wanted it badly. He leaned forward to hear those great words.

But when I heard Charlie's first words... "I accede to all points..." my heart sank, knowing the control Moyer would eventually seek. This organization would not be pacified as the mill managers had supposed. They sought the blood of their opponents in the worst way, and I knew there would be nothing to stop them now, just as Dr. Slocum had described. Charlie was about to cave. But how could he? Charlie was not an easy man to intimidate. Had they gotten to him?

Charlie continued with a forehead of flint, "on the following conditions..."

A pause... and Moyer's finger twitched.

"That every union picketman render his due apology to the individuals and establishments they terrorized."

Moyer looked cross. He turned to Haywood in disbelief. Charlie continued.

"That every Western Federation of Miners man repents of his misdeeds and offers fair restitution for them.

"That every union man, woman, child, cat, dog, parakeet, and flea packs his belongings and leaves the state of Colorado, never to return.

"That President Moyer, Secretary Bill Haywood, Chief Anarchist George Pettibone, and their band of terrorist gun-thugs parade past the Standard Mill on Sunday morning with bands playing and marching girls in tow, saluting all the way to Free Kansas.

"And finally, that Charles Moyer personally sweeps the streets of the filth he permitted to accumulate in our city, sprinkling red and yellow rose petals behind him… buck naked."

Disguised smirks formed on the faces of the mill managers, mine owners, and even the governor as Charlie's rant reached crescendo.

Moyer turned again from best friend to bitter adversary in the twinkling of an eye. I knew the right words had been spoken. And only a man as tough as turpentine could have delivered them.

The words were like the slap of a leather glove across the face of a rogue. MacNeill would not tolerate the acts of an aggressor like Moyer. He had to be stopped and nobody in the room seemed to have the guts to do it. The mess would certainly not be easy to contain, but at least Moyer knew he was no longer free to bully the Colorado City mills. He had finally met a man willing to stand up to him.

The meeting ended abruptly with a partial victory at the Portland and Telluride mills, but with no surrender at the Standard Mill. Although the strikes at those mills would end, and men would return to work, the fury of hell was to follow.

After the meeting, the Portland and Telluride mills which had toed the union line were labeled "fair" mills by the WFM. Every operation siding with the Standard Mill was labeled "unfair." And Moyer turned right around and called for strikes at the Standard Mill and at all the Cripple Creek mines supplying ore to it.

That included me.

The Standard Mill was singled out for an awful beating.

Turns out, the Cripple Creek strikes were only possible because of the unilateral strike provision Moyer had secured years ago, just as Dr.

Slocum had explained. The union did not need a general vote to proceed. One man could call down fire in a single act of retribution. No one spoke to Moyer that way, and he would see that MacNeill ate his words like dirt.

On a Monday afternoon in March, 1903, 722 of my men walked off to strike. Just as I had feared, the trouble had somehow crept up the mountain to Cripple Creek.

Shucks.

"Clark, we're not walking out because of you," one of my men said. "You've been a good boss, and we have no grievances against you."

"Well, stay on then. Quit the union if that's what it takes. I'll make sure you're taken care of. You've been with me since we hoisted with mules. Remember those days?"

"Yes, but… it's not that easy," he said, shaking his head. "They're making us strike because of the Standard Mill in Colorado City. It doesn't make sense, but we don't get to vote on it. They're calling it a sympathy strike, but I think it's stupid. We don't even work down there."

"Yeah, really. Where's the sympathy?" I said.

The Independence, Vindicator, Ajax, Theresa, Elkton, Gold King, and dozens of other mines were affected. Men left their shifts confused by what part they played in this puzzling strike. Cripple Creek men were striking for no other reason than to force the Standard Mill into compliance. A reason they could not have possibly understood.

I caught up with Charlie a few days later.

"Well, Charlie." I began with a morbid tease. "You did it this time. Moyer is no longer your friend. No more picnics in the park and good times for you two."

"Good. He never brought his own lunch."

Charlie clicked his teeth and paused. "This must be tough on you, Jeremiah. You're losing business on account of me."

"I know you're doing what you have to. We'll survive."

"Well don't worry; I've got another meeting with Moyer tomorrow. I'll give him the wage increases and other things, and we'll be loving friends again."

I brightened up. "Oh good."

"Clark, those things don't bother me. A few wage increases? That's nothing. But I will not be bullied into giving them, especially with violence."

"I'll leave my weapons at home the next time we negotiate mill rates."

Charlie smiled wryly. "And then we can all meet in Acacia Park for soda pops and chicken sandwiches. Won't that be grand?"

Just as he said, Charlie negotiated a truce with Moyer. The Black Jack Mine promptly reopened. Others too. Maybe Charlie had apologized for the belittling rant in Denver, but I hadn't heard. In any case, it was cause for celebration in Cripple Creek and Victor. Church bells rang, horns blew, and parades marked the end of the labor battles.

"It's over! The Cripple Creek strike is over!" hollered a man running past the hoisthouse. Men cheered and fired pistols into the air. I was glad to see the conflict end, and so were my men.

They all gathered around to boost my spirits so I took the opportunity to express my appreciation.

"I'm so sorry you've lost wages on account of the strike. I've authorized the paymaster to give $50 bonuses to every man. I hope that will make up for the lost time. Some of you men have been with me since the beginning. I appreciate that. And I want you to know you have a future here."

The men beamed.

"Now, get back to work! Right now." I feigned a scowl. "Just kidding! See the paymaster for your bonuses, and enjoy the day with your families. I'm just happy this is over!"

Springtime and warm weather returned, but the truce was not to last. Moyer called another meeting in May. It had only been three months since the last one, and MacNeill and Moyer were preparing another round of volley fire in Colorado City. The trouble was beginning to make my head hurt.

We met at the Colorado College again.

For more battle.

"Mr. MacNeill," Moyer said, lifting his chin, clearly expecting the negotiations to favor his position. "I have three dozen reports of union millmen who have not received employment offers matching their former positions. These men left in March under strike orders, and have not been offered their same positions since our differences were settled."

He waved the papers in protest.

"In fact, it would seem quite a few more men have not been reinstated to their former posts, but rather rehired to arbitrary positions at your personal discretion. Thank you for rehiring them but I must insist that these men be reinstated to their exact positions prior to the strike. These were clearly the terms of our agreement, and you have not honored them."

"I must sadly inform you, Mr. Moyer, that I am not in your employ nor under your authority," said Charlie calmly, puzzled at the impossible request. "I operate the Standard Mill on a profit and loss basis, and hire and fire to meet those objectives. You will find no such record of that agreement."

"Charlie, just let him have it," I said. "Let him have what he wants, and let's get out of here."

"No." He turned back to Moyer. "That strike caused a lot of financial hardship to this mill. We almost didn't reopen. And it has forced me to reevaluate shift requirements. Another strike like that, and we're out of business."

"Charlie–" I tried to interject. He sounded bullheaded to me.

"No, Clark. Moyer's men made the decision to leave. Fine. Now it's my decision whether they will be reinstated to their original positions, or simply reemployed."

He turned to Moyer. "Contrary to your thinking, I must make those fiduciary decisions for the good of the shareholders of this organization. This is not a socialist empire. We operate on profit and loss here."

"So then, it is your decision to leave those men without employment of their respective skills? What if they get fired because they can't do their new jobs?" pressed Moyer.

"You can attempt to find fault if you like, but I will not reinstate any man unless it makes financial sense to do so, just as any responsible businessman would do. How do you expect me to recover from a strike like that? I've had to reduce staff and move people around. With the new structure, the mill is much more efficient. Anyone would do the same in my place."

MacNeill and Moyer operated on entirely different principles – neither of them compromising. Moyer could not understand the fragile nature of business, and expected the entire strike debacle to blow over like a summer storm. No ill-effects… just start over like nothing ever happened. And MacNeill wasn't offering entitlements, especially to a man he disdained so much. That disdain showed in his eyes and in his voice. Moyer had become too frustrated to deal with the mess he had caused, but refused to acknowledge any responsibility for it. He simply threw up his arms and boiled over.

"Well then, Mr. MacNeill, you leave me no choice. If you refuse to reinstate the union men under your employment, we will take action. I assure you, you and your beloved shareholders will see things my way."

"You listen here–"

"No, you listen, MacNeill; I control the raw materials coming into your mill. I control the mines of Cripple Creek and the ore that comes down that mountain. Did you forget that?"

Charlie flicked him off. "Yeah, yeah, yeah…"

"If you don't believe it, you just watch and see. Labor produces all wealth; and wealth belongs to the producer thereof," shrieked Moyer in an undignified tantrum. Doors banged behind him.

End of meeting.

The next day a union representative stepped into the changing house at the Black Jack Mine and read aloud, "It is hereby resolved by the executive council of the Western Federation of Miners that all union labor in all mines in the Cripple Creek and Victor mining district suspend all working activities."

The men gasped.

"This mine and all others are now in a state of strike until such time as mine owners and mill managers resolve differences with the WFM. No union member is to consort, negotiate, or otherwise contact mine owners or mill operators. This order shall remain in effect until the executive board of the WFM announces a mutually agreeable end of the strike."

With that, the Black Jack Mine, and every other in Cripple Creek, was again under strike orders. This time it was intended to stick.

Chapter Twenty

"LOOK OVER HERE, MR. Whitman. I've got a new stallion!" urged a young miner, as Sam and I exited the Eight Pound Hammer Saloon.

"That boy wants your attention, Sam," I said, shutting the large heavy door behind us. All evening, I had needed Sam's help understanding the strike, but could not pry him from the cards. Sam was quite pleased for having won fifty dollars off a pair of green cowhands, and had spent the last two hours instructing them in the art of poker. Sam never got anxious over little things like labor disputes and strikes, and he'd never even met Charlie MacNeill.

"Jes hold yer dang britches, ya whelp. Give me a danged minute to make water over here. You ain't got no bag o' bones I ain't never seen before. I'm the best judge o' horse flesh out o' Texas." Sam bragged as he pressed up into the bushes along the avenue. The young miner started toward the corner of the saloon before Sam could button his trousers and follow.

"Why don't you call it a night?" I said. "I need to talk this strike over with you in the morning. If we can't keep a small crew until this blows over, we're through."

175

"I know ya got bills, son. But don't worry yerself thin. They can wait. Bills can always wait. I'll see you in the morning, Clark. But I got to see what this kid's flappin' about."

The miner made one last plea for his new mount and then bolted into the alleyway, urging Sam to follow. "Slow down, ya pup." Sam followed hard after the boy as I turned to leave.

Sam must have known the boy, or he would never have followed him into a dark alley the way he did. As soon as he turned the corner, I heard the clank of a twenty-dollar gold piece on the dirty brick street. The boy evidently snatched it up and fled into the darkness. His cap flew off as he escaped into the night, leaving Sam in the dark alleyway. I just stood there, maybe a hundred feet away, wondering what sent the boy off like that. Was this a joke?

An angry voice from around the corner boomed, "Old man… You and your plow hand partner have been a burr in our shoes long enough. How do you like that, scab lover? You got something smart to say now?"

A second later, a peach crate crashed onto the street from out of the alleyway. I took the first few steps toward the dark corner, still puzzled. And then like a spark, I understood why the boy had fled and what Sam was into. Widening my stride toward the corner, I heard scuffling and the sounds of a struggle. More voices… threats… and pounding from at least three men.

"Sam! What's going on?" I hollered. And then sprinted in. By the time I reached the alleyway, Sam was face down on the brick with a knife in his side and a puddle of blood under his head. A white flour sack covered his face and a crimson stain grew rapidly across it. Three men bolted into the shadows, scattering like quail off a field. I had no chance of catching them.

"Oh, Sam!" I yelled, flipping him over.

No response. No movement.

A small crowd of onlookers came out of the saloon at the end of the alleyway. Even at 3 AM, there were plenty. One struck up his miner's lamp for a little light.

"Wake up! Sam, wake up!" His left index finger flicked once at the command, and then nothing. No movement and no breath. By the time I removed the ten-pound flour sack it was soaked red, and Sam was dead. He didn't stand a chance.

"Sam? Sam?" I said, laying over his limp body.

The crowd moved in.

With an ugly strike on, Cripple Creek had become a dangerous place to linger after dark. Sam Whitman learned that a little too late. And I suppose his contempt for union thugs didn't help.

The city of Cripple Creek marked his passing with deep sorrow as the church assembled citizens to his graveside.

"As the deer panteth for the water, so my soul longeth after thee," closed the final chorus in mournful tones. And so, Sam Whitman, the estranged husband of Mabel Whitman, and father of three, was gently laid to rest in the pleasant hills of the Mt. Pisgah Cemetery in Cripple Creek.

A fresh marble headstone had already been cut. It simply read, "Samuel Quincy Whitman. 1903 – Died of beating. A friend to all who knew him."

Two dozen close friends in pressed Sunday black mourned his passing. And another six thousand men, women, and children stood afar off, singing with hushed tones the psalms of grief and displaying their love for the kindly old man on that August afternoon in 1903.

Sam lay in state in a large open casket dressed in the only frock coat he ever owned. His hands were folded over his chest and San Francisco silver dollars covered his soft and caring eyes. He lay ready to be committed to the soil. Not a single citizen could believe what they were seeing.

Old Sam was gone.

They could never have imagined it. Sam was a permanent fixture in Cripple Creek, and to say a quarter of the population knew him was an understatement. He was always cheerful and willing to lend a hand. In addition to his advice to grubstakers, he had always looked in on the widows and orphans with gifts of kindness. They mourned him as though a dearly departed father.

I just left the service to pour out my soul to God. Without care to destination, I wandered into the grassy hillside beyond the marble monuments and past the hundreds of nameless mounds in Potter's Field.

Goodbye, Sam. Tears fell.

I took a long climb through the aspen and spent every tear within me. Then I returned to console those who knew him best. Patricia stood by my side. She knew the full extent of my loss.

"I am so sorry, Jeremiah," she said, crying. "He was like my own father. I just want him back. Why did they have to do that to him?"

The six-foot-tall preacher and undertaker stood over him now, delivering a final sermon to the man we all loved.

"Dust to dust, and ashes to ashes. Naked I have come into this world, and naked I must return. Blessed be the name of the Lord, Amen," he said. An afternoon thunderstorm filled the western skies and a cold drizzle dripped from an oilcloth over the grave site.

My business partner and dear friend Sam Whitman now rested from his labors in a fine plot surrounded by Colorado columbines and sweet grasses which waged their own struggle in the thin alpine air. A swirling cluster of tiny blue butterflies saw to his departure.

The coffin disappeared under the earth. I turned to the men who knew him best and ventured a cautious word. "Charlie, Franklin, Spec, fellas, step over here and we'll let the folks come under the canvas so they can pay their respects. I need a moment of your time."

The small group of mine owners and mill managers gathered under a clump of trees beyond earshot of the thousands of mourning attendees who filed by. Each tossed freshly cut flowers into the open grave and offering condolences to those remaining.

I wiped down my swollen eyes. And then managed a few words to the men standing beside me. "Fellas, this world is an empty shell. A failing timepiece slowly winding down to its final hour. Each one of us will take that final step into eternity one day, but hopefully not as Sam did. This broken world, marred by the sin of Adam, holds nothing for us. Sam was savagely murdered, yet he lives in the arms of his Savior. Even with the events of this week, I am neither anxious nor fearful of what this life has planned for me. In light of Sam's death, I propose a bold plan of action. Please hear me out fellas."

"Go on," the men said sadly. I turned to Charlie MacNeill first.

"Charlie, I'll wager a dollar to a dime your mill won't be standing by next week's time. If allowed to continue, Moyer will have his way down there. He's using these striking miners in a cowardly way. I have heard talk at the Double Eagle Saloon of burning that whole outfit down. Have you fellas heard that?"

"We have," A few agreed. They shivered in the drizzle.

I wiped my eyes again. "Think of it from the striker's viewpoint... the Standard Mill is the only thing standing between those men and honest work. You've got 3,500 angry miners and an entire political party in Teller County wishing to see your hide pegged to a woodshed wall. It surprises me you're even up here today."

"That's right," some of the men said, looking at Charlie.

"It won't be long before one of them slips down there after midnight and tosses a coal oil lamp to that mill. That is what Moyer has driven them to. That's the position he's put them in. They want work and you're in the way. Do you understand that?"

One of the men said, "Maybe we can negotiate with Moyer. We can—"

"No, the time for talk is past," I said. "He's gotten the surrender of the Telluride and Portland mills, right? All the mines are his too. Moyer only needs the Standard Mill to complete a monopoly. The Standard will either fold or be taken out of the way. Either way, a victory for Moyer. His intentions are clear. The evidence is Sam Whitman's body moldering in the grave."

Charlie removed his wet hat. "I understand. But what are we going to do?"

"The way I see it, we've got two choices. Either you surrender to Moyer, or we reopen the mines and mills with non-union labor."

The men stepped back. "Scabs?"

"Or... maybe we can get some of our men to quit the union and reopen with them. If the union gains an iron grip on the mines and mills, the price of labor will go to the moon. That's no good for anybody. We must show them we're not intimidated."

The idea fell on the men like a wet blanket, and I suddenly came to see the folly myself. After all, what leverage could we hope to have? 3,500 striking miners would be a force to reckon with. Reopening without them would invoke their rage and start a war. They had been so conditioned to see the mine owners as enemies that this was the likely result. My heart sank at the silly notion, and I swiftly began formulating an exit from it.

"Or... maybe... we could—"

Franklin Blythe of the El Paso Mine interrupted. "Fellas, I agree. Sam was a good man, and that was a cowardly act against him. There was no call for bludgeoning him that way. That turns my insides something awful and I have never abided a coward. I've had just about enough of this terrorism, and I'd open the El Paso Mine just to put a stick in their eye. These Federation ruffians have got to go."

"That's a little strong," Mac O'Malley said.

"Well, I've seen my share of violence and intimidation. I've tried diplomacy and special incentives to entice a skeleton crew to remain, only to see them sorely mistreated by unionists. Sam's brutal killing is more than I can reasonably stand."

Just as Blythe began building his case, O'Malley interrupted, "Yeah fellas, that's all good and fine. I'd be genuinely high-spirited to reopen the Golden Cycle Mine with strikebreakers just like you. But ye got to know what you're getting yourselves into. Them blokes'll start a war!"

"Go on," I said.

"Like when I fought ol' Lew Joslin in a bare-knuckle fistfight down at Johnnie Nolan's a few years back. It was a fair eighteen rounder with no underhanded work permitted. And yet he dang near killed me. When the last bell rang, I ended up with two broken hands, a busted knee, a bit off ear, and an eye hangin' clean from its socket. And I was the winner! Is that the kind of bare-knuckle brawl you're lookin' to get into? Because that's just what they'll bring. And they won't be as gentlemanly as the Leadville Blacksmith. You won't get a wink and a handshake when it's over. No sir!"

The men winced.

O'Malley lifted a hand. "But I'll tell you one thing right here today. If a horde o' thugs ever tries to take me like they did old Sam, they'll have to pack a lunch."

"I'll take that fight," Blythe said. "We'll either be men of character or spineless creatures to be trod upon at the discretion of a more ambitious lot. Let's step up to the chalk line."

While O'Malley had tried to talk the men out of a bad scrape, he had actually talked them into it instead. No one standing in the circle wanted to be known as one who shirked a bully.

Sherriff Robertson stepped up to the circle. "You boys planning something? Nothing illegal, I hope. You ain't plotting revenge are you?" He smiled.

"You best get on," Blythe said. "You're a unionist and this business don't concern you." Robertson shook his head and walked off.

"Just one thing," I said, watching him go. "This struggle is not against our own employees. If we do this, it is not to make them suffer. It is so they can eventually return to work free of violence and intimidation. Understand? Let's be clear who the enemy is."

Heads nodded.

"Y'all know this won't be Christmas caroling in the park, so gird up your loins fellas, because we got a fight coming."

The next step would be to enlist our own men in the struggle, or to reopen with strikebreakers. The union and their little friend Sheriff Robertson would just have to live with that.

Carpenters spent a fortnight hoisting wooden ramparts around the El Paso and Black Jack mines, and doing the same for the Standard Mill in Colorado City. They constructed eighteen-foot walls of roughhewn Ponderosa Pine. Miners and millmen could operate safely behind them without fear. Picketmen could try to burn us out. They could surround and intimidate. But they would never breach those massive green timbers. Twenty Pinkertons were stationed at each mine and mill, and we boldly announced our plan to reopen and ship ore to the Standard Mill. Anyone willing to join us was welcome – union or not.

This was no small stir for Cripple Creek. Miners knew we were a small lot, and had little chance of bucking the system. After all, the WFM had an iron grip, and a few renegades would not change that.

Most of the men who remembered Bull Hill were still loyal to the union for its battles against the mine owners in '94. But some had come to regret signing over their voting rights. They had given Moyer complete strike control, and to those men, the strike orders at the Cripple Creek mines didn't make sense. After all, they had no beef with the mine owners. And they barely knew that the Standard Mill existed. So why were they striking?

Others just wanted to return to work to feed their families. They didn't care how the conflict was resolved, even if the mine owners took a black eye. And, there were a fair number of younger men who had recently come to the district for work, and had no idea what this was all about.

The politics had become an ugly affair. Even a casual brush with it left one tainted and defiled. Yet the news became the constant talk of the town. Seventy-three saloon and gambling hall owners celebrated as their establishments filled with men hashing out the news from every conceivable angle. Pubs and saloons became the staging grounds of debate, where truth, lies, and uncertainties were the grist for the unceasing turn of the political millstone.

"This means war, you know," an old-timer told me, as we pushed through a rowdy crowd at the Lonely Lode Saloon. "Union bosses don't take strike-busting lying down. They'll come at you with an army. And you ain't got the skilled men you had before the strike. I reckon you can bring in some country hands, but you'll need to teach 'm to wipe their noses. You won't make a dollar, but maybe you'll keep yer mine open. I reckon that's a start."

"You bet I'll keep it open," I said, still looking for a place to sit.

Finding a table in Cripple Creek was no small feat. But, the old-timer, Charlie MacNeill, and I muscled into the crowd at the Lonely Lode just the same.

"You may be right about war," I said, settling in, and ordering beefsteaks and fried potatoes for the three of us. It was the only thing on the menu. "They've had mine owners pinned down since '94. That's a long time to run the rails. They won't let that go over a few scabs at the Black Jack Mine. But it's the Standard Mill that bothers me. Moyer will get his revenge."

"Don't worry about that," Charlie said. "If you reopen those mines, like you said, your fight's up here in Teller County, not Colorado City. They'll forget all about us. This is the big dog's bone yard."

"I guess you're right. They want the Smelterman's Union in Colorado City, but they won't lose Cripple Creek to get it."

The old timer lit a cigar. "Yup, this is their stronghold."

"I can already see the Teller County officials looking forward to some action," Charlie said. "They want to see the mine owners take another licking and be put back into their place. Its 1894 all over again. Except this time they've got the political muscle. They say who's prosecuted and who's not. You no longer have an impartial justice system like they did in '94. Keep that in mind."

The old-timer puffed heavily on the fat cigar. "It's not just that. Have you seen the hooligans they've brought in? They've got a fair stash o' weaponry polished and stacked. Them picketmen is ready for some bloody work. And they ain't yer Sunday Bible tellers neither. This here town is set up fer an old-fashioned high-noon showdown."

"Well, I'm opening up, and so is the El Paso. You watch and see. Get ready for some ore, Charlie. It's coming next week."

And just as I had said, by mid-August of 1903 the Black Jack and El Paso mines opened with two hundred and fifty unskilled men shipped in from Leadville. These were Lake County men of high-altitude vigor, and could be trusted to perform their duties without fail. If all went well, the Golden Cycle was to follow. The experiment at the Black Jack and El Paso mines would lead the way. But if it failed there would be no others.

I met the new men out on the railhead. A band of picketmen did too.

"Columns of four!" the brutish shift boss hollered. "Get in your columns of four." He had brought in the Leadville country men and prepared them for the worst. They were scabs and there was no other way to look at it. None of our employees dared join them.

"When I give the word, you git off these railcars and form up in columns. We're marching in. No talking… no stopping… and no meandering. You'll muster behind those 18-foot walls. And keep your mouths shut. You'll be trained and paid three dollars a day. Some of you will cross that picket line twice a day. And it won't be a pleasant stroll. If you don't care to hazard the line, we've got tents and bivy sacks inside. Now march, you baby eaters!"

The railcar doors flew open.

"You scabs can just turn right around and go home." A gun-thug lowered his revolver on the new men. "You ain't going nowheres today. Not while we're here, you ain't. Pack yer things and git, scabs, 'fore you get what's coming."

The crew boss, Victor Poole and his men stopped dead. They had no other option but to turn back to the railcars. That is until deputy Collins rushed in to save them. The Pinkerton men had been standing guard since midnight, ready for any criminal action.

"Is that you, Minster? Ed Minster? Is that you? Drop your weapon," Collins demanded. "You got to let these men pass. That's the law. If you shoot, we'll gun you down. Now let's go see Judge Hawkins and talk this out. You know we won't tolerate gunplay."

But even Hawkins, who had tried his best to execute justice, was no match for the powerful forces in Teller County. That night he was rousted from his home in Goldfield, threatened and physically assaulted. He did not want to end up like old Sam. The next morning, Ed Minster and his gang went free.

Chapter Twenty-one

September, 1903

THE TELLER COUNTY JUSTICE system insulated union men like Ed Minster from prosecution. And so they repeated the same ugly performances for weeks. All the Leadville men were now forced to bunk inside the tall wooden ramparts. Every judge, lawyer, politician, and policeman in Teller County had caved to union intimidation. Justice became a scare commodity west of Pikes Peak. Although a precious few could see them at the time, the seeds of insurrection were already in the soil. Justice Hawkins toed the line like everyone else.

Hawkins pulled me aside one day. "I ain't your savior in this fight. If you need help with these ruffians you'll need to find it elsewhere. I am sorry. They threatened my wife, you know. I couldn't live with myself if something happened to her. I'm just a man. Not a savior."

As the weeks wore on, our resources with local authorities slowly drained away. Law enforcement had been neutered by the hand of higher powers who had decided it was now time for the unruly mine owners to play ball. No more strikebreakers. No more scabs. And no more operating outside the authority of the union. The noose was tightening, and I knew our only remedy lay with the governor. Hawkins and the other county judges had simply given up.

By the middle of September, 1903, six weeks after Sam's death, we were running ragged. Mines were trying to operate with the few men who remained. The Mine Owners Association finally called a meeting with the governor at the Colorado College in Colorado Springs. An arbitration meeting. We met at the Uintah Street administrative building on Sunday at 1 PM after church services had let out.

The governor opened the hearing and conducted it in a strict legal fashion as he had before. Although he must have been weary of the persistent trouble. Members of the Western Federation of Miners declined to attend.

Officers of the Mine Owners Association and representatives of the mills each recounted their experiences of the past weeks. New testimony of armed insurrection, violence, and government protection was heard without repeat for two hours. The numerous accounts began to blend together into a pool of monotonous disgust. The governor stood to bring closure. He had heard enough.

"Gentlemen, I thank you for bringing this matter to my office. I have long supposed conditions in Cripple Creek would become critical, and this testimony confirms that they have. I have watched the strike with my own suspicion, having daily telegraph reports of violent men and their protection by elected officials. Yes, I know of that character, Ed Minster. You are not the first to relay such news. I am not without my information. But I am slow to act in these matters, hoping for the winds of reason to blow and clearheaded individuals to prevail. It is clear this has not happened."

"No, it has not!" someone shouted from the back. "And maybe you are too danged slow."

The governor ignored him. "You are to be commended for reopening those mines. But whatever in God's green earth possessed you to do so? By George, you have got sand. I will grant you that. But are you sure you know what manner of hornet's nest you've opened up? Well, you're fixin' to find out. That's for darn sure. The Teller County union will not give up this fight without a strong deterrent. I have become convinced of that. So if you're sure you wish to escalate the matter, I possess the forceful means to satisfy you. I just wished there was another way."

I raised a weary arm. "Can you bring in some support? Like you did in Colorado City last year? That seemed to work. The violence cleared up down there... sort of."

"We just need a little help with the hotheads," Franklin Blythe added. "The El Paso Mine is being overrun with them."

"And the Black Jack, too," I said.

Peabody nodded. "Clark, I understand you lost a good man. I am sorry for that. I will agree to dispatch a small detachment of Colorado militiamen under Adjutant General Sherman Bell, but I need your assurance on two matters."

"Okay, we'll do anything."

The man from the rear shouted again. "Yeah, bring in the Rough Riders. They'll run 'em all out!"

"Have that man removed," Peabody ordered. He turned back to me.

"First, I want you to be plumb sure of what you are doing. I will not be politically embarrassed by calling out the militia to squash the grievances of honest workingmen. Do I have your assurance of this? If you have not done your due diligence, then now is the time. I will not proceed until you are confident, and until you have justified the matter with my attorney. We won't be the laughingstock of the country over a few disgruntled ore muckers. Do you understand?"

"Yes. That's only reasonable."

"Next... these troops cost money. The beans and bullets don't just fall off the money wagon. The State of Colorado will not be financially responsible for them. You will. I will levy a four-year bond at $400,000, which the Cripple Creek mines will carry. The mills have given enough. Now it is your turn. Divide the total amongst yourselves. But you will pay the full amount in four years. And I do mean you will pay it. I will expect your assurance in writing."

"Well, the Black Jack Mine can't handle that alone, not even over the four years. We'll need to share the cost somehow."

Blythe looked at me and nodded.

"Okay, we can agree to that. We'll find the backers. And we need the help."

"One more thing," Peabody said. "If I find that this fight is for your own personal gain, I will not abide it. I'll pull those troops right out, and you'll still pay."

"No sir, it is not," Blythe said. "We are just trying to reopen the mines and get our men back to work. The strikebreakers will leave when they return."

"Then it's settled," Peabody finished. "Gentlemen, let us quit ourselves like men. The workingmen of Colorado deserve the full measure of our vigilance. Do not fail them. This is my last word on the matter. Good luck and God be with you."

As the governor quit the floor, the gravity of drawing down troops to defend a few holes in the ground suddenly seemed an unjustified excess. I had just been handed the armies of the state of Colorado and the weight of it was more than I was prepared to handle. My knees dipped. I suppose the saying of a thing is not equal to the doing of it, and the tongue is surely an unruly member. Taking a moment to reflect, I knew Charlie and I had been down this miserable road before. There would be no stopping the union without the show of force. That was a plain fact to everyone by now. We would proceed as agreed.

And so the Colorado State militia marched on Cripple Creek, Colorado in the year of our Lord, 1903. God save the city.

The Western Federation of Miners seized the opportunity to accuse the Republican governor of hiding in the pocket of the mines.

"The mine owners have finally bought the governor!" Charles Moyer complained in a city council meeting, throwing down the Victor Record morning edition. But he didn't see Franklin Blythe and me standing behind the spectators. "We know who is behind this. It's that Black Jack millionaire and his cronies. I'll wring his neck, I swear. The governor of Colorado can be bought for only $400,000."

I just kept my mouth shut because I knew what was coming for Moyer.

By September's end, a thousand troops occupied the Cripple Creek mining district. Townsfolk came out with picnic lunches and steamer chairs to watch the boys drill to the hoarse commands of salty drill instructors.

Most citizens had not understood the need for troops. To them this was just an interesting occurrence not seen every day in the rugged mountains of Colorado. It was certainly worth a chicken salad lunch in the back hills of Goldfield and Battle Mountain. The drill instructors sang out their commands to the delight of watching citizens.

"Hay foot, straw foot, leftie, rightie, low-ah... Take it on the left foot... The mighty, mighty left foot... Left foot, right foot, left foot, right foot," bellowed the drill instructors as green recruits prepared for action, drilling to become a unified fighting force. The young boys scrambled to keep time with drill instructors who might fly in for a heavy tongue-lashing and gut-punch at the sight of any minor infraction. Recruits slept only four hours a night and drilling the rest. The boys were nothing but insects under the boots of c determined old salts, but they would become the most disciplined insects in the territory. If they could only learn their left feet from their right.

Seven hundred such boys mustered in Camp Goldfield, situated one-half mile east of Independence. Another three hundred bivouacked at Bull Hill, El Paso, Black Jack, Golden Cycle, Elkton, and other Victor and Cripple Creek mines. We certainly had the protection we needed now. Ed Minster would just have to seek his amusement elsewhere.

Or face the armies of General Sherman Bell: Roosevelt's finest Rough Rider.

He was not a man to be trifled with as I soon learned at my first meeting.

"Mr. Clark. I have come to do up this anarchist federation. But I will not have your mines provoking a fight. Please release your Pinkerton detectives and deputies. They have done their job. Now it is my turn. Keep your remarks to a minimum. Do your honest work, and leave the law enforcement to me. I will bring a lash down on this rebellious county. Any man who takes his arrest and keeps his mouth shut I will consider an innocent casualty. But I will learn the depths of this rebellious federation. You can work your men any way you see fit, but this district is now under my command. You stay clear of legal matters from here on out, and any further communications with the governor. I will handle that just fine. Do I make myself clear?"

"Yes sir. But can you protect the mines? We're being hit from all sides."

"I've got a thousand men under my command. And a platoon of those are New Boot Marines. They'll train here with us before going to some murder-hole like San Juan Hill to die for God, Country, and their Beloved Corps. Don't cross them or you'll see the brutes that they are. Yes, we can protect your mines."

"Thank you, sir. I understand. We'll stay clear."

Sherman Bell was a man of chosen words and decisive action, if not of questionable character himself. But we needed a man like that. And he was right about my part in the conflict. He would see to the work and didn't need my help. He set to work by first drawing a bead on the Victor Record Newspaper.

The Victor Record seemed to enjoy defaming Cripple Creek mines and portraying the workingman as slaves to malevolent capitalist management. News of the conflict sold like candy canes on Christmas Eve, and the Victor Record benefited by every word they could set to ink. The effect was like a dirty knife in a rotten sore. It only aggravated things.

"Patricia," I said, coming home at a reasonable hour for a change. I was happy for the changes Bell and his men would bring. "Bell's starting in on the Victor Record. I just wish he could do something about the Boston, New York, and Albany papers. Can we send him back East when he's done here?"

"Well, they're taking their stories from the Victor Record, so maybe things will get better," she said. "I know they've had their own stories based on the Eastern millionaires at the steel mills, but that's been over for a while. They need something new, and you gold diggers are it for now."

"It's like they've earned some capital with their readers and they're spending it like girls at a soda fountain. Any wicked-millionaire story, whether confirmed or not, goes to print. And the naïve investors just yank their dollars from the mining stocks. It's really hurting us."

"Well, those investors can't tell the truth from the lie. It's flawed reasoning. Socialism and propaganda. Those Eastern editors aren't out here to see things firsthand, but I don't think that would matter anyway. They love a good story."

"You're right."

"That motto they keep quoting: 'Labor produces all wealth' bothers me the most," she said. "I thought Stratton produced all the wealth up here. At least, when he was alive."

"True. In any case, Bell's the man to set things straight. We're going to be okay after this," I said with a smothering kiss and a big smile.

"You're in a good mood."

"What's for supper? Feed me, woman!"

"Oh, you poor thing. You make me ill." She giggled and deflected my advances with a wooden spoon. "You'll be lucky to get a butter sandwich. Now be quiet."

A second later, she ran shrieking for the safety of the bedroom with me in hot pursuit. I didn't want a butter sandwich.

Under Bell's orders, militiamen arrested the entire workforce of the Victor Record and walked them to Camp Goldfield. Barbed wire bullpens would hold them before deportation to the Kansas state line. Evidently, Bell didn't plan to sit around reasoning with them. He'd handle things his way. And that shocked everyone. Naturally, the editor became a violent opponent of the radical action. From his fallen position in the muddy Goldfield bullpen, awaiting deportation, he let his displeasure be known to everyone within gunshot range.

"This is an outrage! The first actions of an oppressive regime are to suppress the freedom of speech." He pulled at the barbed wire. "I demand a writ of habeas corpus. I demand to be released to the local authorities. I demand a trial by a jury of my peers!" His shrill tone filled the mountainside.

The editor gnashed his teeth as I passed on my way to Bell's tent.

The other newspapermen also could not believe the deportation order. They had been upstanding pillars of society, respected in the community. What madman would have them roughhandedly dragged into a barbed wire enclosure and shipped off to Kansas? They were the ones leading the way in justice for the workingmen who were now losing their jobs to lowdown scabs from Leadville. It was the mine owners, if any, who ought to go to Kansas. For them, the world was turning upside down.

The editor hung from the barbed wire. "Who's in charge here? I want a county judge down here, right now!"

The editor's piercing scream could be heard ringing up the amphitheater-like slopes of Battle Mountain all the way to Altman. You could look down from the Black Jack headframe and see him ranting like a little black rooster.

The editor stretched the wire again, and the swift butt of a Kentucky carbine came across his pale brow. The broken newspaperman crumpled to his knees and ceased his undignified tantrum.

"But that's what the General said. When they cross the deadline and start to climbin' that fence, put 'em down," said the dutiful Marine Corps private. "I don't make the rules, but you got to keep shut while yer in this here bullpen." The boy shifting in fear. He knew what could come next for him, and would not be sleeping his four hours that night.

News of the boy's action reached General Bell that day. He was immediately promoted to Corporal, producing fits of laughter and mockery of the newspapermen who wallowed in the muddy confines. No mercy for them. They would soon be on railcars for Kansas. But news also reached the elected officials of Teller County.

Judge Seeds, the magistrate judge, issued a writ of habeas corpus to permit the employees of the Victor Record to appear before His Honor. All the mine owners, union men, and militia officers were on-hand for the decision.

Judge Seeds passed judgment without deliberation.

"I see neither crime nor trespass for which these citizens have been detained. Certainly, they have committed no crime in exercising their freedom of speech, even if that speech criticizes the unjust occupation of our territory. It is the law of Colorado that militiamen be subject to all local authority, and I am the law here. No staged military coup will circumvent my authority in this court."

A rabble sounded across the courtroom.

Another paid-off judge.

The judge raised his gavel. "By the authority vested in me by Teller County in the State of Colorado, I hereby release these citizens to their own recognizance, warning only that they stay clear of menacing militiamen seeking meritorious promotion to higher ranks. The prisoners are released." Judge Seeds slammed the gavel into the bench and it spun out onto the lacquered courtroom floor.

"Habeas corpus, bunk! We'll give 'em post mortems!" roared General Bell from his tent in Camp Goldfield. "Clark, did you hear that nonsense? Were you there? More rogues than honest men find shelter in habeas corpus. Lieutenant, pick 'em up again and wire the Governor."

"Yessir," he said, saluting.

"I will not have my orders thwarted by that little federation hand-puppet. Pick 'em up again. Hold 'em in that bullpen for ten days, and then let 'em go. Those newspapermen may have escaped deportation for now, but this will inform those rebels who's running things around here.

"I want every union leader, organizer, and sympathizer involved in this rebellion in this bullpen before the snow flies. Put that new Corporal in charge of the round-up. We will see to their safety at the Kansas state line."

Under his absolute rule, the Independence, Vindicator, Findlay, Strong, Joe Dandy, Theresa, Elkton, Tornado, Ajax, and Golden Cycle mines reopened with anyone willing to work, union or not. Militiamen patrolled the streets night and day, enforcing strict discipline and arresting dissidents. 2,900 out of 3,500 miners returned to work, proving to me at least, that our cause was just.

The strike order was never officially retracted. But the men were back to work and happy for it. But Moyer had only just started.

Chapter Twenty-two

November, 1903

"IF THESE COWARDS WANT war, I'll give 'em one!" hollered General Bell. "I was plenty gracious. I gave them fair notice to take their punishment, but they wouldn't have it. Just ask Clark, here. Was I fair? Evidently, they had to have it all. Well, I'll give it to them. I will not abide the likes of this collectivist federation one more day. I swear I will drive every Western Federation man from this mountain by this time next year."

Bell jerked the reins of his mount and galloped off the Vindicator Mine site leaving a scene of devastating wreckage behind.

The once-towering Vindicator headframe and hoisthouse lay in smoldering embers, blown to splinters by another act of cowardice. A satchel charge of nitro had been booby-trapped at the seventh level of the main shaft and detonated as two men innocently stepped off the cage. Another such charge had lifted the massive headframe right off its foundations and deposited it in a burning heap. Charles McCormick and Frank Beck were blown into eternity without so much as a moment's preparation. Now they stood before a Holy God, waiting on His graces.

Hundreds of men milled about the burning wreckage trying to make sense of a senseless act. Each one eyeing another with suspicion. Union and non-union alike had heard the General's wrath and knew the gauntlet was laid. Sides would be drawn. Every man would decide for himself which side he should take.

Violent treachery on one side.

Violent retribution on the other.

"This is getting nasty," one police officer remarked. He lifted a piece of twisted steel. "I'm not sure I care to live in a place like this."

"I agree," said another. "When this is over, I'm going back to Colorado Springs. Hey, look over there. Even the idlers and braggarts are sick of this. It's one thing to hoist a mug in a noisy saloon, partaking of a little one-upmanship. But it's another to cup a hand in the pool of madness itself. Only the desperate partake. And I've got an idea who it was."

"What have you got?"

"It's an engraved metal matchbox I'd seen downtown. Ask around, I'll bet we found a clue. Does the name Poole mean anything to you?"

"No, but that's a good find. You know… The mine owners won't stand for this terrorism long. They will get their revenge one way or another. Whoever he is, he's a dead man."

"This is about that Standard Mill and Black Jack mess, isn't it? Scabs."

"Everybody knows it was MacNeill's doing in the first place. Couldn't keep his mouth shut. He doesn't even live up here."

A telegraph message flew off to Governor Peabody. Arriving townspeople stood shocked and horrified. In one day, our fair city had gone from model of the state to a dark place of terror.

It was easy to sit complacently in one's own home, not allowing disturbing evidence to penetrate. But this was another matter altogether. This came screaming in like a black banshee rooster and could not be waved off. Two more men were dead, and the weight of it hung like a freezing winter fog.

"Who's next?" Patricia asked, that night. "First it was old Sam. Now McCormick and Beck are dead. How many more? None of the ladies will let their men go out."

I steadied her hand. "All three were men of character. How can a man expect to earn an honest wage? You can't even walk the streets at night."

She shook her head. "Despicable."

The governor acted with a proclamation to be read aloud in downtown Cripple Creek and Victor.

"I, Governor James Hamilton Peabody, as the duly elected executive, do hereby proclaim the State of Colorado to be in a state of insurrection and rebellion. A malevolent system of anarchy has infiltrated every level of government and law enforcement of Teller County. Criminals in said county perpetrate crimes upon the citizenry without due process and prosecution. Such conditions defy the laws of the State of Colorado set forth to protect its citizens. They further violate the Declaration of Independence, which guarantees the right to life, liberty, and the pursuit of happiness.

"With this proclamation, I do hereby transfer control of local law enforcement and judicial process within said county to the state militia to dispense as it sees fit. The state militia is hereby elevated above local law enforcement, and is expected to restore law and order at any cost. Any obstruction by Teller County officials will result in immediate prosecution to the fullest extent of the law.

"This notice shall remain in effect until said county may be deemed no longer in a state of insurrection as judged by the Supreme Commander of the militia and this office."

The town crier finished the reading outside the Gold Coin Club in Victor and walked away without a word. He refused questions from the few that had them.

Most simply returned to their homes in disbelief at the act of violence that had been perpetrated upon them. The average man simply could not accept how far we had fallen. Cripple Creek was a proud city of virtue. But now this had happened.

Sherman Bell didn't return home quietly. "You want them out?" Bell said, waving the proclamation to me. "Well, they're going out."

"Yes, I do. But I just want the violence to end. That's all."

"Well, I've got the authority. No defiant judge will impede me now. This is no longer a police action against a loose pack of bullies. This is war, and those responsible will feel the full reach of my fury."

I nodded. "And now you've got the sympathies of the people. This bombing felt like a horse-kick to the head. Townsfolk can now see the wickedness that some will stoop to. They didn't see that before. Even after Sam's death. But now with Beck and McCormick gone, I think we're on a new course. And I think things will get better."

Ironically, as one of the first to seek aid from the militia, I suffered some of the first collateral impact of its actions. Three days after the bombing I was asked to return to the Goldfield bullpens. Victor Poole, my chief engineer sent word from the camp. Nearly a thousand militiamen were now stationed there. It was an intimidating place to venture into.

And it had changed.

Camp Goldfield now had a half-dozen barbed wire enclosures, each detaining idle men awaiting deportation to Kansas and the New Mexico territory. Bell had hunted down and rounded up the worst offenders. Cuffed in leg-irons, the men slowly tramped the muddy enclosures exposed to the raw elements of Colorado weather. They bunked in dirty canvas tents and waited to be shipped off. Colorado would be rid of these scoundrels once and for all, just as Idaho had been decades earlier.

"What kind of Andersonville are you running here?" I asked a militiaman. "It looks like a cattleman's pasture with those black puddles of stagnant water and mud up to the ankles. You keep men penned up like this?"

A man was being flogged in one of the far bullpens.

"Yessir," the armed man answered. "Those are dangerous men, sir. But they don't look it in the mud. They're headed for the desert. We feed 'em the same rations the militia boys have been eating. But it's a hard fall from the lobster and fresh fruit they've been accustomed to getting for their devilish work. Make no mistake, sir. They're desperate men, so watch yourself."

"Well, have you got a man named Victor Poole?" I asked, walking along the six-stranded fence. I hadn't expected the harsh measures, but supposed their deeds justified the treatment. After all, I knew why they were here.

"Who?"

"Poole. Victor Poole. You got him?"

"Yessir, right over there." He pointed twenty yards down the row of bullpens. Dark clouds made the place cold and miserable. I followed him to Poole.

"What are you doing here, Victor? You're a good man. I hate to see you penned up this way. What's going on? What have you done?"

"Now listen, Chief, I never meant no harm to them miners. I just wanted to scare 'em a little. I ain't sayin' I done nothin'. But they got me in here for that Vindicator bombing."

My heart sank. "Oh, Victor…"

"You know I'm a union man, and you keep me on because I do good work. But I've got to take orders like everyone else. You think it's so easy for us union men, but it ain't. I got pressure from more places than you know. If I don't toe the line, they got ways to make me wish I'd had. I am afraid every day of my life. It ain't just you mine owners that's got it bad."

"Okay," I said with a sigh. "What's the verdict?"

"Bell is a fixin' to send me to the New Mexico desert and I'm afraid I ain't never comin' back. Chief, I can't get deported. I'll die out there in the desert if they don't hang me first."

I flinched.

"And I've got a wife and babies to feed. You've got to talk to the judge for me. Will you do that? Will ya?" he pleaded, shivering and wet from the harsh elements of the December air.

I could see terror in his eyes, but knew his conscience ailed him more than any thought of deportation or starvation in the desert. He clearly saw the end of his evil deeds and was in danger of more than the loss of occupation. He had come face to face with eternity and did not like what he saw. Of course, I would help where I could, but he would have to come to terms with any actions he may have taken. It is a fearful thing to fall into the hands of an angry God.

I offered my sheepskin coat for a little warmth.

"Well Victor, if you did what they say, you'll have to pay the price. You know that. Two men are dead and someone's got to pay. There just isn't any way clear of that. If a man's life isn't sacred then this town is nothing but the devil's brooding nest. We can't have that. My best advice is to fess up and take what punishment awaits you. Holding a thing like that can rot a man's gut from the inside out. I'm not saying you did it, but if you did, you best clear the slate before it's too late. Do you understand me?"

"I understand Chief," he said, lifting each foot out of the freezing mud, back and forth, back and forth. "But can you git me out? Tell them I work for you."

"I'll do what I can. I'll see the judge today."

I had promised to do my best, but now began to feel the bite of the cold morning air myself. I managed the trip back into town without the big coat. Victor would fare poorly without it. Next, I went straight to the county courthouse with a single mission in mind: to do what I could for Victor Poole.

I returned to General Bell's headquarters the next day with a writ of habeas corpus, signed by Judge W. P. Seeds, who requested that Victor Poole be presented before His Honor. I felt uncomfortable, as though playing both sides of the game. But this was the least I could do. Poole was a good employee, and I never figured him for a killer. I only wondered who had gotten to him. Nevertheless, I needed him and would stretch my neck out without any misgivings. If I failed, that was one thing, but I had to try.

Bell was already wrestling with a stack of legal injunctions flooded on him by the busy boys in Teller County. This was one task not suited to his fighting-man's nature. He looked up at me, eyed the familiar yellow form I carried, and grimaced.

Seeing his disappointment was all I needed. I knew what would come next.

"Listen Jeremiah, I know you've got a man in the pen. But you know this paper just lets those anarchist judges release a killer back into Cripple Creek. I wish I could offer him due process, but there just isn't any law up here. They'll just turn him lose tomorrow. He'll go off and blow up another mine in the middle of the night like the coward that he is. He's guilty and you and I both know it, even if you won't admit it. He's a union man, and he toes the line. Plus, they found his personal effects at the scene of the crime. I've got two dozen unaffiliated citizens who swear he did it. Have you forgotten that?"

"No, but I thought you could put him under my supervision." Even as I said it, I knew it was wrong. I just didn't want to see him penned up like that.

"I don't think so. He's guilty and that paper just lets him off to do it again. It's a rogue's protection and I will not abide it. Think about what you're doing and you'll understand that we've got to take a hard position here. Obviously, we're not going to hang him without a trial. But we're not going to allow him to linger in the area either. Without the luxury of due process, which no longer exists in these parts, he's simply got to go. Do you understand?"

"I know, I know, I know. This is a mess," I said, tossing the wrinkled paper on the ground. Bell picked it up, smoothing out the creases.

"But for you, I'll wire the governor and see what he wants to do. But just so you know… I'm ready to ship Poole off to New Mexico on the next load. Stop by tomorrow and I'll let you know what I hear." Bell got his telegram the next day.

To Adjutant General Sherman Bell. Stop.
Poole deportation confirmed. Stop.
Habeas corpus denied. Stop.
Evidence overwhelming. Stop.
Next load to NM. Stop.

"Clark, we're going to have to follow through with Poole's deportation, writ of habeas corpus or not. The governor suspended the right of habeas corpus for Victor Poole just as he has for these other two dozen men."

"Humph. Okay."

"Clark, this isn't something new. You know President Lincoln did this hundreds of times with mutinous characters sympathetic to the Southern rebellion. You lived down there in the South and you know it happened, or your daddy did. Sometimes you've got to take the good of the country into consideration ahead of the likes of known terrorists. Do the victims have rights? Poole's going to the New Mexico desert tomorrow and that's final."

"I understand," I said, eyeing the telegram.

"Jeremiah, I am sorry you're losing a man. But you know this is what we're here for. We're sweeping this county clean of insurrection and terror, and making it safe for honest citizens again."

"I know. Half those men don't dare step foot into those mines after what happened. They're afraid they'll be blown up like Beck and McCormick."

"Or, bludgeoned like old Sam. I'm sure you understand that. I am sorry," he said again, looking down, mostly sorry that he had brought up Sam's painful memory. It was only four months back, and I had not fully recovered.

Chapter Twenty-three

December, 1903

THE NEXT MORNING AT 5 AM, four boxcars prepared to leave for the New Mexico border. The vast deserts would receive their human cargo with blistering heat, freezing nights, and barren landscapes. Women and children sobbed quietly in the predawn air, saying their farewells in tears. Angry men shouted and demanded a trial before a jury of their peers, just as the editor had done. This was a common mantra. They all knew no court in Teller County would convict them of any crime. Others, like Poole, stood quietly by their wives and children, kissing them for what could be their final visitation. While I sympathized, I also understood why it had to be so.

Others did not.

"This is military despotism, and there ain't a thing we can do about it," one miner complained.

Bell's brother, Ed walked up to the loudmouth. "Well, that may be true. But it is also the worst form of insurrection where union men can bomb mines, whitecap innocent old men, and then skip free of their crimes. It's an insurrection on the laws of Colorado, and deportation is the only solution."

Bell stepped in next to his brother. "Do you want justice? Show me a fair jury. Or one honest judge. When dealing with a cancer of this sort, nothing short of these measures will produce either relief or permanent cure. We're going to deport you, and that's final."

It was a harsh statement that needed to be carried out by men of conviction. After seeing the sobbing wives and babies, I wondered if I could have done it. Fortunately, others knew exactly where they stood and the job was done.

The next day the Victor Record Newspaper printed a scathing editorial in its morning edition. In light of the vicious bombing, it was not well-received. Most readers felt that such one-sided thinking did not represent our city where citizens enjoyed a fair balance of free-market capitalism and social responsibility. And they had had enough of the ugly work the paper seemed to be protecting. The column clearly demonstrated that the editor of the Victor Record had not gotten the message General Bell was trying so hard to impart. I only hoped for his sake he had secured alternate means of protection. After that article, he would need it.

UNION MEN RAILROADED!

CERTAIN DEATH FOR UPSTANDING MINERS!

Yesterday, December 13th, 1903, the great and powerful State of Colorado suspended a writ of habeas corpus for one of its own citizens in Goldfield, Colorado.

Victor Poole was denied his right to stand before a county judge to be heard for his alleged crimes. It has not been proven in any court of law, nor in the court of public opinion that Mr. Poole had committed any crime whatsoever. He was held without representation and without a trial by jury of his peers. Poole, an upstanding mining engineer of considerable skill and trade, whose wife and three children reside in Altman, Colorado was forcibly deported to the New

Mexico wasteland yesterday at 5 AM. Additional boxcars sit at the Goldfield siding to be loaded at this time.

Good men are treated as cattle. They are herded into dirty cars where they are roughly transported to certain death in the wilds of New Mexico. Their dependents, chiefly women and children will likely never see these men again. It is uncertain what will become of them.

Tactics of midnight search, arrest, and deportation are employed by the so-called state militia who roam the streets at all hours terrorizing our good citizens. It is well-known that such military personnel are the bought property of the Mine Owners Association. They are employed to harass and displace honest miners wanting nothing more than to feed their families, the very same who built this community with their own hands. And the very same who are being herded onto cattle cars today.

First they wanted them back to work. And now they deport them. Shameful.

It can be safely assumed that Governor Peabody sits in splendid pleasure, pulling the strings of militiamen in an all-out effort to gain political control of Teller County. Peabody himself may be the true terrorist of our working class. The blood of these fine men is certainly on his hands, and he may likely be guilty of every crime they are so cruelly punished for. And let the guilt of displaced women and children be upon his head.

The opinion of this paper, and the majority of our citizens as represented by a recent query of mine workers, is that union men must prepare for a terrible battle. It must resist errant government oppression at all cost. Wise men should arm themselves for conflict and resist illegal searches of their businesses and residences. Should Peabody himself enter your home illegally, he must be dealt with at the muzzle of a loaded weapon just as any common criminal.

Even if the allegations be true, in light of the current climate of militia terrorism, it may be no crime to defend one's home territory with desperate measures. Even if those measures call for blood to flow. Such measures as allegedly ascribed to Mr. Poole may merely represent the survival nature in all law-abiding citizens, of which Victor Poole is chiefly among them. After all, one must defend one's homeland with every measure of his vigor. Isn't that also a basic tenet of the principles on which we live?

Bell boiled at the rebellious words. The piece openly encouraged the use of violence against the governor. It encouraged miners to take up arms against the militia. And it disguised a bombing as self-defense. In a fit of anger, he violently stomped the paper into the dirt. Bits of the shredded diatribe drifted in the wind, thereafter to be regarded only by prairie dogs and mice.

"Do they take me for a fool?" Bell vented. He played his next hand with calculated determination. This proclamation followed.

"As the Supreme Commander for Teller County, clearly still in a state of insurrection and rebellion, I do hereby censor the Victor Record Newspaper of all editorial comments. It is strictly limited to factual news only.

"No editorial columns or advertisements criticizing the state of Colorado or the state militia may be printed or distributed. No incendiary communication may be transmitted in any form, including, but not limited to, telegraph, telephone, U.S. Postal Service, or private courier. The consequences of such actions will be the immediate arrest and deportation of the entire newspaper staff.

"I further authorize a thorough search of residences and business offices of all persons associated with, or under the employment of the Victor Record Newspaper and Western Federation of Miners, to be carried out at once. All arms, weapons, and munitions will be seized and retained by militia personnel.

"Any persons without visible means of employment will be arrested for vagrancy and deported from the state. Any persons said to be accused of terrorism or threatening acts will be deported. Any persons found on the streets of Teller County after ten o'clock without a permit will be arrested and deported. These conditions are effective immediately and will be carried out to the letter, without exception."

Bell had laid down his decree. Of course it enraged union bosses and invoking even more acts of violence. Innocent men were threatened and beaten in a continuing display of union defiance. But as Bell had calmly stated, violators were summarily shipped off to Kansas and New Mexico where they could ply their evil acts on the scorpion and rattlesnake. No quarter was given.

Moyer did not sit idle as Bell rode hoof and iron over the organization he had groomed for the last decade. He turned to his eastern allies. If the Victor Record was muzzled, he would look east.

The New England Primary Newspaper obligingly threw Moyer's version of the deportation story out on the front page, to the shock of their readers. But in their haste, they couldn't even get the facts straight.

DESPOTISM IN COLORADO!

ARRESTS AND DEPORTATIONS!

LEARN THE APPALLING DETAILS!

&c. &c. &c.

Complete militia rule was instituted in what Colorado Republican Governor James H. Peabody claims to be a state of insurrection and panic. An untold number of miners of the Cripple Creek Mining District were physically detained and deported to the frozen wastelands of Alaska by Colorado state militia in what is clearly an act of oppressive government control in connection with the ongoing labor crisis.

Some of those detained, including one Victor Puller, have not been extended the basic rights all Americans enjoy, namely the right to stand before a judge and jury of their peers. The right of habeas corpus has been suspended for Puller in what seems an unprecedented bid for political power in the region. Political dissidents are simply rounded up and run out on a rail.

Charles H. Moyer of the Western Federation of Miners, an organization dedicated to the wellbeing of mining labor, is quoted to have said, "This Republican governor, undoubtedly following the lead of the White House administration has overstepped his bounds. The Western Federation of Miners is a peace-loving organization attending to the wellbeing and safety of its members who must toil under increasingly oppressive conditions imposed upon them by a small band of blueblood millionaires.

"This administration clearly favors the wealthy few over the people of its own state. Labor produces all wealth, and wealth belongs to the producer thereof, yet in Colorado, such wealth goes to the mine owners and politicians. Common laborers without the resources to fight the politically-minded stalwarts are merely rounded up for deportation like cattle. No dissent is permitted. Yet healthy dissent is what made our country great. It is a crying shame to witness firsthand."

Mr. Moyer may have a point. It is unclear what course organized labor will take as the state of Colorado places more control into the hands of a select few, and removes it from the common man. Perhaps democracy itself will take a bad fall. Or perhaps the workingman will find smaller and smaller scraps of opportunity than at other times in our great nation's history. Certainly, these acts of indiscriminate deportations would suggest as much.

A former mining investor, J. P. Quincy, is quoted, "I've already sold off all my Cripple Creek mining stocks. I'm not a millionaire and I just couldn't in good conscience support those gluttonous mine owners another day. I can't believe how they've taken advantage of honest workingmen out there in Colorado. It's a disgrace, and I will not reward them another red cent in support of their greedy operations. Let someone else support their mansions and horseless carriages. Don't these millionaires get it?"

Hundreds of investors like Quincy have dumped the oppressive mining stocks for socially conscience securities, which more closely represent the needs of the workingman. Perhaps this is America's social revolution coming in the form of economic reform!

Moyer had scored a home run. In addition to the obvious errors in content, no mention of the Vindicator bombing, beatings, killings, and other acts of cowardice were mentioned in connection with the deportations. No mention of Sam Whitman. Or intimidation of Judge Hawkins. The news article was silent on all those details. Victor Poole's murderous act was cleverly labeled "dissent," effectively disguising it from the reader. After all, Cripple Creek was two thousand miles away and readers simply believed what they read.

"That is how it works," Bell said. "Just leave out half the story."

The Mine Owners Association took their next step to facilitate a safe work environment, free of union men.

Isaiah Jackson of the Vindicator Mine first introduced the tan employment card system, which we would all shortly adopt. It was instituted in direct response to the Vindicator bombing.

Jackson assembled the men of all shifts at the Vindicator Mine for a meeting. Attendance was mandatory, and eight hundred showed up to hear what he had to say. Blythe and I were there for moral support. He had rebuilt the headframe and hoisthouse, which had been reduced to embers, but wanted to assure the men that it was now safe to enter again. Violence would not be tolerated. The tan card system helped.

"Listen up, fellas," Jackson said. "Your shift bosses will be handing out these tan employment cards. We need these signed before you commence your shifts tomorrow. Keep these with you at all times. They will be used to control the men that come and go in this mine. Armed guards will check them at various stations in and around the mines. Have them with you or you will not be permitted entry. These cards will be your lifeline to this mine."

Jackson held up a card for display. Several men heckled.

He looked at them. "However, if you feel in good conscience you cannot carry one, we will no longer require your employment at the Vindicator Mine. We may also ask certain employees to submit to Pinkerton investigations. Again, this is for everyone's best interest in providing secure employment, free of the terror we have seen in recent days."

"You gonna chain us to a jackleg drill now?" a man shouted. Jackson looked down and paused.

"Please remember, two men were killed at the hand of a low-down coward in the middle of the night. That will not stand as long as I operate this mine. I will stand for absolutely no threats or intimidation. If I see so much as a scrap between men, both will be ejected. And you know where you'll go next: straight to Mr. Bell and his deportation machine. There will be no exceptions. I will not abide thugs and terrorists on these premises for one minute. I say this for you honest men to hear. You are safe here now, but the others will be hunted down with every ounce of my energy. You can be sure of that."

Jackson stared at the man.

"No doubt, these cards are an affront to some of you listening to me today because of past associations. You know who you are. So choose this day whether you will retain those associations or abandon them for honest work. That is all I have to say. Thank you for listening. Pick up your cards at the changing house on your way out. We'll be checking them tomorrow at every shift. Good day, and God Bless you honest men."

The tan cards read:

> "I certify that I have no employment with the Western Federation of Miners. I certify that I will have no communications and no association with said organization."

Sadly, the mere presence of the tan card on one's person could mean a beating or even death. This fact sent many skilled men out of the district in search of work elsewhere. Wives simply would not permit their men to carry them for fear of union reprisals. For days, a steady exodus of families clogged the Ute Pass leading down the mountain to Colorado City. It was a sad sight, as the region drained of its skilled labor.

However, by January, 1904, the strong measures were working. Violence decreased and production regained a small foothold. It looked as though we might recover, although in a reduced capacity and with reduced investments for expansion. Perhaps in time we could attract new workers and investors. But for now it was a poor existence.

Ordinary citizens came to understand the need for militia control. They were allowed to retain their firearms after submitting to their registration and a thorough search of their residences.

But desperate men were not so calm, and a daily shipment left for the Kansas and New Mexico borders. Trains stopped within a mile of the state line. Prisoners were escorted up to the line, handed a bindle containing three day's rations, and threatened with maximum prosecution upon reentry. Within minutes, they disappeared into the hazy desert never to be seen again. Families of the deported men were not permitted to receive aid, effectively forcing them to vacate the district.

A thorough and painful purging was under way.

Chapter Twenty-four

March, 1904

"NO! IF YOU FOLLOW through with this, we'll quit. This is madness. Absolute madness!" protested the men at the secret Altman meeting.

"Like it or not, it's going to be done," Moyer had said. "If you can't come up with anything better, then this is it."

"You have become more of a liability than ever," they said. "This is not what we wanted, and we will not be party to such a plan. Count us out!" They shoved their chairs into the conference table and walked out.

I got my sketchy version of the meeting from those who had left in frustration. They had had enough of Charles Moyer and the Western Federation of Miners.

Only Bill Haywood, George Pettibone, and a few others stood by Moyer in his new plan. Those who left the meeting simply could not deny their principles enough to retain their allegiances. Others, whose consciences had been seared with a hot iron suffered no such dilemma. Harry Orchard was one of those characters. A character Moyer had brought down from Idaho.

Orchard hadn't taken up needlepoint to occupy his spare time.

As with all the secret business of the union, word of the meeting got out to mine owners within hours. Nothing was secret for long. Turncoats, traitors, and spies traveled in both camps. This meeting was no exception. I had all the information I ever wanted, but honestly didn't want that much. I just wanted tensions to cool so we could go back to business as usual. The infighting was tearing the industry apart, and I could care less what happened in secret Altman meetings.

The way I heard it, the meeting was a last-ditch effort to formulate a plan to stop mine owners from operating. The mines had been running with strikebreakers and former union men who could no longer tolerate the tactics of their organization. They all carried the tan card. If it continued this way any longer, the union might be eliminated altogether. The Western Federation of Miners had not retracted the strike order and was beginning to look like a paper tiger. Moyer knew something had to be done.

Although browbeaten and maligned, the attendees at the meeting had not come up with anything to combat the effective strategy in force by General Bell. They had lost so much authority and manpower in the district that nothing of substance remained.

But Moyer wanted a new plan. No one was permitted to leave until they had one. Harry Orchard finally presented a devilish idea, and the meeting splintered into irreconcilable groups. Even the miscreants that had been with Moyer since the beginning could not go along with this. This was ugly.

Orchard was no dunce with devices of malicious intent. He had rigged some for Moyer, Haywood, and Pettibone up in Idaho during the labor disputes there. One tripped when a dooryard gate was opened. Another blew up a skipjack full of men. Still another derailed a train. They were very effective in their work. So effective that the three had been ejected from the region. Because of that, Moyer wasn't certain he wanted to go that far again. But in the absence of a better plan, he would use Orchard again.

Naturally, the spies leaked the plan, and I wondered whether to believe it or not. For now, I just wanted to spend some time with Patricia, getting back to normal.

"After that Vindicator thing last November, a lot of the wives are still worried," said Patricia. We shoveled snow from the walkway after a big storm. The boys were inside reading books; they didn't care for the hard work.

"I think things will get better," I reassured her. "Moyer can't go on like this forever. It's a losing battle for him. They've lost so much ground, they'll just give up, I expect. I think they're finished."

"Well, maybe. All the bad ones have been deported. The Victor Record has been censored. Teller County judges are no longer releasing guilty men back into circulation. But that doesn't stop the ladies from worrying. I've heard plenty. They think Moyer is planning something. You've heard it too."

"Yes, I have. I heard about that Altman meeting like everybody else. But I try to keep that kind of talk out of the house. The militia is doing good so I think we're coming out of the worst of it. Maybe we'll even turn a profit next year. Maybe Moyer will see that progress and call off the strikes. I'm trying to get a meeting with him to offer that exact possibility. I think he'll take it. It's good business for everyone."

Patricia stopped and leaned on the shovel. "I'm not so sure." The snow was deep and the work hard and we still had another twenty feet to go. "Any sensible man whose efforts had failed would retreat to build a more positive strategy. True. But I don't think you are dealing with that kind of man. He still thinks you mine owners are the enemies."

"Worse than Charlie MacNeill?" I asked, almost jokingly.

"Yes, I think so," she said. "I guess we'll find out. I just hope things get better so the ladies don't worry so."

I had been pestering Moyer for a meeting every month. But he turned me down every time. I think the tan card system really set him off.

While things were improving for us, I felt it was a mistake to alienate Moyer entirely. After all, balance was still the key to good labor relations. A week after the secret Altman meeting, I finally got mine with Moyer. It was March, 1904. Perhaps after considering Harry Orchard's proposal, he was now ready for an alternative. Maybe we could work things out, I thought. This might be good.

New powder at least knee deep greeted me in my tramp up the hill to the Altman office. My back still hurt from shoveling the last load. As far as I could see lay blankets of snow deposited by the unexpected spring storm. A bold sun now worked to coerce the white layers back into the earth. I remembered the tiny crystal lake at the bottom of Monarch Pass, and how we had skated with Palmer and his railroad crew. I dreamed of escaping to that quiet place rather than where I was actually headed.

The long trudge became a welcomed diversion after months of painful struggle, and I hoped the stroll would never end. The snow covered the ugly mine tailings and abandoned rusting machinery, cleansing everything in simple splendor. It was soft and beautiful and I wanted it to last forever. But the snow-filled road took me faithfully to the top of the hill and deposited me right at the entrance of the union headquarters in Altman. A stirring dread filled my gut – the same feeling I had had on the old freighter's road when we passed the little Altman sign.

A premonition of imminent harm.

Moyer pointed me to his office and began delivering a dose of frigid language I did not expect.

"Clark, I don't have a lot of time for you now. I've got other things I've got to attend to, but I'll tell you one thing right now. And get this clear," Moyer proceeded coldly, venting a full measure of pent-up fury right out of the chute.

"You can buy the governor. You can buy the state militia. You can even buy those low-down scabs you employ. But you don't own Teller County. You never will. We are the party of the people. We will prevail in this labor dispute. If it weren't for the union fighting for the rights of the common man, you greedy capitalists would devour everything they own. You care nothing for the workingman. Your only concern is for your own belly. Go back to whatever mud-hole you came from and work them danged mules some more. Maybe you'll learn some respect for the men who built this district. You're nothing but a hillbilly from Booneville, Arkansas or some such place, and you presume to teach us?"

"Teach? I just came to–"

"I swear, you are the worst gang of cutthroat hypocrites I have ever had the displeasure to lay eyes on. I'll give you a word of warning,

215

Clark. Stay out of my way, or I will squash you. Do you hear me clearly, boy?"

I couldn't believe it. The rhetoric had not died. Even after a year of bloody battle in which Moyer was all but defeated, he clung desperately to it. After hearing it again, I was all but finished with Moyer. He had insulted me again and hadn't even made a pretense of hearing what I came to say. Why he had even accepted the meeting, I'll never know.

"Charles, wait. I know you're mad. I just wanted to meet with you and get things back on track," I began, hoping to apply some diplomacy and bring him back around.

"Without good labor the mines can't make a dollar. But without a fair mine to employ them, you wouldn't have a workforce to organize. I understand your need to protect the rights of your men. That's a noble cause and I'll help you do that. I'm willing to make sure they get fair treatment and steady work. I'll even make concessions to ensure you're satisfied. Concessions you won't get from other mines because we're friends. Please believe me. It's in my own best interest to make the men happy rather than fleeing the district like they have."

Moyer shuffled papers and his face grew fierce. "I don't see where we have any common ground."

"Well, we've got to find some. A house divided against itself cannot stand. If we don't, this shaky business is going to come tumbling down. Neither of us wants that, do we? It's not in our interests to destroy what years of hard work have accomplished."

"Clark, I am—"

"Charles, you're a fine president and organizer. The men follow you. And you're absolutely right about greedy millionaires. Without boundaries, greedy men will take advantage of the workingman. We know that. We need your checks and balances as much as you need our entrepreneurial spirit.

"And yes, I know you've had some scrapes with MacNeill, Tutt, and Penrose over the Standard Mill. I can help with that too. If we work together, we could turn this around. I'd like to try."

216

My reasoning was sound and I hoped Moyer would see things in a sensible light. And privately I was unsure how long the Black Jack Mine could endure the strife. I had seen other operations teeter and fall as a result of the violence. Of course, the steady exodus of skilled men and investors didn't help. A sense of hopelessness hung in the air. If things got any worse the Black Jack Mine might not make it. That was one thing I didn't tell Patricia. I needed this win, and I looked expectantly to Moyer for his response. But Moyer turned a malicious eye to my logic.

"I am completely done with you, Clark. I told you I was busy; I don't have time for this today."

"Then why did you invite me? Why don't we—"

"Stop. Don't try to negotiate me. I can see what you're doing. You're a kiln-dried liar and your kind cannot be trusted. Stay clear of me, Clark. I'm warning you. Or I'll squash you like a June bug on a hot iron rail. Remember Sam Whitman?"

The mention of Sam stuck like a knife in the belly. I staggered back at the sound of it. Everyone knew the union was behind his grisly death, and now the man who likely ordered it flaunted before me. I could either render evil for evil, or hang my head and avoid an ugly confrontation. Descending into aggression would certainly satisfy the feelings I had right now but would never resolve our differences. Sam's death was tragic but I would hold my tongue, however hard that would be.

"Have it your way. But you've got to understand that you're whipped. Your organization no longer holds the power. Your strategy with the Standard Mill has failed and you're taking an awful licking because of it. Most of the miners have quit the union. Your so-called strike has lost its teeth. Even the Portland and Telluride mills in Colorado City have reopened with non-union men. In fact, all the mines and mills are open, even though your strike continues. Can't you see that?"

Moyer looked me in the eye. "I see nothing but a fiend bent on amassing wealth."

"Oh, Charles… I am just trying to make a living. And we need your men. They are good workers and I can't do without them. But if you proceed with your current line of attack you'll auger this district right into the ground. I don't want to see that happen, so let's work this out," I argued, beginning to get red in the face.

"And another thing," I said. "Good miners in Cripple Creek pocket three to four times what they would elsewhere. What do you think the average Joe in Colorado Springs brings home? Or Silverton, Leadville, or Aspen? Your capitalist-oppression argument just doesn't ring true in light of the facts. Nobody is being oppressed. So let's just work though the issues that are bothering you and we'll both be better off. I'll even take you down to the Gold Coin Club and we can toast to success. What do you say?"

"Never! Who do you think you are? Andrew Carnegie? Throwing dirty money around like that. You're nothing; try to remember that, boy. And I will never drink with a terrorist or his bought puppets," Moyer growled, referring again to the $400,000 bond the mine owners had carried for troop expenses to defeat him.

"Charles, I am no terrorist. You know that. I've worked tirelessly in this district since '95 to build a fair industry. Remember? You met me coming in. Yes, I came here a broke Missoura plow hand, but I built the Black Jack Mine with nothing but my own skin. My life is in that ground. My own blood. Just take a look at these hands," I said, holding them up before him. "My money is not dirty and I am no terrorist. I may not be half the man you are but I have fought for everything we have gained here. I have fought for it with my own blood and guts down in those mines. And don't you forget that."

Moyer threw his face at me like a battering ram. "You expect me to believe that innocent farm-boy line? I judge you all as terrorists."

"Well, from that Vindicator incident last year, maybe you are the terrorist." I foolishly added, unable to think clearly.

"Oh, and drawing the militia down on me and arresting and deporting my men isn't terror? That's military despotism. Now who's leading the saints to glory, you hypocrite? I am done with you," he bellowed. He flipped a cigarette at me and marched out of the office, leaving three rough fellows to see to my exit from the building.

The conversation had gone painfully wrong right from the beginning. And now I remembered the last exit from this building, assisted by four angry thugs. I prayed to avoid a repeat, as the harsh language was enough to leave me shaken without the added insult of ejection from the building.

I left the Altman office shaking from the exchange. Moyer had gone into the ether, just as Patricia had warned. He was in no position to change his course of action.

Chapter Twenty-five

MOYER PRODUCED A THOUSAND posters, which he nailed to every building and telegraph pole in the district. The large poster read, "Is Colorado in America?" portraying the American flag with the following black letters on each white stripe.

Martial Law Declared in Colorado!
Habeas corpus Suspended in Colorado!
Free Press Throttled in Colorado!
Bull Pens for Union Men in Colorado!
Free Speech Denied in Colorado!
Soldiers Defy the Courts in Colorado!
Wholesale Arrests Without Warrant in Colorado!
Union Men Exiled from Homes and Families in Colorado!
Constitutional Right to Bear Arms Questioned in Colorado!
Corporations Corrupt and Control Administration in Colorado!
Right of Fair Impartial and Speedy Trial Abolished in Colorado!
Citizens Alliance Resorts to Mob Law and Violence in Colorado!
Militia Hired by Corporations to Break the Strike in Colorado!

He telegraphed the shocking message across the nation within a week. It was clearly intended to draw the last drop of public sentiment to the side of the Western Federation of Miners. After all, how could such grievous acts be perpetrated on U.S. soil? This was America, after all. But Bell and the other Rough Riders were not amused.

"You'll be glad to know he's gone," Bell announced gruffly, only a week after the posters had been hung. "We dispatched his tiresome hide last night with the same rough treatment as the thugs he sponsored. By now, he's trudging the Kansas tall grass in search of a little comfort."

"Really," I said. "On what charges?"

"Desecrating the American flag. Sure, it was only a depiction. But that's the kind of inflammatory nonsense we can do without. And it is a grievous sin to use the American flag so callously for one's own agenda. I won't abide it. Soiling the symbol of the United States of America is to soil the venerable names of those who gave the last full measure of devotion to secure its greatness. I was at San Juan Hill. I saw it draped over their bloody guts. So no… I won't abide it."

"And his right of habeas corpus?"

"Suspended. I told you it's a rogue's protection."

The flag incident had the opposite effect on public sentiment in Cripple Creek. It turned citizens against the union for good. But in the Eastern cities of Boston, New York, and Philadelphia, readers were mortified by the printed words. They had been so indoctrinated with union lies they could no longer see the folly in them. Their reaction was one of renewed anger toward the mine owners. Readers declared with disgust, "Look what new depths those Colorado mine owners will stoop to. Will this madness never end?"

All it takes is a news article.

Investors were not able to discern the truth from the lie. And they were unable to stomach the controversy. They pulled their capital from mining stocks immediately. Moyer had won the battle of the printing press but destroyed any chance of returning to Colorado.

I slapped Charlie on the back. "Well, MacNeill, your prophesy didn't exactly come to pass, but he's gone anyway," I said.

"What prophesy?"

"You remember… the one in Denver… Your little rant?"

MacNeill's eyes widened. "Oh, yeah. The meeting with Moyer and the mill managers before the first strike. 'Your boys really softened 'em up.' Yeah, I remember." He laughed, but then turned grim again.

"Well, there was no fanfare, no horns, no marching girls with rose petals. I just got the word from Bell: a dirty cattle car, a loaf of bread, and a jug of water. But I'm still a little concerned. I think he's the only man that could change the disastrous course we're headed into. I don't see us coming out of this."

"Yep," MacNeill replied. "If Moyer can't have the whole labor movement, he won't permit it to exist at all – no matter where he goes. It's just another Idaho to him. He's gone... but not really... if you take my meaning."

And just as MacNeill hinted, the events that followed his deportation let us know he was still dealing eights and aces from parts unknown. But for now we held the faith, trying to keep a desperately wounded industry from falling into the ditch.

I couldn't spend all my time worrying about Charles Moyer. There was still a business to run. We still had other trouble to deal with. Even little things like hoist clutches needed attention.

"Jack, have you got that hoist operating yet?" I yelled, pacing the hoisthouse floor and shouting commands to all who dared enter. We had burned up a clutch on the big hoist drum which prevented the men on the late shift from exiting the mine at their scheduled time.

Men stuck in the hole. Just like when Black Jack the old mule died.

The smoke and stench of burning asbestos filled the shafts and building. That sent my already nervous mood to an utter tirade. I would not tolerate another minute's delay.

"They're working it," Jack Tinner said. "As fast as they can."

Leaving men in the hole made everyone nervous. It was the one thing above all others that ground my teeth to nubs. I was determined to have the situation rectified at once. But it was more than just the burned-up clutch that had me worked up so badly. The meeting with Moyer had tortured me every night, edging me into tears. His deportation. Fear of failure. The worry. Even Patricia's soothing words could not pull me out of the deep depression. And the broken clutch was the last offense.

"Tinner, I don't care how fast they're working it. Get it done now! I am in no mood for shirkers and dawdlers. I'll fire the whole shift if that clutch isn't finished tonight. Is that clear?"

Frustrated and nervous at the delay, some men walked a half-mile underground, climbed up manway ladders to another drift, walked another half-mile, and then waited for a crowded cage to ascend the final distance. But those who didn't know the way had to wait for the repairs to be made. So they spent their time luring and catching rats. In either case, the entire shift missed the 2 AM train at the Independence Depot on June 6, 1904.

This maddened me beyond words, as I knew the waiting wives would fret themselves sick. The Vindicator bombing had led to that. Patricia knew they still worried. In the coming days, I expected to receive letters heaping blame on the Black Jack Mine for irresponsibility. In some things, there was no winning.

I helped the mechanics scrape away burned asbestos and bolting the massive clutch into place. Dual hundred-ton clutches moved a six-foot drum with three thousand feet of cable coiled around it. When paid out, it could lower the skipjack and man-cages to the very depths of the mine. A licensed hoistman operated the huge mechanism, and by Colorado law was not permitted to speak or eat during the hours of operation. A huge 750-horsepower Ingersoll-Rand steam engine powered the hoist. Many small operations made due with ten to twenty horsepower units, but the daily loads at the Black Jack Mine required the biggest in the district.

The repairs would probably consume another hour. I felt badly that the men had missed the train, but with luck, they could catch the 4 AM. Many had already exited the mine, and with even more time to burn, had gathered around the hoisthouse to watch the massive surgery on the clutches. It was an impressive show of mechanical prowess. The crowd expanding behind me needed an explanation.

"Gather 'round men. We'll have the new clutch installed soon. As you can see, it's a big job. I am sorry you have missed the train. Please offer my apologies to your wives. We're working as fast as we can and I'll make sure you are all compensated for the extra time you've spent here. You men mean a lot to the Black Jack Mine, and–"

Just then the windows all blew out at once and a huge explosion rocked the foundation below us. It roared like a massive dynamite charge, but much louder than the eight-stick pattern used to blow rock, and much nearer the surface. We instinctively covered our faces and hit the deck.

Some fled the hoisthouse in time to see a giant fireball climbing angrily into the northern sky. It rose up from the Independence Railway Depot which lit up like the high-noon sun. Had a boiler exploded? Or an ammunition depot? Everyone ran to the blast.

The southern end of the Independence Rail Depot was completely gone, and the wooden loading dock in a million scattered pieces. A cavernous hole sunk deep into the ground under the smashed building. Its yawning depth reached twenty feet. Fires burned inside the building and outlying areas, threatening the remains of the structure. Men scrambled to learn the cause.

No train sat at the station which ruled out a boiler explosion or locomotive collision. The 2 AM train sat fifty yards up the track nervously puffing white and gray plumes into the night air. The brakeman had evidently stopped short of the explosion just in time. The reason for the wreckage was still not obvious. But I knew it instinctively. My gut told the awful story.

Detached body parts of thirteen men had been thrown in all directions. Blood and shredded flesh dripped from the partially broken overhang. Across the field were torn clothing, lunch buckets, headlamps, tools and twisted steel. A severed hand clung to another man's detached arm. Three fingers of another rolled slowly into the deep cavern under the wooden deck.

Up the hillside lay parts of legs, arms, severed hands and feet. Sections of shattered skulls with singed hair still clinging to them. Crimson stains splattered across the grizzly pattern radiating outward from the large hole. It was a gut wrenching sight. Coughing and vomiting came soon after.

Evidently a twenty-stick charge had been rigged under the wooden platform. And timed to kill every man waiting for the 2 AM train. Newly arriving men said the blast blew out windows all the way to Victor. This was not just a killing; it was a demonstration of force.

"I'll squash you like a bug," I recalled from recent memory. Moyer's twisted image appeared in my mind's eye.

My men approached reverently and thanked me for the burned up clutch. But it was nothing I wished to take credit for. God had saved the men. Not I. I would have unknowingly sent them off to their doom if I could have persuaded Jack Tinner to repair the clutch any faster.

The surrounding area offered a thousand hiding places, covered with mine tailings, wood cribbing, and dilapidated shacks. A man could hide for days. Those guilty men may have been watching from the shadows that very hour. I peered into the thick darkness, but saw nothing.

The entire late-shift of the Black Jack Mine and eight hundred others had crowded the scene. Miner's lamps flashed in a network of frantic confusion, cutting the darkness like swords of light. Every man was crazy with fury and voiced their maddened frustration.

The man-hunt was on.

Lynching, hanging, burning, shooting, dragging, and skinning were the punishments planned for those yellow cowards skulking in the tailings. If they were nearby, they knew justice was coming.

The next morning the citizens of Cripple Creek were livid. Anger had peaked through the fruitless night's search. An angry crowd gathered outside McGunthry's Hardware.

"Come with us, Clark. We're going to clear this up." They demanded immediate action and would tolerate no delays in identifying the men responsible.

Sheriff Robertson promised a complete investigation. But he squandered a full week, allowing scant leads to grow cold. An ignition switch, trip wires, timing wheel, and other evidence had been found in nearby tailings. As that week passed citizens' frustration grew beyond measure. We approached Robertson again for status.

"What is being done to find and capture those responsible," the men of the Citizens Alliance demanded.

Sheriff Robertson looked away evasively. "We have no leads at this time, and I'm afraid we might have to call off the investigation if nothing new turns up. We just don't have anything to go on right now. Check back with me in a week or so. I may have something then. I feel awful bad about this, fellas. I just don't know what else to say."

Robertson was known to be a union-bought man. He would have no true interest in locating the killers. Although the perpetrators were likely unknown to him, he did not expend a great deal of effort to find them either. He had, as suspected, mounted a façade of concern sufficient for the politics of the day but had not acted in earnest to hunt down those responsible. His thin concern for the deaths of thirteen men was not convincing to the enraged citizens who suspected Harry Orchard had probably done the awful deed. They had heard of his work and knew of his secret meeting with Moyer. And for some reason he could no longer be found anywhere in the district.

Telegraphs went out to Boise City and Coeur d'Alene. No sign of him there either.

A larger and more determined group of representatives returned the next week for status. We caught Robertson sheepishly ducking into his office.

"Sheriff, we'd like a word with you regarding the Independence Depot investigation. What do you have for us this week?"

This time we stepped aside to reveal a rope and noose lying in the dirt behind us.

No words were spoken, but an agreement had been reached nonetheless. Robertson shifted in panic. He looked first at the noose, then to the committee, and then again at the noose as it lay hauntingly on the dusty street. He hung his guilty head and returned to his desk knowing he had shirked his sworn duty, and that if he hadn't, Moyer would have skinned him alive. That very hour, Robertson fled the district. Sherman's brother Ed took his place as sheriff.

The cowardly acts at the Vindicator and Independence Depot, and the protective measures by Robertson became a tipping point.

Unauthorized citizen mobs formed to rout the district of every man associated with the WFM. Union men armed themselves for a battle they could never hope to win. Fistfights and shootings broke out in saloons and the streets. Ten citizens for every union man brought swift vigilante justice to the district.

They didn't even need the militia.

"Arm yerselves, boys," a man hollered by torchlight. "I've got two hundred men. These union scoundrels will either consent to deportation or a proper hanging. Start with the Altman and Victor union halls. That's where this all started in the first place. Strip 'm down to the studs; the looters will haul everything off like insects. We've got bullpens and cattle cars for any man who doesn't like it. No union man stays past the midnight toll. Understand? Not a single man."

"What's next?" an eager boy asked.

"When you're done with the union halls, start in on the Victor Record newspaper office," the man ordered. "Smash those printing presses and linotypes. Use sledgehammers, axes, rocks, whatever you've got. Throw the typeface into the street so they get the message. We'll stop this unionism right here, right now!"

Every union sympathizer on the police force was deposed and replaced. Six men were shot and killed in bloody gun battles. Politicians, judges, commissioners, and civil officers were forcibly deposed and deported. The entire county government was overthrown and deported in a thorough coup d'etat. Every remaining union man was arrested and deported. Not a single union man remained to lick his wounds, including Harry Orchard.

Scores of women and children were suddenly left destitute and bereaved of their men. They received minimal care and were expected to leave the district as soon as they could manage. They relied on friends, family, and the Women's Christian Temperance Union to see to their safe retreat. Any union man returning to collect his family was given the choice of public hanging or deportation.

By September, 1904, the city of Cripple Creek was a shell of its former self. It might better be described a ghost town than boomtown.

Any unsuspecting visitor might have concluded that the Great Rapture had just occurred and only the unfaithful were left behind.

News of the riots and lawlessness reached the nation's readers as fast as a crackling wire could hurl it. And again, the halt of investment dollars snapped the district out of any upward trend we had gained, dragging it into a dark depression. Stock certificates became worthless outhouse supplies, spurned by any investor in his right mind. They now hung from rusty nails to be dispensed for baser purposes, one sheet at a time.

We were no longer the darling of the investment community. Mining operations descended into insolvency and consolidation. Mines that had suffered badly since the beginning of the labor wars were finished. Larger operations scooped up the failing mines for pennies on the dollar, or for the price of back taxes, sending their proud owners back to manual labor or out of the district in search of work. Mine executives began their days at the end of a muck stick, clinging to their titles in hopes the depression would end and their positions be restored.

The Black Jack Mine fell just as hard. Credit in Cripple Creek, which had been extended on a seemingly gratis basis, became scarcer than a paying customer. The hoist clutch set us back $15,000. A bill that would normally be settled in a week now lingered for months. So many good men had fled the district that the Black Jack Mine could no longer make profitable production levels.

The monkey show was over.

Chapter Twenty-six

MY STORY IS FINISHED. A warm October afternoon finds me in grim thought amid the quaking aspen. A hint of winter is in the air, but this moment is pleasant, spilling sunshine over my face and shoulders. I need this small comfort and wonder if it was sent just for me for this awful time of life. The hills and valleys are fiery warm. It fills my hurting soul with the tender mercies of God who cares for me.

The rolling mountains of Cripple Creek speak to me like no other place. I have taken an afternoon retreat beyond the racket of mines, mills, and railways. The din of Cripple Creek now seems a hundred miles away. A million golden-red aspen leaves flicker wildly in the sun under a gentle breeze. The stands of aspen form a tapestry of beauty to sooth the soul, and I hear nothing but them.

I lift my eyes to study a dramatic mountainside, which had gone unnoticed in my years in Cripple Creek. Huge evergreens are spiked along the steep slopes, rising two hundred feet above me. A wooded canyon plunges in deep separation. The opposite slope seems only a stone's throw away. Crowning the mountain is a granite outcropping, standing sentry over the dense woods below it. It stands like an obelisk balancing on a base of rock-flow. Rock outcroppings punctuate the steep mountain scene.

I marvel at how this massive lumber supply had escaped the woodmen's voracious appetite in the years of rapid expansion, and it speaks to me. It affirms that while I am laid low, it is well with my soul. And as though caught up in a vision, I permit nature's beauty to interpret my painful feelings.

The stands of aspen and evergreen sway in quiet security. They do not toil, yet they are clothed in majesty. They do not lay up for themselves, yet they are fed. How much more will I also be clothed and fed? My anxieties are no more than an unnecessary hindrance.

But I am entangled in the carnal things of this life, for I have just left the law offices of Smith, Bartell, and Paine, where I reluctantly placed the Black Jack Mine into receivership one month ago. They brokered a sale of the mine to a Chicago firm. The transaction is now complete.

I no longer own the Black Jack Mine.

The operation was slowly forced into receivership during the war with the Western Federation of Miners. Investors fled and debt mounted, even as production fell. Credit was cut off. Bank notes called for payment. Company and personal assets were sold at auction to satisfy creditors in an effort to extend solvency through the final bitter weeks. Half the mines shared similar misfortunes as the war ravaged them viciously. The Independence Depot bombing was the final blow. Thousands of lives lay in ruin, and I am bankrupt. A decade of work is erased. It is enough to shake my faith to its core.

Patricia sits with me to weep before the Lord. With swollen eyes, I gaze out over the fields of aspen, burning red and celebrating their own final days of passion before winter overtakes them in its cruel way. I can sense another message coming.

My days in Cripple Creek had been a summertime romp, but now winter must come.

For everything there is a season, and a time for every purpose under heaven. The sunny skies of summertime yielded their fruit in a generous cycle. But the golden years of Colorado mining are nearing a cruel end.

I recall with fondness the years when we could do no wrong. Simple prospectors held a status among giants. With no greater possessions than a grubstake and a bivy sack, we were regarded as hearty frontiersmen. Thousands of pioneers swarmed these mountain regions, charging the air with reckless energy and producing results beyond imagination.

The buzz and excitement affected everyone, no matter his state or occupation. Shopkeepers and newspapermen, apostles and prophets, suppliers and laborers. Everyone basked in the summertime glow of the Cripple Creek gold boom.

The worn tip of my boot scratches out an arching pattern on the forest floor. Memories of those days warm the soul and bring a small satisfaction to my face. I have run the race and stayed the course. Yet my thoughts are drawn back to our failures as if an unsolved puzzle I am obliged to solve.

Eighteen months of labor wars have swallowed up the wild energy. They took a booming swell, and transformed it into fear, doubt, and uncertainty. The very outlook of our future has changed, where once it was bright and hopeful; it is now dim and uncertain. Where once we saw the future in all its splendor and clarity, we now see through a glass darkly. And where once a mere plowboy with a prospect hole was king, he is now lower than the dust of the earth.

Blind optimism ruled the day, allowing any man with a little grit to succeed. Luck itself was handy for the taking, an essential ingredient for any successful venture. This was the boomtown spirit. This was the spirit of our grand success. But that spirit is delicate. It endures for a summer, but then withers and dies. Winter follows hard on its heels.

One example stands out: the Turn at Bat Mining Company. Stock certificates began trading in 1896 at $10 a share before a lick of soil had even been turned. Credit was extended to two Illinois hatters. The result was a bonanza worth $178 a ton of ore. Debts were paid and stock rose to an astounding $68 by the end of the year. Two ordinary men prospered above their wildest dreams from nothing but a little hope, and dozens were employed in the process.

In our best day, there was room for a thousand such operations. Today they are scarcer than hooves on a horned owl. But I must lay to rest these maddening thoughts and move on with my life.

After many hours in this place, I have come to peace with my affairs. A live dog is better than a dead lion.

I sense the lessons of nature ending. My resting place grows cold and aloof. It is time to leave, having been told all that I will hear today. I will face tomorrow with new determination because His mercies are new every morning.

And so the next morning I rise groggily at four-thirty, at the impatient clang of the alarm. I hastily light the old wood-fired potbelly on which Patricia will fix a ration of flapjacks for a hard day's work. In the cold autumn morning, I miss the indulgences of a feather bed and coal-fired furnace. It is my first reminder of the day that I am no longer the Gold King of yesteryear. I must accept a new routine.

Patricia kneads dough into a thin crust and prepares a potpie for lunch. The warm aroma urges two ravenously hungry teenage boys from their straw beds. They have been spared the harshness of our industry and will tote their lesson books to school for a proper education. I am pleased with this small achievement. No such privilege had been given me in my youth. By five-fifteen, the tiny house is abuzz with voices.

We now rent a clapboard house up the hill from Victor. It is situated in a row of skids pressed hard against heaps of mine tailings. Wooden cribbing holds back a million tons of waste rock above us. A company house – rented to miners for a dollar a day. The odor of hard mineral water leaching through the tailings is a constant blight. Murky water filters down the mountain into delicate little streams. It turns them dark and kills the little trout that live in them. But it is our only drinking water for a half mile.

The little unpainted house, or shack as it were, has two small rooms and two windows. But no running water and no water closet. It sits on a foundation of railroad ties, and leans a little in the east corner where a rivulet of water has undercut the thick black beams. Three steamer trunks stacked against the north wall hold all our worldly possessions. But it is enough for us. We still remember the lowly cabins in Randall's Flats, Missoura.

We share a privy with four families. The path to it is an uncomfortable distance when the urgent need arises. But we will learn to know our neighbors.

The little brown privy is a two-holer. Images of the sun and moon are cut into the spaces above the doors. We will fill the holes and move the privy when necessary. It is a simple system. Crude when compared to the indoor plumbing we were used to. But it serves.

Our small black potbelly stands a scant two feet high. It's set up on a foundation of loose brick at waist height. Although too small for large logs, we can heat the house, prepare meals, and boil a pot for bathing. This morning it teeters on the loose bricks and a bright red glow sprays out from all the little cracks. It is the center of our morning activity and a source of life to us.

A little brown mouse slips through a hole in the floor to take comfort in the warm glow. My wife permits this exception after enduring the pitiful squeaks of its discomfort. I look at her and smile. She evidently cares enough for the little creatures of this world to permit them some warmth – even during our own distress. The mouse sniffs for crumbs and leaves through the same hole it had entered. The floor is swept clean of any morsels it may find, but breakfast has only just begun.

Pages from the Saturday Evening Post and an array of mail-order catalogs adorn the walls. This thin defense stops howling winds from entering. Former occupants have pasted up layers upon layers, and I sit and enjoy the advertising offers.

Merewether's Hardware is offering a new-fangled electric washing machine for $1.38. Or, I can order a pair of leather work boots for two bits. An extra two bits buys the de-luxe steel-toed type. And a postal worker's buggy can be shipped out from Illinois for only $28.50. The harness is extra. Until now, I had not experienced the pleasure of studying these marvelous items, all available from the new Sears and Roebuck catalog. What have I missed?

While buttering flapjacks, sipping coffee, and browsing the advertisements, I wonder if my former employees had rented this very house. If so, the tables have surely turned. With its darkened windows, broken door latch, and drafty clapboard, it is homely but cozy, and everything we need at this time in our lives. It is not, by any stretch of the imagination, a mansion on a hill.

Yet one small luxury remains. A diamond-dust mirror which Patricia refused the auctioneer's anxious grasp hangs oddly out of place on the crooked east wall. It is a portal into our formerly opulent lives. The fixture would still fetch a year's wages. Through the hazy depths of the elegant glass, I see a vision of society ladies gathered in velvet parlour circles. Gentlemen of leisure empty decanters of rich brandy and puff Cuban tobacco. A satisfying wink and a nod send them off to another time. Today, I will focus on the present.

I kiss Patricia and the boys, and step out into the chilly autumn air. If only I were back among the aspen. My gut twists. Petty fears gnaw at me. They are only a slight irritation, but crawl like ants, stirring my disbelief.

Am I really standing here today? Or is this just an awful dream? Have we actually fallen so hard? It seems unreal. I just want to drive the motorcar back up to our hillside mansion and forget this ever happened.

But no. This is my life now.

Hundreds of working donkeys had been released into the wild as the mines failed. Herds can be seen grazing the surrounding hills. They feed on western Grama grasses and rest from their labors. Most are nearly blind from their underground routine. It is commonly said that a donkey has no rights a miner is obliged to respect, but I am attached to these mild beasts of burden. They have served us faithfully. Being in abundant supply, I have taken one for myself. It has become my transportation to the Black Jack Mine where I am gainfully employed, and my sole transportation to all places it may bear me.

I named her Black Jennie. The name conjures years of tender memories. I recall my exodus out of Jackson County, Missoura ten years ago and the faithful service Rosebud and Black Jack rendered. We were friends, laboring shoulder to shoulder, exchanging our sentiments nose to nose.

Black Jennie is a powerful donkey, neither burro nor heavy horse, but suitable for my needs. She plods along at half the speed of my shiny black Ford with the crumpled left fender. It fetched only forty dollars at auction a week ago. Her years of rigor have given her a steady gait for a twelve hour shift. Never too fast but not the least bit slothful.

One such animal made the newspapers when it gave birth to a colt while underground at the Joe Dandy Mine. The little colt was aptly named Billy Thunder Bucket when it went off on a wild kicking rampage, derailing an ore train on its way to the skipjack. The last ore car tipped over the edge and fell three hundred feet to the bottom of the shaft. The crash boomed like thunder, and so the colt was named. Life has a way of prospering even in the worst of conditions.

I mount Black Jennie with a thick Mexican blanket and hemp rope halter. We begin to clump the mile to work in quiet introspection. Whether uphill or down, Jennie does not deviate in her pace. She is in no particular hurry. My efforts to urge her into a lope are fruitless. She has been conditioned for steady work tugging ore cars in the deep passages of the earth. And it is no matter, for I am also in no hurry.

Little curls of dust lift from each clop of the hoof. I am fixed in idle thought when an alarming mood of self-consciousness overtakes me. My face flushes and eyes open into a mild state of alarm.

What if I am seen?

How will I explain myself on this earthly beast of burden rather than atop the extravagant Quadricycle? What will the good folks of high-society say of me should I encounter one on this road? Will I concoct a devilish lie to explain the lowly mode of transportation? Or choose another road to avoid an awkward confrontation? No. Those thoughts of vanity are of no remaining consequence, and I cast off care for my status. I mentally correct myself and resolve to take captive every thought that threatens to deter my course of action. I press onward in one simple mission: to report to work as agreed.

By six, the emerging light from the east stubbornly delays its arrival. It creeps slowly up the long slopes of Pikes Peak. It is also in no hurry. On the western slopes of Battle Mountain, sunhit lags sunrise by an hour and withholds its precious warmth to those tucked behind the cold granite monolith. But the warm rays of sunshine will arrive soon enough.

Up on the cold silhouette of the ridgeline, the electric High-Line trolley speeds along at one-tenth its normal human cargo. The nickel ride no longer seems financially responsible. And not just to me. I count dozens of miners on captured donkeys. An equal number are afoot traversing mountain lanes to their morning shifts. Some appear downtrodden and worried, with heads low. I wonder how many former millionaires now straddle lowly donkeys on this chilly autumn morning. Perhaps they are not so different than me. The nearly empty trolley, once overflowing with rowdy conversation, is a sign of a different time.

I arrive at work thirty minutes early and hitch the donkey alongside fifty others already standing at the feed rack adjacent to the hoisthouse. A bag of oats and watering trough will occupy the animal for the next nine hours. There is no fear of theft. A thousand loose donkeys graze the Independence ridgeline. Their modest forms are now fully visible in the emerging light. They are more prevalent than workingmen on these lonely hills.

A large hand-painted sign at the feed rack strongly admonishes miners to shovel manure from their animals. But I see no evidence of that. Perhaps this is also just another sign of the changing times, with men consumed by their own hard luck, and less interested in the concerns of others.

I give Jack the hoistman a hearty wave. He sighs and waves, knowing my lowly position as a mucker in the mine I built with my own hands. The new owners of the Black Jack Mine do not know me. To them, I am a cog in the wheels of labor. I am a necessary expense with so many others, to re-gin the magic of financial return and attract the interests of investors once again. But I'm happy for the work. Hundreds of others have been deported, killed, or fled the district. Half the mines were liquidated or consolidated. Credit is nonexistent and jobs are scarce. But I have work, and scold myself for the notion that although I am a common laborer today, tomorrow I may return to my former status.

Does vanity ever cease its raging?

Some of the mine executives and owners could not accept the loss of privileged positions when their operations failed. They viewed themselves above the common man and left the district or remained unemployed. One distraught individual took a steam train up to Casper, Wyoming and killed himself. He evidently could not bear the loss of his worldly possessions, and posted a letter to his family before his untimely departure from this world. Other executives held out hope that good times would return. Maybe their skills would be in demand again. That will not be happening, and so I stand here today waiting on the shift bosses for a little work.

"Line up here," the man says. "Drillers, powdermonkeys, muckers, trammers. Line up!"

Jack operates the big hoist that transports fourteen men per trip. It lifts a wire cage with two levels. Seven men to each. Dozens of men are eager to enter the cage and jostle vigorously for position as the white vapor of their exhale paints the frosty air. No man who really needs the work lingers at the rear because the shift boss could bellow out at any time, "That's enough for today," leaving the stragglers without work.

The hoistman prompts the first load to enter, and then lowers the cage for the second. Wayward hands are clipped at the ground level if not promptly stowed. When all the men are loaded, a single bell sounds. The cage drops to its destination – nine hundred feet below the collar. Green Boot miners suck air as it plunges into darkness.

We are let out on level nine. The rough-hewn corridor plaintively summons an audience. "Why have you left me?" it entreats, as if a jilted mistress bereaved of her lover. "Come back." It is difficult to navigate the dark passage without a pang of guilt. My knees dip at the begging question.

My life had been poured out into this very earth. I find it impossible to detach from my romance with it. But I turn a stiff eye and focus on the shift ahead, again putting behind me the awful decline and loss of the Black Jack Mine. I grab a muck stick and a lift to the end of the line. A little black pneumatic train silently transports the crew in complete darkness to the rock face. All sound is muted in a blur of speeding darkness.

Some of the crewmen know I was the owner. An awkward tension lingers. They are unsure how to act. Others are new, brought in from Creede and Bachelor City when the new owners took possession of the mine. No one speaks on the quarter-mile ride to the rock face but I feel the tension.

"Why is he here?" they seem to be thinking. I read their faces as we flash under shafts of light. "Wasn't he the white-collar boss from up in the big office? Didn't he own the place? Why is he sitting here now? He must have done something stupid. If I owned an outfit like this, I wouldn't let them take it from me. That's just pathetic." And so went the assessment of those who had fought the good fight, but lost the war. The failure was not their fault, but common laborers could not have understood that. They are entitled to their opinions.

At the end of the line we exit the little train and assemble tools for work. The pneumatic engine silently reverses direction to the main shaft for another load. The mine is twenty degrees warmer than outside. We shed our coats and roll up sleeves for a hard day's work. I am a mucker, the lowest on the crew, so I wait for drillers to hammer out an eight-hole pattern, and the powdermonkey to set charges and blow rock.

The Black Jack Mine switched from hammer-and-bit to the new 130-pound widow-maker pneumatic drills in '99. Those dry jackleg drills emitted a cloud of microscopic and razor-sharp slivers of rock that cut the miner's lungs to shreds. Dozens of men with rock-on-the-chest suffered agonizing deaths. Once we figured it out, a new water-lubricated method was developed. We switched to the new system as soon as it was available, as did all the mines in Cripple Creek. I personally authorized the $23,000 expenditure, and sat fascinated at the work of the powerful new device. It was worth the money.

But I also remember being one of the first to hand-steel with a four pound hammer-and-bit. Back then we worked with nothing but the light of a single candle.

The pneumatic drill makes an awful racket. It spits water in all directions but takes to the rock with a terrible fierceness. Once a new hole is collared, the bit reaches blasting depth in two minutes. It used to take us thirty. Eight holes are now ready in twenty minutes, and powder is set. The powderman hollers, "Fire in the hole!" Each man turns from the blast, which throws dust and rock into the corridor with a deafening roar. We wait impatiently for the dust to clear.

Once the set is blown, I muck rock into waiting ore cars where it is trammed to the surface by my only inferior: half blind donkeys. And I am responsible for their manure. The crew rests while I load loose rock into one-ton cars. I will load sixteen tons today. The men chatter as though I am not there. A new mucker must earn a position in the pecking order. Although I can perform the most complex tasks of the entire operation, I am esteemed as the least of my brethren. I must earn the right to speak. And given my history at the mine, that is not likely to happen soon.

Work goes quickly and lunchtime is upon us. For a half-hour, we squat at the rock face and eat, happy with the day's progress. I am careful to follow protocol and leave the crust of my Cornish Pastie meat pie in a crack for the Tommyknockers. They are watching. I respect their presence and listen for their knocks deep within the rock walls. Perhaps if I am watchful, I will see the little creatures in their miner's overalls hard at work with tiny picks and shovels, or so the Cornish tale goes.

After lining up at the Red Wagon ore car, we return to work and finish the shift with speed. And after changing from my diggers and tagging out, I mount the little donkey and plod for home. My first day of work is hard but rewarding. A sense of honest work is realized. My tired muscles are unfamiliar with the rigors of hard rock mining, but they will remember.

The financial burdens of the operation are no longer mine to bear. I am able to return to my family without the weight of responsibility pulling at my coattails. This freedom strikes me for the first time in ten years. A little smile crosses my face and helps soften the blow of my weighty loss.

As we clop down the dusty path I consider my new financial outlook. Today was a good three-dollar day. If I work hard and get four days this week, I'll earn twelve dollars. Rent is seven. Food, water, and fuel is four. Supplies and other expenses may come to a dollar. With austerity, we will survive. So much for the raucous nights at the El Paso Club where we spent a year's rent in one week. Those were wild times I will cherish for the rest of my days. I only wish we'd tucked away a silver dollar for a day like this.

Gone is the mansion on the hill, the motorcar, elegant meals at the Gold Coin Club, opera and moving picture shows, fresh seafood, Paris fashions, bullfights, and the exotica available to the Gold Kings of Cripple Creek. But gone are the headaches, the twenty-hour workdays, the fear of financial ruin, and gone are the political dogfights with the Western Federation of Miners. I am on the outside now.

Life is simple.

I hope to see my friend General Palmer again soon. But pulling together the train fare will not be a trivial task. There are other priorities now and Patricia will not permit the leisure of travel when her children must be clothed and fed. I do not fault her. She has been at my side through the best and worst of it.

I consider with selective fondness of the past decade. With all that has transpired I judge it a raving success. In the past ten years, I successfully pulled my family from the jaws of economic panic and crossed the breadth of three states of the Union. I entered the Colorado gold mining business with little more than a dollar to my name. I dug the nuggets myself and built a twenty million dollar empire, which today provides for two hundred families including my own. In that short time I shook hands with the most influential men of our time, and influenced them in a positive way. I have shown my wife and children the finer things in life, allowing them to mingle with high society, if only for a season. We drank of all the goodness this world can offer. We were denied nothing and refused nothing.

I have come to peace with my conditions and learned how to be abased and how to abound. Through it all, I have learned to worship the Creator rather than the creation. And my only earthly compensation is that my children, and theirs to come will remember their daddy once owned the mighty Black Jack Mine of Cripple Creek, Colorado.

Epilogue

CRIPPLE CREEK, VICTOR, AND GOLDFIELD survived the labor wars of 1903 and 1904. But Altman, Independence, and a dozen other mining camps did not. They slowly turned to ghost towns over several decades. Abandoned miner's shacks, wooden headframes, stamp mills, and other structures gave way to the elements in the Colorado backcountry. Their once-busy streets slowly filled with weeds, aspens, and pine trees. Only a few structures survived beyond the 1960's as tourists picked them apart piece by piece.

By 1914, less than a thousand citizens remained in Cripple Creek, and by 1917 Colorado City was annexed to Colorado Springs. The labor wars had done their evil work.

The Short Line only lasted twenty two years. Hard rock mining declined year after year. It became less profitable to operate so it was torn up in 1922 and turned into a scenic byway into Cripple Creek. The gravel road that replaced it exists today.

The Florissant and Cripple Creek Railway, the Midland, and the Florence railways all shared the same fate. Automobiles became affordable to the masses. Ute Pass transformed into a popular resort stopover and Cripple Creek and Victor became quaint tourist destinations. People wanted to see the famous site of the labor wars and the Wild West mining camp of decades ago. Postcards illustrating the gold camps were sent to family and friends everywhere.

Just like the ghost towns, the fossil beds of Florissant were picked clean of interesting artifacts and petrified tree stumps. Only a few remain today.

Charles Moyer, Bill Haywood, George Pettibone, Harry Orchard were tried for their crimes, but no convictions were secured. Clarence Darrow represented them in the 1907 Governor Frank Steunenberg murder trial where they were all defendants and all slipped the noose. Justice was too late for the gold mining business in Cripple Creek. Nothing could stop the downturn that resulted in near devastation for the district.

Cripple Creek and Victor are fascinating tourist destinations today with plenty of history to explore. The Mollie Kathleen Mine provides tours and demonstrations of the hard rock mining methods of the 1890's. The 800-foot C.O.D. shaft is still visible below an iron grate. Many of the brick structures built after the Cripple Creek fire in 1896, and Victor fire in 1899, remain in use today.

Descendants of the lowly donkeys, released after the mining operations failed, still nibble grass along the twisted mountain roads, and at times meander into town to greet surprised tourists.

This story is based on actual events.

Made in the USA
Charleston, SC
10 October 2015